"Are you pregnant?" Travis demanded.

"No, I am *not* pregnant." Lori watched his face. Was that a flicker of relief she saw in his blue eyes? "But I am ready to have a baby now."

"Right this minute?"

His mocking tone irritated her immensely. "Listen, need I remind you that we are no longer married? I'm free to do whatever I want."

"Including making a fool of yourself in front of the entire town?"

"Including parading naked down the middle of Center Avenue should I feel like it!"

Recognizing the belligerent tilt of her chin, Travis silently cursed himself for not having handled this situation better. "This is getting us nowhere."

"I agree. You might as well leave."

"I'm not going anyplace. If you're so fired up about having a baby, you might as well have mine."

Cathie Linz

was in her mid-twenties when she left her career in a university law library to become a full-time writer of contemporary romantic fiction. In 1993 she won the *Romantic Times* Career Achievement Award for Best Storyteller of the Year.

An avid world traveler, Cathie often uses humorous mishaps from her own trips as inspiration for her stories. After traveling, Cathie is always glad to get back home to her two cats, her trusty word processor and her hidden cache of Oreo cookies!

Special thanks to Molly Spradley of Great Falls, Montana, and to Laura Grieve for their able assistance.

Cathie Linz

BABY WANTED

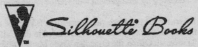

Published by Silhouette Books
America's Publisher of Contemporary Romance

Special thanks and acknowledgment to
Cathie Linz for her contribution to the
Montana Mavericks series.

Text and artwork on page 8 is reprinted with permission from
NEVER ASK A MAN THE SIZE OF HIS SPREAD:
A Cowgirl's Guide to Life, by Gladiola Montana.
Copyright © 1993 Gibbs Smith Publisher. All rights reserved.

 SILHOUETTE BOOKS

ISBN 0-373-50174-9

BABY WANTED

Printed in U.S.A.

MONTANA
Mavericks

Welcome to Whitehorn, Montana—
the home of bold men and daring women.
A place where rich tales of passion and
adventure are unfolding under the Big Sky.
Seems that this charming little town has some mighty
big secrets. And everybody's talking about...

Winona Cobbs: Weddings aren't the only thing the town visionary sees on the horizon. There's trouble brewing in Whitehorn and a whole lot of new faces to account for. Including...

Dr. Errol Straker: Seems this town might be too small for a man of his ambition. But while the doctor is making waves at the county hospital, he'd be wise to watch his back. Or he might just fall prey to the charms of...

Mary Jo Kincaid: It's getting harder and harder for this sweet little librarian to keep a smile on her face. It's a good thing the new doctor has opened his arms to her. Now if she can just keep darling Errol on her side while she takes care of...

Dugin Kincaid: Too bad poor old Dugin's been blinded by love for his wife. Because Mary Jo's got more on her mind than keeping her husband happy. Like a sapphire mine—and murder....

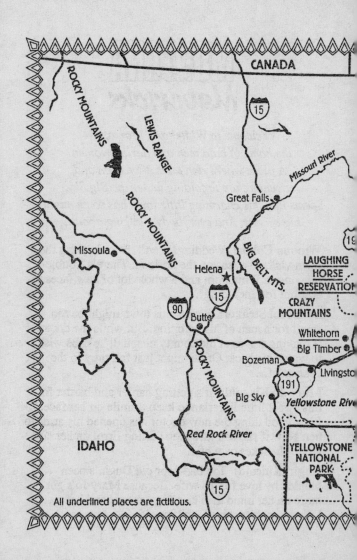

CANADA

ROCKY MOUNTAINS

LEWIS RANGE

ROCKY MOUNTAINS

Missouri River

Great Falls

Missoula

Helena

BIG BELT MTS.

LAUGHING
HORSE
RESERVATION

CRAZY
MOUNTAINS

Butte

Whitehorn

Big Timber

Bozeman

Livingston

ROCKY MOUNTAINS

Big Sky

Yellowstone River

Red Rock River

IDAHO

YELLOWSTONE
NATIONAL
PARK

All underlined places are fictitious.

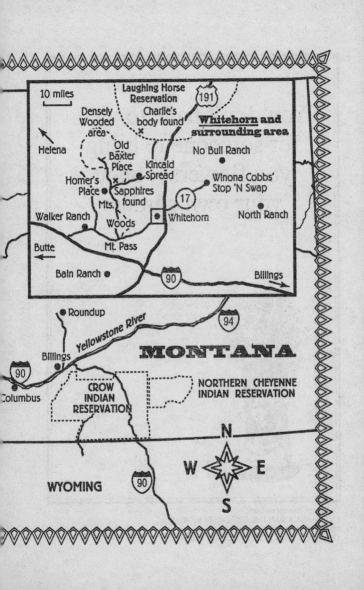

10 miles

Laughing Horse Reservation

191

Densely Wooded area

Charlie's body found ✕

Whitehorn and surrounding area

Helena

Old Baxter Place

Kincaid Spread

No Bull Ranch

Homer's Place

✕ Sapphires found

Winona Cobbs' Stop 'N Swap

Mts.

17

Walker Ranch

Woods

Whitehorn

North Ranch

Butte

Mt. Pass

Bain Ranch

90

Billings

Roundup

94

Yellowstone River

Billings

90

MONTANA

Columbus

CROW INDIAN RESERVATION

NORTHERN CHEYENNE INDIAN RESERVATION

N

W E

S

WYOMING

90

You don't have to wait
for someone to bring
you flowers—plant
your own garden.

Quote and Illustration from:
NEVER ASK A MAN THE SIZE OF HIS SPREAD,
by Gladiola Montana. Illustration by Bonnie Cazier.
Copyright © 1993 by Gibbs Smith Publisher.

One

"I can't believe I did that!" Lori Parker Bains moaned, wishing she could hide under the closest bale of hay.

When Lori had set out that chilly November morning, stoically determined to attend Kane Hunter's wedding, she never dreamed she'd end up in the church basement along with the stored props for next month's Christmas pageant, rolling in the hay with...

"We *both* did it," her ex-husband, Travis, languidly murmured from right beside her.

"It was a mistake," Lori declared, her voice as unsteady as her fingers as she sat up and hurriedly sought to redo the button front of her deep purple dress, which Travis had so recently undone.

There was a moment of utter silence. Then Travis muttered, "Damn right it was a mistake." His curt statement was punctuated by the sound of him angrily zipping his slacks, the noise adding an emphatic exclamation point to his words. Cursing under his breath, he sat up and jammed his feet into his expensive gray snakeskin boots.

Staring at him, Lori saw Travis as if for the first time, as if he were a seductive stranger who'd just taken her innocence. The teenager she'd married had matured into a hard man, and she was struck dumb by the sheer physical impact of him—tall, strong, mysterious. A woman's fantasy of a cowboy lover. His rippling muscles were formed by hard work on his ranch, not by any workouts in a fancy gym.

She blinked, willing herself to remember that this man was her ex-husband and therefore not suitable material for her fantasies.

"We're divorced, for heaven's sakes," Lori stated in that logical tone of voice she used on her patients. "Have been for five years."

"And six months, but who's counting," he said.

"It was the wedding," Lori insisted, tugging loose bits of hay from her short blond hair. "And the champagne they had at the celebration beforehand."

"Which you barely touched."

"You had enough for both of us," she retorted.

"Sure, blame it on me. You're real good at that, Lori," Travis mockingly noted. He wasn't about to admit that the reason he'd been so pleased to toast Kane Hunter's wedding was because the good doctor was marrying Moriah and not Lori. Travis was all too well aware that Kane and Lori had been more than just working associates—the two had been dating before Moriah had returned to Whitehorn. The one time Travis had seen the doctor kiss Lori on her front porch, he'd wanted to tear Hunter's tongue from his throat.

For her part, Lori ignored Travis's accusation. As a certified nurse-midwife, she was used to assisting with new beginnings, new life. But she didn't want a new beginning with Travis. There was no new life to be had in their relationship. *So why did you just make love with him?* a persistent voice in her head demanded.

"It was just sex," Lori muttered.

"Damn good, incredible sex!" Travis retorted.

She couldn't argue with him there.

"Besides, you were the one who started this by crying," he reminded her.

"It's not my fault," she said, defending the teary-eyed state that had sent her scurrying down the steps into the empty basement while all the other guests boisterously took off with the happy couple for the reception being given elsewhere. All the guests except for Travis. "I always cry at weddings," she added. But she'd cried *more* at this one.

Because Kane's wedding to Moriah put a final nail in the coffin of Lori's dreams—her dreams of settling down and raising a family with Kane. Deep down, Lori knew she was crying more for the lost dream than for Kane. She knew he belonged with his first love, Moriah.

But it was hard—damn hard—to be sensible and to maintain a stiff upper lip when you saw the wave of reality sweeping away the sand castles you'd so lovingly built. The future she'd thought she'd have was gone, her plans washed away. She'd been alone again. Until Travis had taken her into his arms and comforted her and kissed her...and made love to her.

"You didn't cry at our wedding," he reminded her.

His words made her pause. Her hesitant gaze settled on Travis's face. The only illumination in the crowded basement came from the exit sign over the door leading to the steps, and from the single frosted window high up on the wall.

The winter sunlight coming in through that window transformed his face into a study of shadows and angles. His jaw was as uncompromising as the nearby snow-covered mountains. His hair had been recently trimmed and just brushed the top of his ears on the side, falling to the collar of his shirt on his back. In the summer his light brown hair was streaked with blond, turning it golden, but now that winter was beginning to grip the countryside, the color was a little darker. She knew he'd been a towhead as a kid; his dad had shown her boxes filled with photos.

A beam of watery sunlight landed on his hand as he reached for his sheepskin jacket. She knew that hand as well as her own. She knew he'd gotten the scar between his thumb and index finger at the tender age of six, when he'd tried to rope his first calf. Those lean fingers of his had been the first to ever touch her intimately.

Looking at his broad back, Lori wondered where she and Travis had gone wrong. They'd been high school sweethearts. He'd sat next to her the first day of her freshman-year English class, and when he'd turned those incredible blue eyes of his her way, *kabang!* She'd fallen for him like a baby grand piano pushed out of a tenth-story window.

To her amazement, he'd seemed to fall for her, too. They'd dated steadily until graduation and gotten married in early August. It had seemed meant to be. Fate. Her destiny.

Travis was absolutely right; Lori hadn't cried at her own wedding, which had taken place in this very church. She'd been too euphoric, too excited. Her dreams were coming true. It had been the happiest day of her entire life. A perfect ten.

Less than six years later, her happily ever after was over—done in by reality. Not by infidelity, or any other momentous rendering. No, it had been done in by things like overwhelming workloads, lack of money, lack of time together. They'd grown apart.

Lori had always hated that phrase. She was a firm believer in fixing things that went wrong. But how could you fix something too vague, too ethereal to put your hands on? She only knew that the love she and Travis had shared had somehow melted like the winter snows in the spring, leaving emptiness behind.

Immediately after the divorce, Lori had moved away from her hometown of Whitehorn to the big city of Great Falls, Montana. There she'd continued her work as a registered nurse, in the delivery room of one of the city's larger hospitals, while also going on to specialize in clinical midwifery skills. She'd stayed in Great Falls almost three years, and by the time she'd left, she'd passed the rigorous certification process that made her a CNM—certified nurse-midwife—and was working at a well-respected birthing center in the city.

Almost three years ago she'd returned to Whitehorn to join the small medical team at the Whitehorn Family Practice. In addition to that, one day a week she worked with Dr. Kane Hunter out at the Laughing Horse Reservation, doing prenatal clinics. She'd returned to her hometown because she'd felt needed here.

She'd known she would run into Travis; Whitehorn was too small for her not to. But she'd managed. Quite well. Until now. Now she'd fallen off the wagon big-time. And they hadn't even practiced safe sex. Her face burned at the memory. After all the speeches she'd given to young women, after all the pamphlets she'd handed out... "I can't believe I did that," she repeated, her moan even more distraught this time.

"*We* did it, and which part can't you believe?" Travis countered. "The part where you came apart in my arms or the part where you dug in and demanded more?"

"The part where you didn't use a condom," she snapped back furiously.

"There was never a need when we were married."

That was true. They'd both been virgins when they'd gotten married. And the threat of AIDS wasn't something they'd worried about. For birth-control purposes, Lori had taken the pill in those days. "We aren't married anymore," she curtly reminded him.

"I didn't come down here expecting this to happen," he growled.

"We should have stopped."

Her eyes caught his intensely blue ones and she looked away. There were too many memories in his eyes for her to deal with now, memories of the passionate explosion they'd just shared. Things between them had ignited faster than a brush fire.

"Twenty-twenty hindsight is useless," Travis stated. "And if you're worried about communicable diseases," he added bluntly, "there's no need. I got a clean bill of health a few months ago at the hospital's blood drive."

"Same here," she said.

"I'm not in a high-risk category," he told her curtly.

"Neither am I."

"You mean you haven't...you and Kane didn't...?"

"I'm not talking about that with you," she said.

"You talk about sex-education stuff with half the population of this county," he reminded her.

"You're not asking for factual information, you're asking for personal information."

"We just made love, Lori. I think that gives me the right to get personal—"

"You think wrong," she interrupted. "You often did," she angrily tacked on. Her emotions were a jumble of contradictions, too mixed-up to untangle at the moment. She only knew there was no going back. First and foremost she felt the need to protect herself, to reduce her vulnerability. "I've got my own life now. My own dreams. And they don't include you."

Shooting her a look fiery enough to incinerate the entire building, Travis grabbed his black felt Stetson, turned on the heel of his custom-made boots and walked out.

Two weeks later, Lori grimaced as she approached the Whitehorn County Hospital staff room. Her period had come, along with the attendant cramps, and she'd been feeling weepy all day.

Why? She turned thirty today, but that wasn't the reason for her emotional state. The weepiness was caused by the fact that, with her period coming, she now knew she wasn't pregnant. There had been a good possibility that she might have been after her interlude with Travis.

It was only now that she realized how much she'd been secretly contemplating the idea of having a baby, savoring the possibilities since she and Travis had made love. Not the possibilities with Travis; she knew better than that. But to have a little baby of her own to love... The tugging appeal of that had crept up on her and stolen into her heart.

Since becoming a midwife, Lori had helped and guided more than two hundred mothers in delivering healthy babies. She'd seen the miracle of birth firsthand and up close. But she'd never experienced it herself. She'd always had to hand the baby over—into its mother's loving arms. She'd never been able to keep any of the infants herself. She'd never had an infant nursing at her own breast. And she wanted that. Wanted it badly.

Blinking away the threat of tears, Lori took a deep breath before entering the hospital's staff room. A nice, calming cup of hot tea was called for here....

"Surprise!" a dozen people shouted all at once, swarming around Lori. "Happy birthday!"

Lori knew she had to look as stunned as she felt. The staff lounge, so recently decorated for the upcoming holidays, had additional birthday decorations festooned from the walls.

Molly, a nurse who worked with Lori at the Whitehorn Family Practice, hurried to her side. "I guess you thought we forgot about your birthday, huh?"

"I'd just as soon have forgotten *my* thirtieth birthday," someone in the group good-naturedly noted.

"We wanted to surprise you," Molly continued excitedly.

"You certainly did that," Lori noted with a wobbly smile.

The next fifteen minutes were filled with laughter and the mocking black humor so often found among those in the medical profession. It was reflected in their presents to Lori—a pair of bifocals, a T-shirt that said Thirty Isn't Old...for a Tree! and a funeral wreath with the words *May your youth rest in peace, Lori!* written on the black-ribbon banner.

Dr. Errol Straker put a temporary damper on the celebration when he made an appearance. He carried a lot of weight in the small hospital and he never let Lori forget that fact. He also disapproved of nurse-midwives, and his subtle and not-so-subtle verbal cuts reminded Lori that her professional battle for equity wasn't over by a long shot.

Some might actually consider Dr. Straker, with his silvery hair and brown eyes, to be a fairly good-looking man, albeit an unbearably superior one. He was in his mid-forties and wore power as if it were indelibly starched into his white lab coat.

"I heard you girls were having a party back here," Dr. Straker noted with a joviality that Lori knew to be fake. He often used that tone when preparing to deliver a real zinger. Boldly walking over and cutting himself a piece of cake, he then turned and asked, "So who's the lucky birthday girl?"

"Lori," someone replied.

Straker's laser gaze settled on her, his expression one of indulgent condescension. "Ah, our little rebel midwife. Well, enjoy things while you can, Lori." He patted her on the shoulder. "The future is always filled with uncertainty, isn't it?" He smiled again, this time like a wily ferret, and then thankfully was gone, taking his pilfered piece of cake with him.

"Imagine Straker the Streaker putting in an appearance," one of the nursery nurses murmured, using the supercilious doctor's nickname.

"He probably just wanted to sample the air we poor peons breath," someone else replied.

"Not to mention sampling the cake," the secretary from Admissions added.

With much laughter, everyone hurried to sample some of the delicious devil's food cake provided by Molly, who possessed a chocolate thumb where baked goodies were concerned. The intricate holiday gingerbread house on display back at the Whitehorn Family Practice was another of her creations.

"You look depressed," Molly noted as she joined Lori in a relatively quiet corner of the room. "I hope the presents didn't make you feel too bad. You know how this gang is...."

Lori shook her head. "It's not that."

"What then?"

"I know it sounds like a cliché, but I'm starting to feel my biological clock ticking. And it's sounding like a time bomb about to go off," Lori said a bit morosely, while brushing a crumb of chocolate cake from her trademark lavender lab coat. "I'm thirty already. A lot of my patients have two kids or more by the time they're my age."

"And they look twice your age. You may be thirty, but you look like you're barely out of high school."

"That's not an advantage in my profession. It's a little difficult to inspire trust in my patients when they keep asking me how old I am," Lori noted.

"Then I'd think you'd be glad to reach this milestone age."

"I am. Sort of. I just thought that I'd have a family of my own by now. Look at Kane. He's only four years older than I am and he's already got a teenage daughter."

"Which he didn't know about until recently. Are you upset that he and Moriah got married?" Molly asked.

"Not the way you think," Lori replied. "The timing wasn't right for Kane and me. We were just about to move on to the next step in our relationship when Moriah came back. Now we're friends, nothing more. But I confess I liked the idea of having a family, and I do envy him that."

"If you don't mind my asking, why didn't you and Travis have kids?"

Lori shrugged. "We thought there was plenty of time for that later. We were only nineteen and living out at his dad's ranch. Travis was working long hours to save the ranch after his dad had a stroke. I was working and trying to go to college. We wanted to wait until our future was more secure before bringing a new life into this world."

"That was probably a wise decision on your parts," Molly said. "Divorce is hard on kids."

It's hard on adults, too, Lori wanted to say, but didn't.

"It's good that you're not so bitter about your divorce that you've given up on marriage altogether," Molly noted.

"Who says I haven't?"

"Well... you said you wanted a baby."

"You're a nurse, Molly. You know that you don't have to be married to have a baby. There are plenty of other options, from personal life-style choices to medical choices."

"You mean like artificial insemination?"

"What a fascinating discussion," Danette declared from their side.

Lori silently groaned at having one of her least-favorite people in the entire hospital overhear them. Danette was right up there along with Dr. Straker on her Top Ten Pains-in-the-Derriere list.

"So you want a baby and you're considering artificial insemination, Lori?" Danette continued. "That's a drastic step, but I can understand that it must be difficult for you... what with Kane dumping you to marry his true love and all."

"Kane didn't dump Lori," Molly exclaimed, loyally defending her.

"Yeah, and if you believe that, there's some land over on the East Ridge I'd love to sell you." With a scornful smile, Danette dumped her paper plate in the garbage and sailed out of the room.

"Don't let her upset you," Molly said quickly.

"I'm upset with *myself* for letting her overhear us," Lori replied.

"Danette does what she wants. No one *lets* her do anything. No one can stop her."

There was no stopping Lori's beeper from going off, either. It looked like another baby was ready to come into the world, and she was needed to help it on its way. Another baby that wasn't hers....

Sunday afternoon, Travis stopped at the Hip Hop Café for a nice big slice of freshly baked cherry pie. His housekeeper, Tex, was a sweetheart, but she never had gotten the hang of baking a good pie. Her efforts resembled cindered wood rather than flaky dough. Even the barn cats, who normally ate anything, disdained eating it.

He'd no sooner settled on an empty swivel stool at the counter when Virgil, the latest cook and general jack-of-all-trades, said, "So, have you heard the news?"

"What news is that?" Travis countered, sliding off his sheepskin gloves to warm his hands around the cup of coffee Virgil had just poured for him, to go along with his pie. Although Virgil might be relatively new to the Hip Hop's payroll, he was well known in Whitehorn, having lived there all his life.

"Why, the news about Lori and the baby," Virgil replied.

"Whose baby did she deliver this time?" Travis asked, before taking a sip of coffee. The temperature outside was almost zero and the wind cut through a man like a knife.

"I'm not talkin' about Lori deliverin' other folks' babies. Word is that she's interested in havin' one for herself."

Travis choked on his coffee, burning his mouth in the process. Grabbing the paper napkin Virgil handed him, he glared at the older man before demanding, "What are you talking about?"

"Word is that Lori is in the mood for... *nestin'*," Virgil said, with a meaningful lift of his bushy eyebrows.

"Nesting?" Travis croaked.

"That's right, boy." Virgil called every male in Whitehorn under the age of fifty "boy." "Her hormones is workin' overtime. She's not gettin' any younger, ya know. Let me tell ya, I know how these gals get when they feel the call of Mother Nature." He shook his balding head. "They get bitten by the baby bug and *wham*—they have to have one of their own and ain't nothin' gonna stand in their way. I know, son, that's how I got caught by wife number two."

Virgil was currently between wives, having recently been divorced by number four.

"What makes you think Lori wants a baby?" Travis demanded.

"Shucks, boy, the news is all over town. She just had a birthday the other day, you know."

Travis did know. He always remembered her birthday, and he knew this was a big one.

"Anyways," Virgil continued, "she up and announced she wanted a baby. Word is she's lookin' for a likely candidate, if you get my drift. I heard it straight from Lily Mae, who heard it from Sally, the cashier at the Roxie Movie House, and she heard it from that little gal workin' as a police dispatcher, who heard it from a nurse at the hospital, who was there—"

"This town gossips too damn much!" Travis interrupted him to growl. Tossing down three bucks for his coffee and uneaten pie, he grabbed his gloves and stormed out of the café.

Outside, he yanked open the door to his red pickup with more force than necessary. Jumping inside, he slammed it hard enough to rattle the entire truck. Seconds after reaching for the ignition key, Travis switched on the heat and radio, turning both knobs to full blast and keeping them there during the forty-minute drive back to the ranch, hoping the wail of Garth Brooks would keep his mind off the disturbing news he'd just heard.

Lori... nesting? It couldn't be true. Could it? It would sure explain her behavior at the wedding, a nagging voice in his head pointed out. Was that why she'd made love with him? In the hopes of having a baby? What if she were pregnant already?

No, if she were pregnant, she wouldn't be announcing the fact that she wanted a baby in front of one and all, would she? Travis squinted against the sunlight bouncing off the snow-covered ground and pouring through the windshield as he drove south on Route 191. God only knew what Lori would do these days. He certainly couldn't figure her out. He still wasn't even sure how he'd lost her in the first place. He only knew he had.

And then she'd cried in his arms after Kane Hunter's wedding and he'd thought...hell, he'd thought that maybe there was a chance for them again. She still had a powerful effect on him, that was for sure.

But their roll in the hay had been just that, nothing permanent. Unless there was a baby concerned. He hadn't used a condom and he had no idea if she was still on the pill.

As he drove beneath the hanging wooden sign for the Triple M ranch—his home—and the pickup's heavy-duty tires rumbled over the metal cattle guards, Travis was no closer to finding answers to all his questions. And that aggravated him. Five years and six months after his divorce and he still couldn't get Lori out of his mind.

Muttering under his breath, he slammed into the ranch house with the force of a winter storm.

Tex McClintock looked up from the chili she was cooking for dinner and inquired, "Golly, who put a bee in your bonnet?"

"No one."

"This is *me* you're talking to. Tex. The woman who knew you were lying when you said you had nothing to do with putting salt in the sugar bowl on April Fool's Day when you were nine." She waved her wooden spoon at him. "I know when you're lying, Travis."

Tex was the closest thing Travis had to a mother, his own having died when he was only a toddler. Tex had been his father's housekeeper, while her husband, Slim, was the ranch foreman. "You think a woman could want a baby so badly she'd do something stupid?" he asked her.

"Depends on the woman," Tex replied.

Taking the wooden spoon and sampling her chili, he nonchalantly murmured, "Say it was Lori we were talking about."

Tex lovingly slapped his hand and regained possession of her wooden spoon before replying. "Well, the desire to have babies is a real strong one. It's Mama Nature's way of ensuring the continuation of the species. And after delivering so many beautiful babies, I guess I wouldn't be surprised to hear that Lori wanted one of her own."

"Well, *I* would be surprised," Travis angrily declared, smacking his gloves against his thigh. "What could she be thinking of? What's wrong with her?"

"Hormones are a powerful thing.... Hey, where are you going?" Tex demanded as Travis turned on his heel and headed out of the kitchen as stormily as he'd entered it.

"I'm going to talk some sense into her."

Lori was in her bathroom, sitting on the closed lid of the toilet and singing along with Linda Ronstadt while threading shower-rod holders onto the new chenille shower curtain she'd just received the day before from a catalog company. When she'd seen a picture of the shower curtain, she'd known it would be perfect for her bathroom. The white background and pink flowers matched the old-fashioned look provided by the cast-iron tub with its claw feet.

Lori ordered a lot of her furnishings and other things from catalogs. Aside from the fact that Whitehorn wasn't exactly the shopping capital of the world, she didn't have the time these days for shopping.

She was in the middle of securing the last holder when she heard pounding at her front door.

She frowned. Patients contacted her through her answering service and beeper, not by knocking on her door. Usually. But then Lori knew from experience that *usual* wasn't always the case around here.

"I'm coming," she yelled as she hurried from the bathroom and headed for the front door. "I'm coming, I said. Hold onto your...horses...." Lori's voice trailed off as she opened the door and was confronted by a cold blast of frigid air along with a hotly furious Travis.

"What's with this ridiculous story I heard about you and your hormones wanting a baby?" he demanded.

Two

Lori looked at Travis as if he'd taken leave of his senses, only to realize that he was looking at her in exactly the same way. "What on earth are you talking about?"

"It's not true then?" He heaved a sigh of relief as he stepped inside and closed the door behind him. "I knew Virgil had to be spouting hot air. I even told Tex that you wouldn't do anything that crazy, hormones or no."

"Have you been drinking?" Lori demanded suspiciously.

"No, although you'd sure drive a man to it," he retorted. "Are you saying the rumors aren't true?"

"Depends what the rumors are."

"There are lots of them, all revolving around you, hormones and a baby."

Lori closed her eyes and pictured herself strangling Danette. For that's where these rumors had come from. And like a game of telephone, by the time whatever it was that Danette had said made the rounds of Whitehorn, it no doubt bore little resemblance to the truth.

Opening her eyes again, she was about to try and explain how things could get blown completely out of proportion in situations like this, but Travis spoke first.

"Are you acting so crazy because you're pregnant?" he demanded. "I mean, we didn't use any birth control when we made love. Is that what this is all about? Are you pregnant?"

This time when Lori closed her eyes, she imagined herself strangling Travis instead of Danette. She silently counted to sixteen before opening her eyes and glaring at him. "You have some nerve, you know that? You come over here, uninvited, pounding on my front door like a maniac and then making these wild and incoherent statements...."

"Forgive me if my protocol is a little off," Travis retorted sarcastically. "I'm not used to dealing with women and their hormones."

"That much is painfully clear."

"I'm a rancher, not a damn mind reader. Just answer my question. Are you pregnant?"

"No, I am *not* pregnant." Lori watched his face, gauging his reaction. Was that a flicker of relief she saw in his blue eyes? Her earlier irritation flared into anger. "That pleases you, doesn't it? After all, a baby would get in the way of those grand plans you have for that ranch of yours. But be careful, Travis. After a lifetime devoted to that piece of land, you might end up dying an old man without having anyone to pass it down to, because you were too damn busy taking care of business instead of living life!"

"A man can have kids well into his sixties," Travis said. "Women aren't as lucky."

His salvo hit home. "Women in their fifties are getting pregnant," she retorted. "Even having twins. But I don't plan on waiting that long."

"What's that supposed to mean?"

"That I'm ready to have a baby now."

"Right this minute?"

His mocking comment irritated her immensely. "Listen, need I remind you yet again that we are no longer married? I'm free to do whatever I want."

"Including making a fool of yourself in front of the entire town?"

"Including parading naked right down the middle of Center Avenue should I feel like it!"

"Fine. Go ahead and get yourself arrested for indecent exposure." Recognizing the belligerent tilt of her chin, Travis silently cursed himself for not having handled this situation better. Trying to make amends, he quietly said, "This is getting us nowhere."

"I agree. You might as well leave."

"I'm not going anyplace. If you're so fired up about having a baby, you might as well have mine."

"Don't do me any favors," Lori retorted instantly.

Frowning, Travis noted that once again his words had gotten away from him, like a runaway horse—tumbling him from the saddle of control. The realization didn't improve his mood any. "There's still something between us," he growled. "You can't deny it, not after what happened in church two weeks ago."

"It wasn't in church, it was in the church *basement,*" she immediately corrected, her face turning red at the memory. "And it was a mistake. A momentary flash of insanity."

"Right," he noted scornfully. "Like your current plan isn't just as insane? A single woman having a baby?"

"Who said I'd stay single?" Lori calmly countered.

Travis looked as if he'd been poleaxed.

"Are you saying you plan on getting married?" he demanded.

"I'm saying I'm keeping *all* my options open," she stated.

"What kind of options?"

"None of your—"

"Business, yeah, I've heard that one before," he said.

"You've heard, but you don't *listen.* A recurring problem of yours," she noted tartly.

He ignored her last comment, doggedly going on. "So these options include what? Marriage?"

She nodded.

"And what else?" he pressed. "Medical stuff? Test-tube babies?"

"It's called intrauterine fertilization."

"I don't believe this." His blue eyes flashed at her.

"Modern medicine is making some unbelievable things possible," she agreed, deliberately misunderstanding him.

"That's not what I'm talking about and you know it. So what . . . you're going to start interviewing studs from here to Billings for the job of sperm supplier?"

"Maybe. It's none of your business. We're not married anymore, so you've got no cause to be ordering me around."

"Someone's gotta talk some sense into you."

"No, they don't," she said calmly.

"Your hormones have gone off the deep end."

"Really? And what do you know about hormones?"

"I know they make women do crazy things," Travis declared.

"Do go on, Dr. Bains," she invited him mockingly. "This is really most fascinating."

"Can the sarcasm," he snapped back.

"I will when you can the BS. Your hormones have gone off the deep end," she mimicked before rolling her eyes. "Puhlease!"

Shifting uncomfortably, he muttered, "You're the one with all the medical know-how, not me."

"Well, you can go on home, reassured that my hormones are just fine."

"And that you've given up this wild idea of having a baby, right?"

"Wrong."

"What's it going to take to get you to see how ridiculous the idea is?" he asked in exasperation.

"Why is it ridiculous?" she countered.

"Because it takes two to make a baby."

"Gee, no kidding," Lori noted with mocking, wide-eyed shock.

He shot her a fiery look.

"I know it takes two, Travis," she said. "Thanks so much for worrying about me." She patted the shoulder of the thick sheepskin coat he wore. "You may leave now."

"Not on your life. Not until I talk some sense into you."

"I've got plenty of sense."

"Yeah, right. So what you are going to do? Take out one of those personal ads? 'Hormone-driven woman looking for good genes'?"

"I might," she said militantly.

"I'll believe that when I see it." Travis tugged his hat down even farther and yanked open her front door.

Travis did see it. Oh, the personal ad in the *Whitehorn Journal* was discreet enough. It didn't actually have Lori's name on it, but he knew it was hers. The words were branded into his brain: *Looking for a good man—DWF, nonsmoker with sense of humor and medical background looking to start a family ASAP. If you are a healthy nonsmoker interested in same, contact me.*

"Did World War III break out?" Tex inquired dryly, popping her head around the doorframe.

"What?" Travis murmured absently.

Strolling into the room, she said, "You were studying the paper so closely I figured something earth-shattering must have happened. Nothing short of World War III would keep you from digging into your supper once I told you it was ready."

"I'll be there in a minute," Travis said.

"That's what you said ten minutes ago. Food's getting cold." Seeing him fold back the paper into a neat square, Tex frowned. "Since when have you taken to reading the personal ads?"

"Since Lori placed one."

"No kidding." Tex tried to look over his shoulder, but since she was almost eight inches shorter than he was, she had to make do with looking around his arm until he finally gave in and handed the paper to her. "So which one is hers? All I see are numbers listed, no names. Ah, here's one that says 'Howdy.' That's nice and friendly. Let's see what else it says.... 'DWF'—what's a DWF, for heaven sakes?"

"Divorced white female."

"'—Looking for the simple life,'' Tex continued. "'I love to cuddle in front of the fire on cold nights—'''

"That's not Lori's ad."

Tex tried again. "''Looking for a cowboy. I love water sports and welding—'''

"No, that's not it, either. This one is hers." He jabbed the spot with enough force to almost knock the paper from his housekeeper's hands.

"How can you tell?"

"Because of the wording. Who else in this town would place an ad like that?"

"Well, it sure is short and sweet," Tex said. "Makes sense, since most papers charge by the line. Lori always was cautious with money."

Travis made some kind of growling noise that Tex simply ignored. "So I guess this means you weren't too successful talking some sense into her during your last visit, huh?" she continued.

"That's an understatement," he muttered.

"You two ended up at each other's throats again," Tex guessed.

"She's an incredibly stubborn woman."

"Are we gonna eat tonight or just leave the food on the table looking pretty-like?" Slim inquired from the doorway.

"Travis is upset because Lori placed a personal ad in the paper," Tex told her husband.

"An ad for what?" Slim asked.

"A stud," Travis said curtly.

Frowning, Slim said, "Lori's breeding horses?"

"No, *she's* thinking of breeding…having a baby," Travis replied.

"By golly! And she's putting an ad in the paper about it?" Slim shoved his hand through what little hair he had left and then shook his head in bewilderment. "Modern times. I don't understand 'em. Not at all."

"What happened when you went over there to talk to Lori?" Tex asked, as she steered the two men toward the dinner table in the huge kitchen. The ranch house didn't have a dining room.

"She claimed that nothing she did was any of my business because we're divorced. Claimed she'd walk naked down Center Avenue if she felt like it."

Slim looked ready to choke on the bite of steak he'd just swallowed, while Tex nodded knowingly and said, "You egged her on, didn't you? That's what happened."

"What are you talking about?"

"You *dared* her to take out an ad."

"I did no such thing," Travis exclaimed.

"You tell her she couldn't?" Tex questioned.

"Damn right I did."

Tex gave a see-what-I-mean shrug. "Same as daring her to do it."

Travis shot a glance at Slim, as if seeking male reinforcement.

"Don't look at me," Slim said with a shake of his head. "Women are a law unto themselves."

"A law that oughtta be illegal sometimes," Travis muttered.

"What's so complicated?" Tex countered. "You'd do the same thing if someone tried bossing you around."

"I wasn't bossing her around," Travis declared.

"You told Lori she couldn't do it. Looks like she proved you wrong." Tex nodded at the paper, now sitting beside his dinner plate.

"So you're saying she only placed that ad to make a point? To prove something to me?"

"Could be."

Travis practically heaved a sigh of relief. "Then she's not serious about this."

"Now, I wouldn't go that far. It appears to me that Lori is serious about having a baby."

But Travis wasn't listening to her anymore. "And since she's not serious, then what I should do is call her bluff."

"How do you figure that?"

"She says she's looking for some good men, right? I should just call her bluff and send her a few prospects." Seeing the look on his housekeeper's face, Travis added, "Not serious prospects, of course. Just a few guys to make her see the error of her ways."

"Convincing yourself that a bad idea is a good one is a *bad* idea," Tex declared, using one of her favorite home-spun bits of advice. "Now eat."

"Lori, we haven't seen you at rehearsal," Virgil said, catching her as she ate a hurried meal at the Hip Hop Café during her dinner break from the family practice.

Personally, Lori thought that Lily Mae's unofficial title for being Whitehorn's town gossip was in jeopardy, as Virgil was coming in a close second these days. His new position as cook put him right in the hub of things, just the way he liked it. As the recently appointed interim choir director, he took his job very seriously.

"Lily Mae," he called to the older woman sipping coffee in a booth a short distance away. "Have you seen Lori at rehearsal?"

Lily Mae shook her head, the bouncy curls on her head a brassy color that could only come from a bottle. "Why, no, Virgil, now that you mention it, I haven't seen her at rehearsal."

As music director, Lily Mae pounded on the piano while Virgil directed a chorus that made the off-key nuns from *Sister Act* sound like pros.

"What rehearsal might that be?" Lori inquired, playing dumb. It sometimes worked with Virgil and Lily Mae.

"For the Christmas pageant," Virgil replied. "It's only two weeks away."

"Less than two weeks now," Lily Mae came over to his side to correct him.

"What with that flu that's goin' around, folks have been droppin' like flies," Virgil declared.

Lori wondered if the overwhelming combination of Virgil and Lily Mae simply wasn't too much for the poor souls in the chorus.

"I'm sorry to hear that," she murmured sympathetically.

Virgil promptly made his move, leaning over Lori's booth like a vulture eyeing its terrain. "That's where you come in, Lori. We need a soprano. You're it."

"I'm not a soprano," Lori said. "I'm an alto."

"You're close enough," Virgil declared. "Rehearsals are at seven tonight."

"I'm working tonight," Lori protested. "I have patients to see."

"Fine," Virgil said. "Come tomorrow night. We're gonna be rehearsin' every night 'til we get things right."

At that rate, they'd be rehearsing until doomsday, Lori silently noted.

"Chorus is a mighty good place to look for fellows," Virgil stated, before Lily Mae belted him in his Santa-size belly.

"Ignore him," the older woman told Lori. "Men can be so... obvious sometimes."

Lori was well aware that Lily Mae's methods were more discreet but equally effective. Little went on in this town that either Lily Mae or Virgil didn't know about. Lori could only pray that neither knew what had gone on in the basement of the church after Kane's wedding. She didn't think anyone knew—other than herself and Travis, of course.

Since then, Lori hadn't been able to drive or walk past the church without blushing. Even looking at the nativity scene, and its abundant hay, made her feel like sinking through the frozen December ground.

She needed to make amends. Maybe this was God's way of getting retribution—by making her sing in Virgil's chorus. If so, she'd pay the price. And then maybe she'd stop feeling so guilty and could get on with her life.

Well aware of Lily Mae's intent stare, Lori restlessly smoothed her short hair behind one ear, making sure in the process that her garnet stud earring was still in place. She'd already lost one of her earrings—an amethyst one—in the church basement that fateful afternoon with Travis. She'd forced herself to stop by the rectory last week and ask if anyone had turned it in. No one had.

Rings and bracelets just got in the way in her line of work, so the only jewelry Lori wore were earrings. And that amethyst pair had been her favorite.

"You seem upset, dear," Lily Mae observed. "You know you can tell me anything, don't you?"

Right, Lori thought, and as soon as I tell you, you'll turn around and tell all of Whitehorn.

"I was on your side in that awkward situation with Kane, you know," Lily Mae continued. "Don't get me wrong, Moriah seems very nice and all. But secretly, I was hoping you and Kane would somehow work things out. After all, the two of you had so much in common—both of you working in medicine the way you do."

"Kane belongs with Moriah and their daughter," Lori said.

"That *was* surprising news, wasn't it? You know, I thought it was unconventional to have that get-together before the wedding, with the champagne and all. But then I told myself that Kane had been unconventional by having a baby sixteen years before he married the mother."

"Kane didn't know about the baby," Lori said, defending him.

"I know that. I wasn't saying anything bad about Kane. Some in town would, given his background, you know. But I'm not like that."

No, Lori would give Lily Mae that much: she was an equal-opportunity gossiper. The fact that Kane was a Native American wouldn't make him a bigger target as far as she was concerned.

Lily Mae then changed the subject, a favorite tactic of hers. "You know, Lori, someone said they saw that handsome ex-husband of yours pounding on your front door a few days back."

"Really?"

Lily Mae nodded.

Lori noted that Virgil had returned to the kitchen, apparently trusting Lily Mae to get the goods out of her. Well, they were both in for a disappointment.

"My gosh, will you just look at the time," she exclaimed, with a glance at the large numerals on her easy-to-read watch. "I've got to get back to the office. Patients to see. Just put dinner on my account, Virgil," she called out.

"Hey, you don't have no account here!" Virgil called back.

"I do now," Lori said with a grin.

"Only if you're at rehearsal tomorrow night!"

"Deal," Lori agreed. "And remember, Virgil, *don't have no* is a double negative—which means it's a positive."

"Oh yeah? Then how come double negatives in my checking account don't work that way?" Virgil countered with his own brand of logic.

Shaking her head, Lori decided to leave before his comments actually started making sense. Travis had her mixed up enough as it was....

Three

"You'll think I'm crazy," Lori's eight-month-pregnant patient, Sarah Sutton, said.

"No, I won't," Lori replied, setting down her chart and giving Sarah her undivided attention. "Listen, I just came from the Hip Hope Café, where I actually agreed to take part in the Christmas concert."

Sarah, who clearly knew what Lori was letting herself in for, just shook her head in disbelief.

"I know, I know. So trust me, nothing you say will make me think you're crazy. Besides," Lori added with a grin, "after all this time, I've heard just about everything."

"Okay, well, I know it may sound silly, but I've been playing tag with the baby. When I feel Junior moving around and kicking down here—" Sarah patted her protruding stomach "—then I gently push back where the baby just pushed me. It's a game we play."

"I think it's very clever of you. Sounds like fun," Lori noted somewhat wistfully.

"Sounds like you wouldn't mind having one of these—" Sarah patted her large tummy again "—yourself."

"I've been giving it some thought," Lori admitted.

"You'd make a great mother," Sarah said. "You're so empathetic and patient."

"Thanks. I really appreciate you saying that."

"I'm not just saying it, that's the way I feel. I can't tell you what a difference it's made having you as my midwife. I went to Dr. Straker for my first pregnancy, before you came to town, and let me tell you, the difference between you two is like night and day."

"Completely different bedside manner, hmm?"

"Dr. Straker doesn't even *have* a bedside manner. He's not there long enough. He barely made it to the delivery room in time to catch Erica when she came out. And in all the months I went for prenatal visits, he never spent more than five minutes tops with me, whereas you take the time to answer my million questions and you don't make me feel dumb for asking them."

"That's because there is no such thing as a dumb question."

"Tell that to Dr. Straker."

"I have," Lori noted with a grin. "I don't think he appreciated hearing it."

The truth was that Dr. Straker didn't appreciate Lori's existence, period. It was nothing personal. She was sure he'd have felt the same way regardless of what nurse-midwife was in town. When she'd gotten the clearance to become affiliated with the hospital, Straker had almost blown a gasket.

To this day he still didn't accept her. Instead, he was forever trying to irk her into an argument by saying—among other things—that women who chose to give birth with a nurse-midwife were practicing child abuse.

Lori had done well in biting her tongue, countering his absurd comments with factual data supporting the fact that midwives had an excellent record of safety. She'd even quoted a study published in the prestigious *New England Journal of Medicine.* It made no difference.

Personally, Lori thought that, aside from him being an autocratic demigod, Straker saw her as a threat to his economic turf. She was horning in on his territory, delivering babies he felt should be his to make money on. So he got back at her in little ways, like showing up at her birthday party at the hospital.

Still, whatever drivel came out of his mouth, Lori hadn't let Straker egg her on—unlike Travis. Maybe that's why

Travis had been able to get to her—because she had used up her limited reservoir of tact at work and had little left to apply to her own private life.

There Travis was again, sneaking into her mind, darn his hide! Clicking off her personal thoughts, Lori stated, "Like I said, Sarah, there's no such thing as a dumb question."

"Thanks. I appreciate the fact that you never make me feel like the meter is running, like I'm just a number on a chart and that I should get a move on because there's a waiting room full of people wanting a second of your time."

"That's because you're not just a number on a chart and I don't have a waiting room full of people," Lori replied with a grin. "For one thing, not everyone feels comfortable with a nurse-midwife yet. And I only accept the number of patients I can do justice to, which means I schedule appointments accordingly. I like to spend time with my patients. I *need* to spend time with them, to see how their pregnancy is progressing. Speaking of which, how about lying down so I can check out Junior?"

Sarah rearranged herself from a sitting to a horizontal position on the soft, oversize couch that made the examining room look more like a sitting room. "Have I told you how much I prefer this comfy couch to that cold examining table?" she said as she pushed her maternity top up and her slacks down a little so that Lori could measure her abdomen.

"I believe you may have mentioned it once or twice," Lori murmured, writing the fundal height on Sarah's chart before putting her hands gently on Sarah's abdomen, feeling the size and position of the fetus.

"I like this floral pattern couch cover better than the striped one you had on here last week," Sarah noted absently. "Where do you come up with these ideas?"

"From catalogs." Using a fetoscope, Lori listened to the baby's heartbeat. "I like this beat! Nice rhythm, easy to dance to," she teased, using an American Bandstand classic description. "Want to listen?"

On earlier visits, Lori had already taught Sarah how to listen to the *swish-swish* sound on the specially designed stethoscope.

"I half expected to hear a soccer game going on in there, the way the baby's been moving lately," Sarah said, before handing the fetoscope back to Lori.

Sarah had opted not to have an amniocenteses to determine the baby's sex. Since her pregnancy was a healthy, normal one and progressing right on time, Lori preferred not to order more tests than necessary or the parents felt they needed.

"You know, I really like the what-do-you-call-it... the holistic approach you take," Sarah continued as she rearranged her clothes and sat up again. "I mean, you tie in my physical condition with my emotional one. Straker's approach was entirely from the waist down. It was as if I didn't exist as anything but a baby carrier. And as for emotions... hah!"

"So how about those emotions, Sarah?" Lori asked with a grin.

"I still feel ugly sometimes. Okay, a lot of the time. I feel like a beached whale every time I sit down. And I can't get comfortable anyplace, not even in bed. And speaking of bed, my husband is acting like I'm made out of glass again."

"Have you tried cuddling, like I suggested last time?"

"Who can cuddle with a whale?" Tears came to Sarah's eyes.

"A whale lover," Lori replied, sitting on the couch beside her and handing her a facial tissue. "And that hubby of yours is a whale lover if ever I met one."

Sarah grinned, her tears forgotten. "My emotions are still all over the map. Is that normal?"

"Perfectly normal," Lori assured her. "Why don't you bring your husband in for our next appointment?"

"He'd be too embarrassed to talk about us not making love."

"He won't have to talk about it. I will," Lori said with a grin. "Don't worry, I'll smoothly work it into the conversation, just like I did when he was worried at the beginning of this pregnancy. That worked pretty well, didn't it?"

Sarah nodded.

"Okay, then, it's a plan."

They talked several minutes longer before Sarah left. "Remember to keep your daily journal going, recording your feelings and the movement of the baby."

"I won't forget," Sarah promised. "It's my favorite part of the day."

Sarah was her last patient of the evening. After completing her notes on Sarah's chart, Lori checked her watch. A little before nine. Still time left to stop by the hospital to see how Mary Red Deer was. Kane had twisted a few arms at IHS, Indian Health Services, to get Mary admitted to Whitehorn County Hospital.

"What are you doing here?" Danette belligerently demanded as soon as Lori got off the hospital elevator. Danette was a stickler for hospital rules and was religious about enforcing them. Her zeal for paperwork, filled out in triplicate, no less, was only one of the things about Danette that drove Lori crazy.

"I'm here to see Mary Red Deer."

"She's not your patient. She's got a *doctor* looking after her."

"Chill out, Danette," Lori advised with a grin. "Hypertension can shorten your life." With a cheerful wave, she headed down the hallway toward Mary's room.

"I'm putting this in my report," Danette called after Lori.

"Be my guest."

Even though Lori had been there that morning, Mary was clearly glad to see her. "So when do I get sprung?" the young Native American woman demanded as she breast-fed her baby girl, Kate.

Lori checked the chart at the end of her bed. "Tomorrow morning sound soon enough for you?"

"Really?"

"I suspect that's what Dr. Hunter is going to tell you."

Kane had called her in on this case from the beginning, feeling that, at fifteen going on sixteen, Mary needed some extra moral support. While her youth and poor health made her a high-risk patient, and therefore one that Lori needed to refer on to a physician, the teenager had taken a liking to Lori during the prenatal clinics out at the reservation. They'd clicked together, even though their circumstances were very different.

At sixteen, Lori had been a sophomore in high school—a cheerleader going steady with Travis, the football team's star running back. An only child, she'd been on the honor roll and had gotten to borrow the family car on weekends.

At sixteen, Mary was one of eight children. She lived with her mother, grandmother and siblings, in very crowded conditions—everyone jammed into a trailer that should have housed half as many people as it actually did. She'd dropped out of school once she'd discovered she was pregnant. Throughout her pregnancy, Lori had suggested that Mary continue studying and eventually go for her GED.

"What's the point?" Mary had asked. "There aren't any jobs for people like me anyway."

While some in Whitehorn might turn away from the conditions at the reservation, Lori did not. She only wished there was more that she could do, besides assisting Kane once a week in a prenatal clinic. It was all very well and good to tell a woman that she needed to eat lots of fresh vegetables and fruit for a healthy diet, but such things didn't grow on trees—at least not in Montana in December, as one Native American woman had dryly noted.

Lori wasn't alone in doing volunteer work at the reservation. Along with volunteering for story hour at the Whitehorn library, Mary Jo Kincaid had done some work with the kids on the res, and Melissa North, the owner of the Hip Hop Café, was known to drop off food baskets regularly.

Jackson and Maggie Hawk had made remarkable strides in the past two years, but there was so much more that needed to be done. Conditions might not be as bad at the Laughing Horse Reservation as on some others, where the unemployment rate could run as high as ninety percent, but they were bad enough.

"You can't solve the world's problems," Lori's mom used to tell her. Still did, in fact, whenever she called from Phoenix, Arizona, where she and Lori's dad had moved shortly before Lori had gotten divorced.

"Maybe not, but I can try to fix things in my little corner of the world," Lori always replied.

Yet she hadn't been able to fix things with Travis....

Lori frowned. There he was, finagling his way into her thoughts once more!

She forcefully reminded herself that she couldn't afford to become vulnerable to him all over again. She still hadn't completely sorted out her reasons for making love with him. Being frank with herself, she admitted she was working hard not to think about him. Obviously not hard enough, however.

The professional in her took over. "So how's the breast-feeding going?" Lori asked Mary. As a health-care giver, Lori was interested in the entire pregnancy-birth experience, including encouraging new mothers to breast-feed immediately after delivery. As a woman, Lori longed to experience that bonding between mother and child herself.

"Fine. I was worried that it would hurt. But it doesn't. I position the baby the way you told me. She eats a lot! And often, too. Thanks for talking to me about all this."

"No problem. One of the most harmful myths about breast-feeding is that since it's a natural function, it will just come naturally to a new mother. It doesn't, so you need to ask questions. And remember that demand creates supply, so the more often Kate nurses, the more milk you'll have. If you have any questions, call me or call the consultant listed on the information sheet I gave you."

"You know, there are already so many kids in my house." Mary sighed. "I don't know where we're going to put Kate when I go home. My mom says we can empty a drawer and use it as a cradle. If it was good enough for me and my brothers and sisters, I guess it's good enough for my baby."

Lori knew that often in cases of teenage pregnancies, the mothers came to resent the babies for depriving them of their freedom to do as they pleased. But Mary had already had the responsibility of taking care of her younger brothers and sisters while growing up. Her pregnancy had been unplanned; the father had been killed in a car accident. Mary had told Lori she'd had intercourse with him only once, thinking nothing could happen the first time. Reality had proved her wrong. Lori had given her a quick course in birth control for future reference—facts, not fiction.

"The most important thing your baby needs is your love," Lori murmured.

"Love...and breast milk," Mary impudently added, before turning serious as she touched a fingertip to her baby's thatch of dark hair. "I know I said I didn't want another baby around the place. But this one is mine. It makes a difference, you know?"

Lori didn't know; she could only imagine—imagine what it would be like to have a baby that was part of you, that had come from your womb, nestled beneath your heart.

She blinked away the sudden threat of tears and vowed that someday soon she'd have a baby. Her own baby. And while she outwardly smiled and joked with Mary, she was making a silent vow to keep moving onward toward her goal of becoming a mother herself.

The next morning at the family practice, Molly and Lori were sharing a cup of coffee before the patients started arriving for the day. Lori had just tugged on her lavender lab coat over her black jeans and hot pink sweater, while Molly regaled her with the story of how she'd narrowly saved her gingerbread house from certain destruction.

"Little Billy had his hands on the gumdrops—you know, the ones around the base? He yanked two of them off before I could stop him. Luckily, I prevented him from stealing the peppermints from the windows," Molly said.

Lori thought the gingerbread house, an elaborate confection Molly created every year at this time, was a work of art, from the candy-cane front-porch pillars to the cotton puff coming out of the chimney. "I hope you moved your masterpiece to safer ground."

"You bet I did. I put it on top of the bookcase in the waiting room. Had to stand on a chair to do it, and then it took two of us to get it up there. Even Michael Jordan would have a hard time reaching it now."

"Good. I love your gingerbread houses. Maybe even more than the kids do."

"That reminds me, have you thought any more about the conversation we had on your birthday?" Molly asked. "About having a child of your own?"

"I've done nothing but think about it," Lori replied. She propped her chin on the heel of her hand and, with one finger, absently fiddled with her pink ice stud earring. It was her favorite thinking pose. "Danette, meanwhile, appears to have done nothing but *talk* about it. Would you believe that even Travis heard the gossip? He came pounding on my front door a few days ago, fit to be tied and laying down the law. Claimed he was there to talk some sense into me, but all he did was bellow. And darned if he didn't end up provoking me into placing one of those personal ads in the paper."

Molly's eyes widened with this news. "Travis suggested you place an ad in the newspaper?"

"No, of course not. He just dared me into doing it."

"You mean you actually did do it?"

Lori nodded and twirled her earring with her finger. "The ad ran yesterday."

"So, have you gotten any replies yet?"

"I don't know. The paper has a special 900 phone number for people to leave messages and make their replies. I haven't had time to check in there yet. I'll have to see."

"Call now," Molly urged.

"Now?"

"Sure. Why not? You've still got a few minutes before your first patient comes in."

"Okay. I suppose I might as well get it over with." Lori stood up and reluctantly called the number the newspaper had given her. Using the touch-tone phone, she followed the prerecorded directions to retrieve the messages for her ad's ID number. There were already more than a dozen replies. Some of them made her blood burn, some made her laugh, some made her eyebrows rise at their creativity. One sounded suspiciously like Travis. By the time she was done, Lori had a notebook filled with several phone numbers.

"Wow," Molly exclaimed, clearly impressed by the quantity of notes Lori had made. "You got all those messages after just one day?"

"I have a feeling Travis made half those calls to aggravate me," Lori muttered.

"How would he even know you placed the ad? Your name wasn't on it, right?"

"Right. You're right. I'm probably just being paranoid."

"So what's this note about corn syrup?" Molly asked, trying to decipher Lori's handwriting.

"One of the more-creative messages."

Reading further, Molly's eyes widened. "I'll say. Maybe you should pass that one on to me."

"If I did, your mother would shoot me."

"If you don't, *I'll* shoot you," Molly retorted with a grin.

"Don't get cocky, kid," Lori said in her most professional voice before ruining the affect by giving Molly a hug. "Come on, we've got patients to see."

After work that evening, Lori stopped by the post office to mail a Christmas box to her parents in Arizona. With the holidays so close, the line was long and it seemed to take forever. Her luck didn't improve as she ran into Travis, who was in town checking his post-office box.

"This isn't going to work, you know," he said, when she acted as if she were going to walk right past him without saying a word.

"What isn't?"

"This scheme of yours to drive me nuts. I know that's the only reason you went ahead and placed that ad."

"You flatter yourself."

"Are you denying that you did it because I said you couldn't?"

"Of course I deny it."

"Well...the only other explanation would be that you've taken complete leave of your senses."

Leave of her senses... His husky words echoed in her head. Senses...of touch, remembering the feel of him moving his hand over her skin in the church basement; of sight, remembering how he looked lowering his head to caress her breast with his wicked tongue. Visions flashed in her head like Polaroid shots, frozen for eternity. Her fingers thrust into his golden hair, her head tilted back as he slid into her...

"I know exactly what I'm doing," she croaked, through lips that had grown dry from the sensual pictures playing in her mind's eye.

"Well, if this is what you want, far be it from me to stand in your way."

His mocking tone of voice snapped her out of her daydream. "How generous of you," she noted sarcastically.

"In fact, I'll do whatever I can to help you."

She eyed him with extreme suspicion. "Meaning what?"

"Meaning I'll see what I can do to send a few likely candidates your way."

"Yeah, right." Lori didn't take Travis's threat seriously. "I'll believe that when I see it." She tossed his earlier words back at him—and lived to regret it, just as he had.

* * *

The knock on her door came three days later, on Sunday afternoon. A grizzled cowboy stood on her front step, his battered hat in hand. "Afternoon, ma'am. I'm here about the job."

"Job?" Lori repeated in confusion.

The man nodded, gave a smoker's pack-a-day, hacking cough, and then said, "Travis told me you was looking for a virile, able-bodied man. Here I am."

Four

"Excuse me?" Lori said, certain she couldn't have heard the man correctly. He'd pronounced virile as *vee*-rile.

Staring at him more closely, she recognized him as a ranch hand who'd worked off and on at Travis's ranch for some years now. The man was sixty if he was a day, and his coughing prevented him from replying to her question.

Taking hold of his arm, she ushered him inside. "You need something for that cough. I was just about to make some tea. Would you like a cup?"

The man nodded gratefully and followed her into the kitchen, which, luckily, was in good shape for visitors. Lori was still dressed in her cleaning clothes, in fact—jeans and an old red flannel shirt that had gone pale from so many washings. Her earrings were turquoise flowers.

"So...what's your name?" she asked the grizzled ranch hand.

"Granger."

"Well, Granger, your boss has a twisted sense of humor," she told him as she fixed him a mug of tea.

He took the proffered mug cautiously. "I don't like getting in between fighting married folks. Good way to get your head shot off."

"Travis and I aren't married. We're divorced. Have been for years."

"Look, I don't want to know any of the details. Travis just told me he'd excuse the four hundred bucks I owe him from our poker games if I'd show up here and say what I did."

Lori heaved a long-suffering sigh. "How many other men is he going to send over?"

"Darned if I know."

"Let me put it this way—how many other hands owe him money?"

"Don't rightly know, but one thing I can say is that Travis is a damn good poker player, if you'll pardon my French, ma'am. Wouldn't surprise me if a couple guys were in the hole to him."

"Great," she muttered.

"Would you mind a suggestion from a man who's been around long enough to know better than to give advice?"

"Go ahead."

"It never pays in the long run to rile a man like Travis."

"You mean a stubborn, mule-headed, anachronistic throwback to the Dark Ages like Travis?"

"Yeah, well...that's not rightly the way I'd put it," Granger said, "but I reckon it's close enough."

"Rest assured that it's not my intention to rile Travis deliberately. It just seems to happen. Now may I return the favor and give *you* some advice?"

"Didn't give no advice. Just gave a suggestion, that's all," Granger stated.

"Fine, a suggestion then. Cut down on the cigarettes. They'll do you in," she said bluntly.

"I'm as hardy as a horse." His claim was cut short by his hacking cough.

"A horse with emphysema maybe," Lori countered. "Think about it, okay?"

The grizzled cowboy nodded reluctantly.

"And try drinking some hot lemon toddies for that cold." Lori knew men well enough to know that calling it a toddy, rather than saying it was a hot lemonade, made it easier for them to swallow, somehow. "Add a touch of honey," she reminded him, as she led him to the front door.

"Will do. Thank you, ma'am."

"And one more thing. You tell Travis you paid your debt in full, and if he gives you any grief, you come to me. What's so funny?" she demanded.

"You sure are a feisty little thing."

Lori grimaced. "*Feisty* isn't my favorite word," she said.

"Heard it a lot, have you?"

She nodded. "It comes with the turf. You have to be a stubborn cuss to be a midwife."

"It's that hard birthing babies, huh?"

"No, it's that hard dealing with other people's prejudices about midwives. Birthing babies is a piece of cake next to that," she noted with a tired smile.

"Good luck to you," Granger said with a chivalrous nod of his head.

"Same to you, Granger."

Lori was on call most evenings. One of the two physicians at the family practice did cover for her on alternate Fridays and special occasions. She could still remember how thrilled she'd been when she'd first gotten her beeper. She'd fastened it on the belt of her jeans and felt like she'd arrived.

Three years and many interrupted hours of sleep later, the thrill was gone—but not the responsibility. She always double-checked the batteries each morning to make sure her beeper was working, and today was no exception.

The device was quiet as she headed out of town Monday evening to pay Winona Cobbs a visit at her unique place of business. Located about twenty miles northeast of town, the Stop 'N' Swap was something of a local landmark. It had certainly been there for as long as Lori could remember. Some called it a junkyard. Some called it a treasure trove. Winona called it home.

Along with selling everything from porcelain sinks to Studebaker hubcaps, Winona also put up the best honey in the state. Lori's supply was running low. Besides, she liked visiting Winona. The woman had a way about her. And she invariably found things for Lori that she didn't even know she needed. Like that neat wooden table that Lori had ended up painting white and setting in her bathroom.

Winona was special, all right, which is why Lori had brought along a Christmas present for her. Reaching out, Lori touched the small wrapped present—a pair of rose-quartz-crystal earrings—on the car seat beside her to make sure she hadn't left them behind.

Her headlights were the only beacons in the wintery darkness. As she cautiously pulled into the lane leading from the highway to Winona's place, Lori was glad of the fact that her vehicle had four-wheel drive. She'd have gotten stuck in the snow for sure without it. Winona's drive wasn't exactly in the middle of any snowplow's route.

Winona greeted her warmly, sitting her right down in her dining area and getting her a cup of tea sweetened with her best honey. A garish plastic cactus almost as tall as Winona served as her Christmas tree. The thing was decorated with tiny lights, while a tinfoil star was precariously perched on top.

"I can't see killing a tree just to haul it inside for two weeks and then toss it out," Winona stated. "And I think those fake ones are depressing. But I like this one. Thank you for the present." She carefully set it under the cactus. "I'll save it for Christmas Eve, if you don't mind."

"I don't mind. It's just a little something—a thank-you for all your help. That table you gave me last time I was out here was perfect, just like you said."

"A little paint made it look a lot better, right?"

Trying to relax and keep her mind off Travis, Lori nodded, looking around. A dog Lori hadn't seen before was curled up near the small couch, while four or five cats were snoozing on the couch itself. Winona was forever taking in strays, especially at this time of year.

Short and stout, Winona had the kind of internal energy that defied age. No one knew exactly how old she was, and she certainly wasn't saying.

"Something's wrong," Winona abruptly stated in that unique voice of hers.

Startled, Lori's gaze shot back to her. "Are you getting a premonition?" she asked, aware that her friend was known for having psychic abilities.

Winona shook her head, her gray hair flying in every direction. Sometimes she kept it in a braid, but even then strands were forever coming loose.

"Then how can you tell that something is wrong?" Lori asked.

"Body language," Winona replied bluntly. "If you grab that teacup any tighter, it's going to break," she noted dryly. "A blind man could see that you're more than a little uptight."

"You could say that." Laughing ruefully, Lori loosened her hold on the mismatched tea set—the cup fine porcelain with a rose pattern, the saucer earthenware, with pears painted around the edge.

"You want to talk about it?" Winona inquired.

Lori shrugged. "I wouldn't know where to start."

"The beginning is usually a good place."

"The beginning, huh? Well, let's see . . . I had a significant birthday a short while ago and it got me to thinking—thinking about what I want out of life."

Winona nodded, absently fingering the large amethyst crystal she wore around her neck. "I sensed that you'd reached a crossroads."

"There are just so many choices."

"More choices than when I was your age," Winona acknowledged.

"Do you ever regret the decisions you made?" Lori asked.

Winona shook her head.

"What about children? Do you ever regret that you didn't have any?"

"Not really." Winona shook her head again. "Some folks are cut out to be parents. And that's all well and good. I guess I'm just not one of them. But you are, aren't you?"

Lori nodded.

"So what are you doing about it?" Winona asked.

"I'm considering my options. And arguing with people about them."

"People?"

"Mostly Travis," Lori admitted.

Winona nodded. "I sensed as much. A lot of negative energy—although that could just be due to the dry air in here," she added. "All I have to do is walk across the trailer and I end up getting shocked with a spark as long as my finger. We're talking some powerful static electricity around here! I've often wondered if it might affect my psychic abilities one way or another. But back to you and Travis. What are the two of you arguing about? Having a baby?"

"Yes. Well, not exactly. That is to say, my decision to have a baby shouldn't affect Travis one way or another."

"You don't want to have his baby?" Winona asked, sounding surprised by this news.

"We're divorced. It's not a good idea to have a baby with your ex-husband, Winona."

"I wouldn't know." Winona frowned and stared just above Lori's head, as if she saw something fascinating there.

"What is it?" Lori demanded. "Are you getting another premonition?"

"Hmm? No, I was just staring at that spider on the ceiling there. Blasted things bite, you know."

So much for Winona's psychic input, Lori thought to herself.

As if sensing her discouraged mood, Winona patted Lori's hand comfortingly. "Things will all work out, you'll see. You'll get that baby you want."

"How do you know?"

"Because I know you. And I know how much determination you have when you discover what it is that you want.

Deciding what you want may be the hardest part for you,'' she astutely observed. "But once you make up your mind, there's no stopping you. Look what you've done with your work, going off to the big city and learning to be a mid-wife.''

"Some people aren't as pleased by that as you are.''

"What people?''

"Dr. Straker, for one.''

"He doesn't qualify as a person. He's an arrogant little toad,'' Winona stated.

"You won't get any argument from me there.''

"He's been giving you a hard time?''

"I'm not exactly at the top of his hit parade.''

"The idiot has no taste. He actually had the nerve to haggle with me over Harry.''

"Harry?''

"The moose head. The one I keep above the cash regis-ter in the store. Straker tried to get me to sell him Harry for a measly nine bucks. I told him he could put his money where the sun don't shine, 'cause my Harry ain't for sale. He hasn't shown his skinny butt here again—Straker, not Harry.''

Lori couldn't help it; she cracked up. "Oh, Winona, you're so good for me,'' she gasped, wiping tears of mirth from her eyes. "You've got your head screwed on right.''

"Why, thanks!'' Winona beamed. "Not many folks 'round here would agree with you, though. 'Bout me hav-ing my head screwed on right. Everyone sees me differ-ently, but they think I'm a character.'' Winona popped a wad of chewing gum into her mouth. "And I like it that way. So don't go spreading no rumors 'bout me being nor-mal, got that? Might be bad for business,'' she added with a grin.

"Your secret is safe with me,'' Lori assured her with a wide smile.

"And yours is safe with me.''

"The fact that I want a baby isn't exactly a secret.''

"Maybe not, but the fact that you're still attracted to Travis is." Seeing Lori's startled look, Winona sat back and smiled smugly. "I'm psychic, remember?"

"I think that static electricity is giving you false readings," Lori retorted.

Winona shook her head, the amethyst crystal she wore gleaming in the light. "Nope. I can feel it. You and Travis making sparks. Feels like old times, huh?"

"Do the words *Been There, Did That* mean anything to you?"

Winona shook her head again, popping a bubble in her chewing gum at the same time.

"Travis and I are a thing of the past. I'm certainly not going to make the mistake of getting hooked up with him again."

"There's no fighting fate," Winona said, her tone of voice making it plain that there was no more to be said.

"No fighting fate, huh?" An hour later, Lori was still muttering under her breath about Winona's words. Even though she was now back in town and was in fact grabbing some groceries for dinner, she still couldn't get over Winona's unshakable conviction about Travis.

As if thinking about him was enough to make him appear, Travis strolled into the food market. Lori was actually glad to see him—and she told herself it was because now she could confront him face-to-face. She hadn't forgotten Granger's appearance on her front step yesterday.

"Nice try," she stated as she wheeled her cart past Travis in a smooth curve that would have done a figure skater proud.

Travis gave her an innocent look that didn't fool her for one second. "Sending your hired hand over yesterday afternoon," she elaborated, at his deliberately baffled expression.

"Oh, that. I was just being helpful."

"So how many other helpful prospects are you sending over?" Lori inquired, while selecting a head of lettuce from the fresh produce piled nearby. "Perhaps it's time to put up that sign I've got."

"What sign?"

"The one that says I shoot every third solicitor, and the second one just left."

"We picked that sign up near Glacier when we were on our honeymoon."

"Did we?" She set the lettuce into her cart and started inspecting the tomatoes. "I don't remember."

"Liar."

"I beg your pardon?" she said haughtily.

"You *should* beg my pardon, after the shenanigans you've been up to these past few weeks."

Turning, with a tomato in hand, she said, "How many times do I have to tell you—"

"You can tell me until your face turns blue." Reaching out, Travis brushed his index finger over her lips. "Won't make a bit of difference."

Lori clung to the poor tomato with both hands now, bruising the sensitive object with her grip. It was that or *lose* her grip, as Travis created magic with the simplicity of his touch. She was standing in the middle of a public place—a crowded food market, with canned Christmas music blaring in the background while the cashier called for a price check in Lane One. Lori heard all this, yet it seemed distant somehow. The imminent anticipation of his touch put everything else on the back burner. He circled her bottom lip and skimmed his fingertip across the curves of her upper lip.

She stared at him as if caught in the headlights of an oncoming eighteen-wheeler. *Yeah, and you're likely to end up as road kill if you keep standing here like this,* a mocking inner voice came to her rescue by saying. What on earth was wrong with her? Why was she letting Travis get to her this way?

Look at him, she ordered herself. Look closely. Take note of that expression in his eyes. He's pleased he's getting to you. He's doing this deliberately.

Just as deliberately, she opened her mouth and bit his caressing finger—not hard enough to hurt him, but firmly enough to let him know she meant business.

Travis, curse his black soul, just grinned at her and brought his finger to his mouth as if he intended to taste her teeth marks on his skin.

"This isn't the first time you've put your mark on me," he noted in a husky voice. "I seem to recall a certain incredible incident in a church basement about three weeks ago—"

"Hush!" Lori looked around nervously before grabbing her cart and heading toward Aisle Two.

"What the matter?" Travis demanded, hot on her trail. "Are you ashamed of what happened?"

"I don't want everyone in Whitehorn knowing about it."

"Oh, that's rich. You don't care that everyone in town thinks you've gone off the deep end."

"They do not. Winona is on my side."

Travis snorted. "Like she's a pillar of society dos and don'ts."

"Winona is a very wise woman."

"Who runs a junk shop out of her front yard."

"That's just one of many things she does."

"Yeah, she also reads your future by the lines in your forehead, too."

"She does not!" Infuriated, Lori punched Travis in the arm—not doing much damage, thanks to the thick sheepskin jacket he wore. "She happens to have many talents, including harvesting the best honey in the state. Oh, I don't know why I even bother talking to you. You're impossible. Winona is as sane as Homer is."

"Homer is just a loner," Travis said defensively.

"Who thinks he was kidnapped by aliens."

Travis sidestepped that one by saying, "He knows these hills better than anyone else."

"Except for Winona."

"You two gonna stand there jawing all day or are you gonna get out of the way of the corn chips?" Virgil demanded. "Geez, a man could starve waiting for you two to stop arguing." Grabbing a handful of corn-chip bags, the cook from the Hip Hop Café made a quick getaway.

"Homer is a changed man since his daughter came back," Travis stated, returning to his defense of the town eccentric—one of them, anyway. "Having family changes a man."

"And a woman," Lori noted quietly. "That's why I aim on getting a family—a child—of my own."

"A baby isn't something you add to the shopping list like a gallon of milk," Travis argued. "It's not something you pick up at the market."

"I know what it takes to have a baby," she retorted, "and believe me, I mean to do whatever is necessary to reach my dream." Pivoting her shopping cart in a 180 degree turn, Lori left him speechless in the snacks aisle.

The next prospect showed up on her doorstep the following evening. Like the previous one, this candidate stood with his hat in hand. Unlike the previous one, he didn't look old enough to drive, let alone shave. His fingers, nervously twirling his hat, were trembling—from terror more than from cold, she suspected.

A chinook had been blowing all day, bringing with it the tantalizing taste of spring. It was a fake promise, of course. Winter hadn't even officially begun yet. The warmer weather lulled you into a false sense of security—right before walloping you with a subzero cold front or half a foot of snow.

Kind of like her relationship with Travis, Lori noted. The passion they'd shared had been a tantalizing taste, but a false one.

Because there was no going back. Lori was a different woman now than she had been when she'd been married to Travis. She could only move onward.

"Ma'am?" The young cowboy's voice cracked, forcing him to clear his throat and try again. "Ma'am, I'm here about the job."

"Don't tell me, let me guess," Lori said wryly. "Travis sent you, right?"

The boy gulped, his Adam's apple leapfrogging in his skinny neck, before nodding.

Lori took pity on him. "Come on in and have a cup of coffee. Don't worry, I don't bite."

"No, ma'am."

"No, you don't want coffee?" She'd never met a cowboy yet, regardless of how young, who refused a free cup of coffee on a winter's night.

"No, ma'am. I mean, yes, ma'am. Coffee would be nice."

Coming inside, the youth wiped his scuffed boots five times on the mat before venturing into the room. The now nearly crumpled hat remained a permanent fixture in his hand.

"So how much did you lose to Travis in your poker game?" Lori asked conversationally.

"Seventy-five dollars, ma'am."

"My name is Lori. 'Ma'am' makes me feel old enough to be your grandmother." There was an awkward silence as the youth gulped his coffee. "So what's your name?"

"Tommy, ma'am. I mean Lori, ma'am."

She sighed. Had she ever been this young?

Ten minutes later, Tommy had relaxed enough to shyly ask for Lori's advice on his love life and a certain sixteen-year-old girl she knew. Lori had a knack of making people open up and confide in her, to trust her with their hopes and fears. That ability made her a better midwife.

When the cowboy left a short while later, his hat still in hand, he had a relieved grin on his face. Lori had promised to break the ice on his behalf with the girl of his choice.

Half an hour later, there was another knock on her front door. It was Homer. "I'm here about the job," he said.

Five

Lori couldn't help it. She freaked. "Not you, too!" she ranted. "Travis has gone too far this time! I don't believe him. And I don't believe you. How could you agree to do this? You must owe him money big time for him to have gotten to you, too. Well, let me tell you that this has gone on long enough!"

When she finally had to pause to draw in breath, Homer bluntly declared, "I have no idea what in tarnation you're talking about. I'm here about that handyman job you mentioned a few months back. Said you wanted a couple of rooms painted and some shelves built. You remember that?"

"Oh." Lori felt like sinking into the carpet. "Right. Of course, I remember. I'm sorry I misunderstood, Homer."

He shrugged. "You still want the work done or what?"

"Yes, of course I do. Are you going to be able to take on the job?" Lori was well aware that Homer worked to his own timetable and no one else's.

Homer nodded. "I could use the money, what with the holidays coming up."

"Are you sure you've recovered from that bout with pneumonia you had?" she asked in concern.

Homer's nod was impatient this time. "Don't go fussing over me. My daughter is doing enough of that already. I don't need any more mollycoddling."

Sensing that the man's pride was at stake here, she said, "In that case, when would you be able to start?"

"Tomorrow soon enough?"

"Tomorrow will be fine. Shall I give you a key so you can get in while I'm working?"

Homer nodded again.

"I've already bought the paint," Lori proudly stated, pointing to the cans she had stored near the front door.

"'Calypso'?" Homer read from the label in disbelief. "What kind of a name is that for a paint?"

"I picked it because of the color, not the name of the paint," she said somewhat defensively. "It's a lovely shade of rose."

"Humph." Homer's snort was often mimicked but never duplicated. No one else could produce the same element of disgruntled disapproval.

After seeing Homer out, Lori was about to close her front door when she heard what sounded like a cat's meow. Going out onto the porch, she peered into the front yard. She saw a startling pair of luminescent green eyes first. Then, as her own eyes adjusted to the darkness, she saw a small cat sitting a good distance away, poised as if to race off at a second's notice.

The look in the cat's eyes caught at Lori's heart, and she found herself going inside, opening a can of tuna, pouring some into a plastic dish and putting it out on the lawn. "Here, kitty, kitty," she softly called. The cat didn't come when called, of course, but Lori hoped she'd come back and eat some of the tuna later on. The poor thing had looked half starved.

Reluctantly going back inside, Lori started brooding again about Travis's outrageous behavior in sending over 'prospects.' She hadn't had the heart to have young Tommy take a message back to Travis—the kid had been trembling in his boots as it was. No, it wasn't fair to involve others in this battle of wills between herself and Travis. Her ex-husband had her so rattled she'd almost bitten poor Homer's head off. The old man probably thought she was crazy. Which was just what Travis wanted.

Staring at the phone, she decided to call him. Recognizing his voice as he said hello, she skipped the pleasantries and got right down to business.

"Stop this nonsense, Travis," she stated.

"I will if you will," he smoothly countered.

"Were you this impossible when we were married?" she muttered, half under her breath.

"Why don't you tell me? You never did say why you took off."

She shifted in her seat, uncomfortable with this topic of conversation. "We were smothering each other."

"I didn't feel smothered."

"Well, *I* did," she said.

"I thought you said I spent too much time working on the ranch. How could I smother you if I was never around, the way you claimed?"

Lori rubbed a line on her forehead. "I don't know."

"So you don't even know why you divorced me?"

"We wanted different things."

"Seems to me that we wanted the same things when we were in that church basement."

"You're never going to let me forget that, are you?"

"Damn right!"

"There's no talking to you," she sputtered. "Just stop sending over your ridiculous prospects."

"I'm just helping you out in the stud-sperm search."

"Your two guys don't qualify," she retorted.

"I do," he drawled.

She hung up on him. How had her life gotten so complicated?

As she wearily got ready for bed, she realized she was no closer to finding an answer to that or any of the million questions buzzing around in her head. Travis's challenging her about her reasons for divorcing him brought old insecurities to mind. Because she still didn't know exactly where she and Travis had gone wrong. She couldn't point at any one incident, one fight, that had been the turning point.

And that made it difficult, for how could she learn by her past mistakes if she didn't know exactly what they were? It was scarier for her not to have something definite to pin their breakup on.

Yes, they'd grown apart. The question was why. Because he'd been trying to save the ranch, while she was trying to get her nursing degree? Or because they'd been trying to make ends meet and kept coming out on the short end of the stick, with the unpaid bills never seeming to go away?

Had they broken up because Travis was stubborn and old-fashioned, because he didn't want her having a life of her own, because it felt as if he didn't give her room to grow as a person? Or was it that they wanted different things out of life? It was true that Travis was happy as a clam out on the ranch, never leaving for weeks on end, while Lori found she needed to interact with people more.

On the heels of those thoughts came the fiery memory of their lovemaking a few weeks ago. Other men just couldn't compare to Travis—didn't even come close. But good sex didn't make a good marriage.

So what did make a good marriage? There was clearly no such thing as a perfect relationship. Maybe love just complicated things. Maybe it was better to have respect for one another, to share the same values and want the same things in life. Maybe that was a better foundation for a lasting relationship than the volatility of passion or the frailties of love.

But that's what she'd thought she had with Kane—a common background in medicine, along with friendship and respect. That relationship hadn't worked, either.

Lori had been burned, not once but twice, by two different men in two totally different kinds of relationships. Which left her feeling scared that maybe she wouldn't be able to sustain a successful relationship with any man. And if that was the case, then she might never have a baby the usual way.

Logically, she realized that, these days, thirty wasn't that old to be having her biological clock ticking. But she was tired of waiting for Mr. Wonderful to come sweep her off her feet; she wanted to have a baby *soon*. As she fell asleep, her last thought was of holding an infant of her own in her arms.

Lori spent Wednesday morning making a house call on a patient, Kaye Ingalls, who has having a hard time with morning sickness. "I was ready to kill my husband yesterday!" Kaye declared.

"What did he do?"

"He thought was was being helpful by cleaning out the fridge. Next thing I know he's waving an open can of salmon under my nose, wanting to know if it was still good. Two seconds later I was racing to the bathroom to throw up. I've done nothing but throw up since I got pregnant. And don't tell me to grin and bear it!"

"I wasn't about to," Lori assured her.

"And crackers are the pits."

"I have a few more tricks up my sleeve. First off, try eating several small meals instead of three large ones. That way you'll keep some food in your stomach at all times."

"Keeping food in my stomach doesn't seem to work," Kaye moaned.

"Because your nose is getting in the way. Not anatomically speaking, of course," Lori said dryly. "Avoid odors that upset you—and keep note of which ones do bother you, so you can avoid those in future. Perfumes, cleaning solutions, fish—all can have strong smells and hit you the wrong way."

"The smell of scrambled eggs makes me green just thinking about it."

"Then don't cook scrambled eggs, and avoid anyone who is cooking them."

"That means avoiding my husband."

"Only when he's cooking eggs," Lori said with a grin. "Get plenty of rest, but don't get into a rut. Get out and spend some time with a relative or a friend, to try and keep your mind off the nausea."

"The nausea isn't in my mind!" Kaye declared.

"I know it isn't. Unfortunately, we still don't know much about the cause of morning sickness."

"If men had this, we'd know the cause and have a cure by now," Kaye muttered.

"You're probably right. But for now it's a disease of theories. Some think it's caused by hormone levels, others by vitamin deficiencies. But no study has been conclusive. We have been making strides in treating the symptoms, however. In fact, I've brought something for you."

"I'm nervous about taking medication," Kaye said.

"That would be a last resort. Try this instead." Lori handed her a small paper bag.

Opening it, Kaye exclaimed, "Lemon hard candies?"

Lori nodded. "Helps with a lot of my patients. I also had one woman who swore by watermelon-flavored lollipops, so you see, we can try a number of things besides crackers."

"Thank heavens!"

"You might also try sipping some ginger tea, or try peppermint tea, if you prefer. I'll check back with you tomorrow afternoon and see if you're feeling better. And if you should get the urge to eat anything, even if it may seem strange, eat it. It's important at this point that you don't go off your feed, so to speak," she said in rancher terminology that Kaye, a rancher's wife, could relate to.

"Thanks, Lori."

Lori's next stop was the No Bull Ranch, home to Maris and Luke Rivers. Maris had been her friend since they'd been kids. Maris had had her share of sorrow—her first husband, Ray, had been a lazy, irresponsible, no-good rodeo rider who'd died while driving under the influence, plowing his pickup into a cement pier. Maris had been left a widow, in debt up to her eyeballs.

A weaker woman would have given up. But Maris was the strongest one Lori knew. She was a no-frills kind of person—what you saw was what you got.

And what Lori saw when Maris opened the door was a woman who radiated happiness. Not only had Maris found love in the form of Luke Rivers, who'd originally come to the ranch to recoup a debt owed him by Ray, but now the happily married couple had a baby—Clay, Lori's godson.

Maris held Clay in her arms as she opened the door. "Hold still, you little rascal," she said. "Lori!"

"I hope you don't mind my dropping by without calling first. I was out this way visiting a patient—"

"Get in here. You know you don't need to call." Maris was dressed in her customary worn jeans and a T-shirt, her long, honey-brown hair gathered in a ponytail.

"I wanted to drop these by. Here, I'll trade you." Lori handed Maris the bag filled with Christmas presents she'd brought along, while taking the baby in exchange.

"You've been going overboard with those catalogs of yours again," Maris noted.

But Lori wasn't listening. She was nuzzling Clay, inhaling the sweet smell of baby.

Seeing what she was doing, Maris said, "Sure he smells good now, but you wouldn't have wanted to get within three feet of him a few minutes ago. Whew!" She waved her hand under her nose.

Lori smiled but made no reply. The truth was, smell or no, she wanted one of these little miracles. In fact, for the first time in their long friendship, Lori envied Maris. Envied her *deeply*. Because Maris had what Lori wanted most. A family.

"I'm glad you stopped by," Maris was saying. "I haven't seen you in a while."

"I can't stay," she replied, afraid that if she did linger, Maris would pick up on the jealousy bubbling deep within her. "Do you know how lucky you are?" she murmured.

"Sure, I do," Maris said, clearly thinking Lori was putting her on.

Although it hurt to do so, Lori handed Clay back before she gave in to the temptation to hug him and never let him go. "I've got to get going."

"Wait! Don't forget to take your present." Maris handed her a small box. "Sorry it's not wrapped very fancy. I was never very good at that kind of thing."

Lori knew that what she wanted most—a child—was something that Maris couldn't give her. But it was something Lori could have—providing she wanted it badly enough. And she did.

When Lori found herself out near Travis's ranch after making another house call nearby, she decided to pay her ex-husband a little unannounced visit. She couldn't let him continue to get away with this—she'd found another prospect waiting for her when she'd left her house this morning. Like Granger, the man had been old enough to be her grandfather. This had to stop. Her anger overrode her nervousness at returning to the ranch for the first time since the divorce.

The place hadn't changed much. The ranch house had received a new coat of white paint since she'd left five years ago. And Tex had finally gotten her way in painting the window shutters red to match the barn, instead of black. Smoke was coming out of the chimney in the gabled roof, which meant there was a fire going in the huge fieldstone fireplace in the living room.

Tex greeted Lori at the back door. "What did Travis do now?" she asked in resignation.

"He's trying to drive me crazy," Lori declared.

"He claims the same thing about you," the housekeeper noted with a smile before turning and heading back to her oven filled with cookies.

"Well, he's wrong," Lori stated, automatically tugging off her Wellington boots in the mud room. The earthy smells

of wet leather, horses and denim mixed with the more tantalizing scents of Tex's home cooking—and she was always
cooking something—were familiar. "I'm just trying to live
my own life. And he's getting in the way."

"Men," Tex muttered. "You can't live with 'em and you
can't shoot 'em."

Lori had to smile at this often-spoken observation. The
older woman had been at the ranch the entire time of Lori's
marriage. Tex had been there; maybe she could give Lori
some insight into what had gone wrong. "I think Travis and
I fight now more than we did when we were married," she
noted ruefully.

"Beware of puppy love, it leads to a dog's life."

Lori attempted to translate. "You mean you think Travis
and I were too young to get married?"

"Maybe just too young to *stay* married," Tex said.

The differentiation struck Lori as being an important one,
something that hadn't occurred to her before. At eighteen
and nineteen, had she and Travis been too young, too im-
mature to handle the required give-and-take of a marriage?
Staying married was hard work at times, especially those
times when the aura of romance had been vaporized by the
harsh light of reality.

"How about a cup of my famous hot chocolate and some
sugar cookies before you go out and strangle Travis?" Tex
interrupted Lori's thoughts to say. "We don't get that many
visitors."

At her words, Lori felt a flash of guilt for not having kept
up her relationship with Tex. The two of them had been
close while Lori had been married to Travis. But since her
return to Whitehorn, Lori hadn't done more than say hi to
Tex when she'd seen her in town.

But it had been an awkward situation all around. After
all, the older woman's first loyalty lay with Travis. She'd
practically raised him, his mother having died when he was
just a toddler.

"You're fretting," Tex stated. "I can always tell when you're fretting, just like I can always tell when Travis is lying."

"Does he do that very often? Lie, I mean?"

"Only if he thinks he's protecting someone he loves. Travis is a good man, Lori."

"I know that. He's also an impossible one."

"Can't argue with you there," Tex acknowledged with a slow smile. "Go on, I can tell you're dying to talk to him. We'll share that cup of cocoa another time. You'll find Travis out in the barn. Try not to get too violent out there, though. Slim is getting too old to be dragging any unconscious bodies back into the house."

Lori found Travis pitchforking new hay into an empty horse stall in the barn. The unseasonably warm weather continued, with the temperature currently in the low fifties, turning the barnyard into a muddy quagmire. Lori's Wellingtons had protected her from the worst of the mess. Her irritation protected her from Travis's charm as he looked up from his work to grin at her. "Well, this is a surprise. To what do I owe this honor?" He was dressed in his customary work clothes of jeans and a white T-shirt covered with a denim shirt. Resting one arm on the pitchfork handle, he looked devilishly handsome.

"I'm here to tell you to lay off," Lori stated.

"Lay?" His gaze wandered to a bale of hay nearby.

Lori felt herself blushing. She knew what he was thinking as clearly as if he'd put his thoughts in skywriting twelve feet high.

"Stop that," she muttered, flustered by his ability to get to her without him even saying a word. All he had to do was look at her with those blue eyes of his, a smoky look filled with the promise of passion and remembered secrets.

"Stop what?" Travis murmured, his voice as seductive as his stare had been.

"That." Her voice was a whisper now.

"Make me," he dared her.

"I'm not that gullible,"

"No? Well, maybe *I* am." And then he kissed her.

Six

Lori should have been prepared. But she wasn't. Not for the rush of magic, the feeling of rightness, the incredible surge of passion. Until that moment, she'd hoped that her memories of their fiery lovemaking a few weeks ago had somehow been blown out of proportion.

But that hope died an instant death as he nibbled on her bottom lip, coaxing her to part her lips—which she did. The thrust of his tongue erotically mimicked the plunging possession of their lovemaking, making her want things... making her want *him*.

Forbidden. She knew Travis was forbidden fruit. But as he hungrily probed very curve and corner of her mouth, she was helpless to resist the raw pleasure coursing through her.

She'd *never* been kissed the way Travis kissed her. Passionately. As if she were the reason he drew breath. As if she were the only woman in the universe for him.

His kiss was a sensual declaration of possession and intent. It was hot and intimate, bold and demanding. Her tongue met his in a slick reunion, a tempestuous tussle with no single victor.

Murmuring her name, he tugged her closer. Now she was pressed tightly against him, from shoulder to hip. His hands eagerly shoved aside her denim jacket in their impatient quest to cup her breasts. The pink Oxford shirt she wore provided little protection against the potent power of his touch.

Lori shivered with unmitigated delight. It felt so good for him to be caressing her this way. She pressed closer as one kiss slid into another, each one wetter and rougher than the last.

For there was nothing gentle about the need coursing through her. Nothing subtle about the way her nipples tautened against the thin cotton of her shirt. Her breath caught as he intensified her pleasure by brushing his thumbs over the sensitized tips of her breasts. Her knees weakened, forcing her to lean into him in order to remain upright.

Her hips were now cradled by his as he rubbed against her in a motion as old as time itself. She felt him throbbing against her, knew his need, for it was mirrored by her own. It was wild and powerful, all-consuming.

"Yes, sweet darlin'," Travis whispered in a raspy voice. "You can feel it, too. You want it, too."

His use of that old-time endearment brought Lori to her senses faster than getting dunked in a horse trough filled with cold water.

She wasn't eighteen any longer. Travis couldn't kiss her into agreeing with him. She was her own person now.

Jumping back into the fire with him—tempting though it might be—was the worst thing she could do at this point in her life. It hadn't been easy leaving Travis once. Lori wasn't sure she had the strength to do it again. And five years of marriage had proved that they couldn't live together. They hadn't been able to make a go of it, despite the great love they'd had for each other in the beginning.

Now Lori didn't know *what* she felt for Travis. She didn't want to feel anything. *"No!"* The word was as much for her own benefit as for his, and she shouted it even as she pushed him away. "No," she repeated. "I'm not going to do this. I'm not going to let you con me back into bed with you."

"This is no con," he retorted, taking her hand and placing it on the taut placket of his jeans. "It doesn't get realer than that, sweetheart."

She yanked her hand back, furious with herself for the spark of arousal his outrageous action had instigated. "What is this—a game for you?" she demanded.

"You're the one playing games," Travis countered. "Starting with placing that stupid ad in the paper."

"It wasn't stupid," she declared. "I've gotten a lot of response from it."

"I'm sure you have. You walk into half the bars between here and Billings, and you'd get the same response."

"You have the subtlety of a bull," she snapped before turning on her heel and storming out, feeling as if she'd done this scene a million times before, which of course she had. Perhaps not a million, but a number of times during the later years of their marriage she'd gotten too angry with him to even stay in the same room.

"Good luck with that stud-sperm search of yours," Travis called after her.

Lori told him what he could do with his stupid phrase in the most unladylike of terms.

She was practically shaking with anger as she drove out of the yard, taking pleasure in the fact that the spin of her wheels threw up a wash of mud that hit Travis smack in the chest.

But by the time she reached the main road, Lori felt guilty about her temper tantrum. Of course, Travis would try the patience of a saint—that went without saying. But she shouldn't have let him get to her the way he had. And she certainly should *not* have let him kiss her. That had been a really dumb thing to do.

Once he started kissing her, she should have stood there like a fence post and not responded at all. Instead she'd melted faster than snow during a thaw. Not very bright. What had she been thinking of?

The bottom line was that she hadn't been *thinking* at all, of course. Who could when they were being kissed senseless? When they were having their heart stolen?

Not heart, she reminded herself. This was merely a physical remainder of their marriage. She and Travis had been attracted to each other from the time they'd first met in high school. There were bound to be some residual aftereffects

from that. And that's what happened when he kissed her.
She got caught up in residual attraction.

Yeah, she liked that term; it made it seem like something
in the past, something that she could get over. She'd made
great strides since her divorce. She wasn't going to start
backpedaling now.

But she'd also missed a lot—missed having someone special there to share good news with, to cuddle with at night,
to look after her when she was sick, to care for her and
about her.

As she drove on, the radio played a song that asked who
picked up the pieces when two fools collide. Lori decided
that described her and Travis in a nutshell: two fools who
kept colliding.

It didn't make sense that she'd been able to keep her distance for the past three years, only to step into quicksand
now. Of course, the secret had been to *keep* her distance.
She should try to do that again. Forget Travis; stay away
from him. Banish him from her thoughts and concentrate
on her goal of having a baby.

With the day going as badly as it had so far, Lori should
have known better than to stop at the bank after work that
evening in order to use the automated teller. But she was out
of money, and she needed to pick up some stuff for dinner.
To her dismay, the machine made a meal of her cash card.

"Spit it out," she shouted, banging the front of it with the
palm of her hand. To her vivid imagination, it seemed as if
the machine simply belched and began digesting her card.

Great. Now what was she supposed to do? The bank was
closed until tomorrow.

There comes a time when it's wise to admit defeat and live
to fight another day, she reminded herself as she marched
back to her four-wheel-drive station wagon. The car already had almost 100,000 miles on it, and she planned on
keeping it for another 50,000. They didn't make this model
anymore, but she loved it. At least her car was still depend-

able. More dependable than any man—even ones that kissed as incredibly as Travis did.

"I've never heard 'Jingle Bells' sung as a ballad before," Lori told Virgil at rehearsal later that evening. "It's very...innovative."

"I wanted to give it that Frank Sinatra touch, you know?" he replied.

Virgil had sounded more like Tiny Tim on steroids than Frank Sinatra, but Lori didn't have the heart to tell him that.

"Okay, listen up, the rest of you." The straggling group of maybe twelve people were huddled around the food table like cows in a blizzard. "After my 'Jingle Bells' solo, we go right into... Doggone it, someone moved my notes. Lily Mae, did you touch my notes?"

"Of course not."

"He can't hit a note to save his life, can he?" Molly whispered from beside her.

"What are you doing here?"

Molly shrugged sheepishly. "I got roped in, too. I fought as long as I could."

"Ah, good—another soprano," Virgil declared. "Go stand over there." He pointed to the right side of the church.

"The rest of the sopranos are on the left," Lily Mae reminded Virgil, who glared at her.

"I knew that. I was just testin' to see if anyone was payin' attention."

Lori was amused to see that Travis's young ranch hand, Tommy, was chatting up the girl of his choice over a dish of decorated Santa cookies. Clearly he was only here because she was. The advice Lori had given him the other night seemed to be working.

"Looks like a case of love," Molly noted.

"'Beware of puppy love, it can lead to a dog's life,'" Lori answered, quoting Tex.

"Who told you that?"

"A wise woman."

"Wise woman? We've only got wise men in this pageant," Virgil noted. "No wise women. The school is doin' that part of things, anyways. All we have to do is sing."

"Hopefully on key," someone added.

"Who said that?" Virgil demanded, looking around as if searching for the ghost of Christmas past. "Did you say that, boy?"

Blushing, Tommy shook his head.

"I don't go for any insubordination in my chorus," Virgil warned. "If any of you can't take that, then you'd better leave now."

When everyone immediately went to get their coats, Virgil barked, "Get back where you were! I'm not done with you yet. We still have to practice 'Joy to the World.'"

"'*Oy* to the World' would come closer to the truth," Molly noted with an irreverent grin. "Why do I get the feeling that this year's pageant is going to be the most embarrassing yet?"

Embarrassing would have been getting caught in the church basement in the clutches of your ex-husband, Lori silently noted. She still skittishly avoided going too close to the basement stairs—as if they might actually reach out and lure her into further temptation.

The truth was that Travis was the one doing the tempting. She was the one trying to be good. Without much success, as that fiery kiss this afternoon had proved. At least she hadn't fallen into the hay and made love with him again.

There were so many reasons why she'd made love with him the first time, after Kane's wedding. She'd been feeling unloved and unwanted, for one thing. Travis had dispelled those feelings, only to arouse a hornets' nest of other emotions.

"Come on, snap to it!" Virgil ordered as the singers slowly made their way to their appointed spots. "Okay, Lily Mae, hit it."

Everyone winced as Lily Mae pounded the piano, hitting the wrong keys and creating a noise that sounded about as bad as a moose in heat.

"Oh, dearie me, I had the page upside down," the woman exclaimed, finally realizing something didn't sound right. "Let me just fix that...." She turned the pages right side up and tried again. "There, that sounds better."

His beefy arms poised in the air, Virgil gave the motion for everyone to begin. They did...at about three-second intervals of one another. "No, no, no," the director exclaimed, looking frustrated enough to tear out his hair, had he any left.

"How did he get this job?" Molly asked out of the side of her mouth.

"The previous director moved out of town last month," Lori replied.

"I can see why with this bunch," Molly returned. "Probably couldn't face the thought of having to do another Christmas program."

"Talkin'?" Virgil demanded. "Are you two gals talkin'? I don't allow talkin' durin' rehearsals. Tell them, Lily Mae."

"Virgil doesn't allow talking during rehearsals," the woman dutifully repeated.

"Now if you two are done, maybe we could get goin' on this next song. We don't have all night, ya know. From the beginning..."

History repeated itself.

"Maybe you should count," Lily Mae suggested.

"Count?"

"You know, the way Lawrence Welk did."

"An' ah-one, an' ah-two, an' ah-three!" Virgil did a memorable Lawrence Welk impression that cracked everyone up.

"Any other bright ideas?" he demanded of the pianist, who huffily turned her nose in the air.

The third try was the lucky one, with everyone starting off together. Not on key, however.

"That's better," Virgil said. "But we need some more baritones." He looked at his watch. "They're late."

"Who's late?" someone asked.

"We are," Travis said from the back of the church. "Sorry about that."

Lori stared at him in amazement. The only place Travis ever sang was in the shower. What was he doing here? And how had he known she'd be here? She hadn't said a word to him about it when she'd been at the ranch earlier that day. She hadn't said a word to Tex, either.

"I brought along some reinforcements," Travis added, motioning to Tex and Slim beside him.

"Good," Virgil declared. "We need more volunteers."

"Volunteers?" Molly whispered. "I thought we were drafted."

"We were drafted," Lori agreed, her eyes on Travis. "And conned."

"What are you talking about?"

"Travis."

"What about him?"

"He's here to drive me crazy."

"Come on, Lori. Don't you think you're overreacting a little?"

Lori shook her head. "You just wait."

Travis, of course, took perverse pleasure in ignoring Lori during the whole rehearsal. Lori was sure he did it on purpose, just to make a liar out of her.

The sound of his voice did funny things to her. No doubt that was due to the fact that she kept picturing him singing in the shower. Naked. With nothing but droplets of water sliding down his body, from the powerful breadth of his broad shoulders, over the muscular expanse of his chest, down to his naval and inward, toward his pelvis....

The next thing Lori knew, she was three beats behind everyone else in the chorus.

"Pay attention!" Virgil barked.

Lori saw Travis's lips curve upward and knew he was laughing at her. She sidled closer to the tall man on her left and was pleased to see Travis frown. Good. She didn't want him thinking he could control her. That she turned into mush whenever he kissed her. That wouldn't do at all. He was a false fantasy, one she'd tried already, and it hadn't worked.

Sometimes it worked, a traitorous voice inside reminded her. *Sometimes it worked as wonderfully as it did this afternoon, and it ended with a powerful surge of satisfaction instead of this lingering, restless yearning.*

Residual attraction, Lori told herself, overriding that other voice inside of her. *Residual attraction.* She silently repeated the phrase over and over as if it were a magical incantation. Thank heavens the last song was completed.

"We've been rehearsing for a week and we don't sound any better now than we did then," someone noted in a disheartened voice.

"That's because you're not doing it right," Tex declared. "You can lead a horse to water, but you can't make him drink." Seeing everyone's blank look, she explained, "You can force all these people to join the chorus, but you can't make them *want* to sing. They have to want it themselves. Course, for all I know, they might want to sound like a bunch of sick calves."

A dozen voices were raised in protest.

"No? Then let's get down to business here. This pageant is only three days away, folks. It's time we showed what we're made off. Now straighten up and act like you're proud to be here, proud to sing in front of your neighbors. Act like you know what this holiday is about, like you're singing with joy." Lifting her arms, Tex said, "When I lower my hands, you all start singing your hearts out. Together and on key. I know you can do it. Now you gotta prove it to yourselves. Are you ready?"

Lori noted that the entire chorus nodded, herself included.

"Okay, then let's get this show on the road." Tex lowered her arm and the chorus sang like…a chorus. What they lacked in harmony, they made up for in enthusiasm.

"Better," Tex noted appreciatively. "Much better."

"I thought so, too," Lily Mae agreed.

"That's *my* job," Virgil complained. "She's takin' over my job." He clutched his baton close to his bulky body, as if fearing Tex might yank it right out of his hand.

"Stop your complaining," Tex retorted, not the least bit intimidated. "It worked, didn't it? I got 'em singing, didn't I?"

"Only because I got 'em warmed up," Virgil retorted. "Slim, can't you keep your wife under control?"

"Nope," Slim replied. "Besides, she's got a better voice than anyone here."

"Go on and stop your bragging," Tex chided her husband lovingly.

"I wasn't bragging, just stating the truth," Slim replied, giving her a hug.

"If she's got such a great voice, how come she's never sang in the chorus before?" Virgil countered.

"'Cause no one asked her before," Slim replied.

"Well, then, if you think you're so good, why don't you sing somethin' for us, Tex?" Virgil's invitation was laced with mockery.

"Why, thanks, Virgil. I believe I will. I don't need any accompaniment, Lily Mae." Taking a deep breath, she started singing "Amazing Grace," and by the time she was done there wasn't a dry eye in the place.

Lori stared at the woman in amazement. Even after having lived with Tex on the ranch those five years of her marriage to Travis, Lori had no idea the older woman had such a magical voice. She wondered if Travis had known.

Lori's thoughts were interrupted by the sound of applause, as everyone showed their appreciation of Tex's crystal-clear voice.

"Thank you kindly," Tex said, before turning back to Virgil with more advice. "They're not troops you're leading into battle. So stop treating them as if they were."

"Maybe you should lead us, Tex," someone said. Lori thought it might have been Tommy's girlfriend.

"Nah, I'm busy enough on the ranch. Besides, it wouldn't be fair to Virgil here. He's put in a lot of work already."

"If you think you can do a better job, then go right ahead," Virgil suggested, clearly not expecting her to take him up on his hollow offer.

She did. "Well, then, I will, Virgil. Thank you." Tex took the baton from him and turned back to the chorus. "Okay, let's start again, from the beginning."

"Did you know Tex could sing like that?" Lori asked Travis after the rehearsal. She had to say something, or risk making a scene by continuing to ignore him completely as they left the church. She'd decided that the topic of Tex was a safe-enough one to pursue.

"Sure I knew."

"Then why didn't you suggest that she join the choir sooner?"

"Tex can be downright prickly about suggestions. Reminds me of another woman I know." Travis gave Lori a meaningful look.

Lori ignored his reference. She wasn't about to let him taunt her into talking about that kiss in his barn. There were times when silence was golden, and this was certainly one of them.

Seeing that he wasn't going to get a rise out of her, Travis switched tactics. "Christmas is just around the corner. What are your plans for the holidays? Aside from singing in the pageant Christmas Eve."

"How did you know about that?"

"What do you mean, how did I know? You're standing right here next to me after rehearsal."

"No, I meant how did you know that I was here at the rehearsal? And why did you suddenly decide to participate? You've never sung in public before."

"I don't know. There were times after you left when I sang in a couple of bars. Course, I'd had a few beers too many at the time."

Lori felt a hidden fault line in her heart give way at his words. She knew Travis rarely got drunk. And it hurt her to think she'd caused him such pain that he'd gone and tried to drown his sorrows.

Regret softened her defenses and prompted her to stop questioning his motives about joining the chorus. Instead, she answered his earlier question about her plans for Christmas.

"My parents invited me to fly down there for the holiday weekend, but I can't leave town right now. One of my patients is due any time."

"So how are you going to celebrate?" Travis asked.

"I'm stopping by the hospital in the morning to take part in their gift distribution for the patients."

"And after that?"

"I thought I'd spend some quiet time at home."

"You're welcome to come out to the ranch and celebrate the holiday with us," Travis said.

Lori immediately shook her head. "No, thanks."

He looked stung by her swift refusal, but there were simply too many memories for Lori to spend Christmas Day out at the ranch. Look what had happened this afternoon.

As if reading her thoughts, Travis said, "How long do you think you can keep running from the past?"

"I'm not running from it," she replied. "I just don't want to relive it again."

Cupping her cheek with his hand, he softly said, "Was it so bad?"

"Not all of it." Feeling herself slipping back into his spell, she quickly reached for words as a lifeline to haul herself out again. "You shouldn't have kissed me this afternoon."

"If you feel that way, you shouldn't have kissed me back."

"I didn't kiss you back." Her denial didn't hold water, even with her. Her innate honesty made her say, "Okay, so I did. But it was a mistake," she immediately added.

"You know, I'm getting tired of being referred to as a *mistake*," he growled, reaching for her.

This time Lori was prepared and she slipped out of his grasp. "And I'm tired of you thinking you can kiss me and make me do whatever you want."

"Did you ever consider the fact that I might be kissing you because I can't help myself?"

"No."

"Well, consider it." Leaning down, he kissed her once, gently and briefly. "We could make beautiful music together," he whispered in her ear, his husky voice laced with laughter and temptation.

"Only in the choir," she retorted.

"I don't think Tex would approve if I seduced you in the choir," Travis solemnly noted.

Staring into his blue eyes, Lori felt for one moment as if she were seeing a juxtaposition of the old Travis and a new one, the result being a man she was tempted to get to know better.

Who was this big cowboy who looked down into her eyes, his black Stetson shadowing his face? Was he the man she'd married a lifetime ago? The man she thought she'd known so well? Or was he a dangerous stranger, a man determined to do whatever it took to get what he wanted? For all of that, did he *really* want her, or was he just playing a game with her? Who was this man with laughter in his eyes and mischief on his mind, tempting her to make "beautiful music" with him? Was he an ex-husband out for revenge because she'd divorced him?

Lori didn't know. And she wasn't sure it was wise to find out.

Seven

Lori was still muttering under her breath as she attempted to let herself into her house a short while later. The white mist formed by her breath in the cold air seemed to mock her as she struggled to unlock the stubborn dead bolt on her front door.

She knew the perfect cure for what ailed her: a bowl of caramel corn and a good video. Not a holiday video—that would remind her of Christmas carols, which would remind her of the rehearsal and Travis. She needed a distraction.

Once inside, she kicked off her boots and headed right for the TV and the new set of *Poldark* tapes she'd ordered from the public-television catalog. The historical romance set in the beauty of Cornwall was just the thing to get her mind off her difficulties—otherwise known as her ex-husband.

As she slid the tape into the VCR, Lori noticed that her plants near the window were looking rather wilted, so she detoured long enough to water them, grabbing a bag of caramel corn in one hand and the watering can in the other.

While Lori didn't have a green thumb by any stretch of the imagination, she was rather proud of the fact that a philodendron had survived her move from Great Falls. That and an English ivy were the only long-time residents on her plant stand. African violets came and went. So did Boston ferns. But those two plants had survived, somehow.

She was much better at catching babies than she was at keeping plants. Since returning to Whitehorn, she'd been able to follow the progress of the children she'd helped bring into the world. Some of the early ones were walking and talking now, little people in their own right. She'd see them playing in the park and remember how she'd been there in the beginning. But she'd missed all the time in between.

Recently, each time she passed by the hospital nursery she was overcome by an almost overwhelming need to pick the little babies up and cuddle them. Sometimes she did, only to discover that when she set them back in their bassinets, the emptiness inside was even larger than before.

She'd felt the same way this afternoon, while holding Clay. The pain of giving him back had felt like having her heart torn out right down to the roots.

Absently snipping off a dried leaf on her philodendron, Lori smiled sadly at her horticultural analogy. But it was an apt one. Since her birthday, her desire to have a baby had grown tenfold and was now as deeply rooted as her five-year-old philodendron.

She'd already caught herself thumbing through some of the larger catalogs and lingering over the baby stuff. She'd even dog-eared a couple of pages and marked the things—a quilted two-in-one changing-and-stroller bag; a baby activity mat with a mirror and attached rattles—that caught her attention.

"Enough daydreaming, already," she muttered to herself. She returned her brass watering can to its home beside the plant stand. "I'm going to cuddle up with some caramel corn and get transported from the wilds of Montana to the wilds of Cornwall."

At first, Lori thought the meowing was on the video tape soundtrack. Turning down the volume, she clearly heard the sound of a cat...coming from her front door.

Pushing aside the floral-print, denim curtains and peeking out her living room window, she found the black cat sitting on the windowsill staring back at her. "Oh, you poor kitty." While the days had been warmer than usual, the nights were below freezing. "Are you ready to come inside now, kitty?"

The black cat meowed again.

Lori hesitated a moment, uncertain whether to go and open the door or just open the window. She didn't want to scare the cat off. She ended up opting for the window. It slid open smoothly, and the cat stayed where it was.

"Here, kitty, I'm not going to hurt you," Lori crooned, holding out her fingers for the stray to sniff. To her surprise, the cat began purring and butted her head against Lori's hand in a blatant appeal for some petting. "It's cold out there. Don't you want to come in?"

The cat stared at her as if she understood Lori's every word. Then she looked at the inviting room and appeared to make the decision to move inside. A moment later the stray jumped from the windowsill to the couch to the floor. Lori quickly closed the window and watched as the cat did a thorough inspection of every square inch of the living room.

Hoping that she'd eventually be able to convince the animal to come in, Lori had earlier in the week gotten some dried cat food as well as kitty litter and a litter box. "Are you housebroken, I wonder? I hope so," Lori said as she prepared the kitty box for her new house guest.

The cat, although somewhat bedraggled, still managed to give her a haughty look before making use of the box and answering Lori's question.

Meanwhile, the video tape was playing, albeit with the sound turned off. The cat leapt to the top of the TV set and settled there. That's when Lori decided on a name for her. Demelza. The name of the spunky heroine of *Poldark*.

"Demelza," Lori said, trying it out loud.

The cat immediately stopped her grooming and looked at Lori, as if to say, *Yes, what do you want?*

"It's a big name for a little cat," Lori noted thoughtfully.

Demelza, looking completely unconcerned by this worry, settled herself more comfortably and closed her eyes in an expression of such feline contentment that Lori had to smile.

"Well, Demelza, it looks like you've found yourself a home," she noted ruefully before settling on the couch and enjoying the rest of the *Poldark* episode.

After a day like today—from her secret pain at holding sweet little Clay, to the passionate kiss Travis had given her in his barn, to the ATM eating her cash card, to Travis showing up unexpectedly at the rehearsal tonight and kissing her again—it somehow seemed fitting that Lori should end it by taking in a *black* cat, the traditionally superstitious sign of bad luck.

But Lori wasn't traditional, and she had a feeling Demelza was going to bring her good luck, not bad.

Lori's bout of good luck began the next morning, when she stopped at the bank on the way to work. She'd tried to call in her complaint about her eaten-cash-card episode, but she'd been told she had to report it in person. The good luck came in the good-looking form of David Asher, branch manager at her bank and handler of any customer problems.

David proved to be so nice that Lori forgot her earlier aggravation with the bank's card-eating machine. David had dark hair and brown eyes—kind brown eyes. He was different than most of the men in Whitehorn. He had a more worldly air about him than the ranchers and cowboys in this area.

They got to talking, and she discovered he'd been transferred to Whitehorn from Billings a few months ago, but was originally from Great Falls.

"Really?" Lori said. "I lived in Great Falls for a few years. In one of those Victorian houses over by Gibson Park."

While filling out the necessary forms to claim her cash card, they talked some more. Then Lori realized that time was getting on, and she had to get moving or she'd be late for work.

"Would you be interested in having dinner sometime, so we could continue our discussion?" David suggested. "I'm going home to Great Falls for the holiday, but I'll be back right afterward. How about dinner on Monday?"

"That sounds like a nice idea," she agreed, as he escorted her from his office across the lobby toward the bank's front door. "I'm on call, so we'd have to eat here in Whitehorn."

"No problem. Seven sound okay?" he asked.

"Fine."

"I'll pick you up at your place, then," David said.

She nodded.

By now they'd reached the bank's glass door, which he opened for her. "See you on Monday evening. And I hope you have a Merry Christmas!" he called after her.

"Thanks. You, too." To herself she softly added, "Things are looking up. David may be just what the doctor ordered."

The next two days before Christmas Eve flew by for Lori. All the kids in Whitehorn were disgruntled over the lack of snow, which had completely melted and had not yet been replaced. She'd managed to get some baking in, an annual tradition for her, and was pleased with the way her trays of Florentines and spritz cookies turned out. They tasted even better than they looked. She'd been nibbling on them all day, too uptight to eat a proper meal.

At ten that night, Lori started getting dressed for the midnight candlelight service. She'd decided on black suede pants and a softly ruffled white blouse. Her garnet stud earrings provided a bit of holiday color. While putting them on, she remembered that she'd lost yet another earring and suspected she'd lost it in Travis's barn when he'd kissed her. She hadn't asked him about it, though, because she was trying to avoid him. Not easy to do with them both in the choir.

The truth was that Lori had been half hoping she'd be working tonight, and therefore wouldn't have to sing in the pageant, but her beeper remained quiet. Still, she had a position at one side of the choir, so she could make an early exit, should duty call.

She arrived at the church to find most of the choral group already there. Like her, they were dressed in black and white. Virgil had tried getting everyone to put on red-and-white choral robes, but Lily Mae was no better a seamstress than she was a pianist, and the robes made them feel like they were in a circus rather than a church.

As the time drew near for them to make their entrance, a pale-faced and trembling Tommy moaned, "I think I'm going to be sick!"

"Nonsense," Tex declared. "You've just got a case of stage fright." Putting her hands on his thin shoulders and looking him right in the eye, Tex said, "You can do this." Turning to face the rest of the now-jittery chorus, she added, "You can *all* do this."

"Are you nervous?" Travis murmured in Lori's ear.

"I wasn't until you asked me that question," she muttered in reply, wondering how he'd managed to sneak up on her that way.

Sliding his hand down her arm, he took hold of her fingers.

"What are you doing?" she demanded suspiciously.

"Checking to see if your hands are shaking." Travis lifted her hand closer to get a better view, while caressing it with a callused fingertip at the same time. "Hmm, shaking just a bit, but not too bad."

Her slight trembling was magnified by his nearness. "I'm the one with the medical training, remember?" she said unsteadily.

"I'm not likely to forget."

"Places, everyone," Virgil ordered. "Time to light your candles."

The chorus was to enter with their lit votive candles, stopping at each pew to light the candle of the person sitting at the end, who would then pass the flame from candle to candle down the row.

"What if I trip and set everyone on fire?" Tommy said in a shaky, squeaky voice.

"Nothin' to worry about, boy," Virgil assured him. "We've got a medical person standin' by in Lori here. Now get movin', everyone!"

Lori didn't remember much else after that, except that no one tripped and no one was set on fire as they made their way down the center aisle of the candlelit church.

Standing in front of a crowd and giving a workshop on birthing techniques, or speaking to a group of prospective parents in a childbirth class was one thing. But standing in front of half her hometown and singing—even with a dozen other people in the chorus with her—was scarier than she'd thought. Over and over, Lori found her panicked gaze searching out Travis on the other side of the chorus.

Their eyes would meet, and he somehow gave her courage. One time he actually winked at her. She was amazed at how easily he adapted to performing in front of a crowd. It wasn't something she'd have expected of him.

Tex's performance of "Amazing Grace" brought tears to Lori's eyes, and to those of everyone else in the congregation. Virgil had wisely decided to shelve his solo Sinatraballad version of "Jingle Bells" until he'd "polished it up some," as he put it, adding "there's always next year." In exchange, Tex had returned his precious baton to him and, with it, his duties as interim choir director.

During the final carol, "Joy to the World," Lori was overcome by the beauty of the moment—the goodwill of the season, the spiritual meaning of the holiday, the hope for a better world, the belief that miracles were possible. The church was decorated beautifully, with garlands of evergreen and boughs of holly draped everywhere. The congregation all held lit candles, and the sight was a moving one as the air became filled with the mingling scents of fresh pine and burning wax.

It was a smell Lori remembered from her childhood. One that brought with it the memories of Christmases past—staying up late and going to church with her parents; feeling the anticipation of Santa's visit the next morning; wearing a new, red velvet skirt her freshman year in high school and hoping Travis would like it; sitting in the second pew from the front as a new bride of six months.

She'd gotten married in this church, something she hadn't thought about lately. Here she was all these years later, caught up in the hope and faith of the moment, yet feeling somehow isolated from it all. Who knew what this next year would hold for her? Six months ago she'd been sure she'd known what her future would be. With Kane, who was now sitting out there in the congregation with his new wife and his daughter. Emotion rolled over her like a tidal wave as she swallowed back the sudden onslaught of tears.

Once the service was over, she gathered her coat and headed for the door.

"Lori, wait up!" Travis called, before getting waylaid by the pastor.

Knowing she was too vulnerable to talk to Travis again on this most magical of nights, she hurried out into the darkness alone. It was snowing lightly—looked like the kids would have their wish and get their white Christmas, after all. Lori could only hope that her wish of having a baby would also come true.

"And have you been a good little boy this year?" Lori asked the urchin with the broken leg.

"Just give me the present," the boy demanded, yanking it out of her hands.

"What do you have to say to Santa's helper?" his doting mother prompted him as he tore open the wrapping paper.

"She looks stupid in that elf costume," the boy declared, before focusing his attention on his present.

"I'm sorry," his mother said with a wispy smile. "Roger hasn't been himself since the doctor put that pin in his broken leg. It's the pain, you know."

It was the kid, not the pain, but Lori didn't have the heart to tell the hapless mother that. Brats like spoiled-rotten Roger almost made Lori think twice about her plans to have a baby. Almost, but not quite.

Straightening her pointed brown elf cap, Lori moved on to the next patient in the children's ward. This little boy was a sweetie, and his grateful smile warmed Lori's heart. It made dressing up in this ridiculous costume, complete with red-and-white-stripped tights and pointy slippers, worthwhile.

Virgil was playing Santa this Christmas morning. He was a natural for the role, since he didn't need any extra padding to fill out the jolly red costume.

Danette, who didn't like holidays messing up her precise hospital schedule, was playing the role of Scrooge to perfection. Molly was spending the holiday with her family. Mary Red Deer had been released from the hospital in plenty of time to spend the holiday with her family. Before she'd left the hospital, Lori had given her an adorable flannel sleeper for little Kate, plus a tin of homemade cookies and a basket of fresh fruit for the rest of the family.

All in all, Lori was feeling pretty good. As if sensing that, Dr. Straker showed up, looking prepared to burst her bubble.

"So, have you delivered any babies in barns lately?" he mockingly inquired.

"Some very good role models have been delivered in barns," Lori replied. "Carpenter, born in Nazareth. We celebrate his birth today. Ringing any bells, Dr. Straker?"

"Two thousand years ago, midwives may have been a good idea, but in today's high-technology world—"

"They're an even better idea," Lori inserted.

"I certainly wouldn't want my child born anywhere but in a hospital," Danette inserted with a sniff.

"Some women feel that way, which is why I'm affiliated with this hospital and assist with births here," Lori replied.

Dr. Straker's face tightened with disapproval, his bushy eyebrows meeting over the bridge of his nose. Danette's face wore the feminine version of the same look.

"I meant with a *doctor* in charge of my care," Danette clarified.

"Oh, I see, I'm sorry I misunderstood. A lot of women prefer having continual care and support throughout the labor process, not someone just moseying in when the baby has crested."

"Nurse Bains believes in positive energy and singing and chanting rather than relying on medical technology," Dr. Straker told Danette with a we-know-she's-nuts grin.

"Midwives believe that labor should not be interfered with merely to make things more convenient for the physician's schedule," Lori said.

"They also believe in the tooth fairy and Santa Claus," Dr. Straker noted before slapping his patient's chart on the counter for a nurse to file. "Well, I've got to go. It's been nice chatting with you girls."

Lori gritted her teeth until her jaw ached. She reminded herself that she was fighting a war here, a war she was doomed to lose unless she maintained her control. The career she'd chosen entailed fighting against the reputation that midwives were either superstitious hillbillies or New-Age hippies.

Lori knew that it was in Dr. Straker's own self-interest for him to discredit certified nurse-midwives—and her in particular—because given an informed choice, more patients would chose to have their baby with Lori and her care-giving ways than with Straker and his high-priced, low-compassion arrogance. In these days of escalating health-care costs, CNMs were a cost-efficient way to go, and Straker felt threatened by that fact.

Lori's control regained, it was soon shattered again as Danette said, "So how's your test-tube-baby idea doing?"

* * *

"Home at last!" Lori muttered as she closed the front door behind her. "Merry Christmas, Demelza," she crooned as the black cat wound itself around her ankles. Before Lori had left that morning, she'd set out a dish of tuna for Demelza as a holiday treat. Lori had also called her parents early that morning to wish them a happy holiday and to thank them for the box of Christmas presents that had arrived the day before.

Lori had always loved the holiday season. It was her favorite time of year. She enjoyed decorating her house and her tree, which was filled with angel ornaments she'd collected over the years. The elaborate, handmade wreath on her door was one she'd purchased at the Victorian Christmas Bazaar in Great Falls. The doorway leading to the living room was ringed with Christmas cards, many of them including the photos of babies Lori had delivered over the years.

Memories of Christmas past inevitably came to mind in a random sequence—a Christmas morning she'd spent at the birthing center delivering a healthy baby boy, named Jesus in honor of the holiday; a golden-haired doll she'd wanted all year long and had finally found under the tree Christmas morning, delivered in a burlap sack bearing the unfamiliar script of Santa Claus; opening the tiny box from Mason's Jewelry to find a beautiful engagement ring from Travis.

Lori's reflections were bittersweet. She'd certainly never expected to spend Christmas Day alone. "I guess it's you and me, Demelza," she whispered to the cat as it jumped up on her lap and rubbed her wet nose against Lori's hand. "Just you and me."

"You and me will have to go out fishing this spring and try out your new rod," Slim said as Travis admired the present his ranch foreman had gotten him.

"It's a beauty," Travis murmured.

"Speaking of beauties, that turkey in the oven is just about done," Tex declared from the doorway. "Give it another half hour or so and it should be just perfect."

"Finally!" her husband exclaimed. "I'm so hungry I could eat a bear."

"You have eaten bear and didn't care for the taste of it, as I recall," Tex retorted.

"I'm not keen on buffalo steak, either," Slim admitted. "You agree with me on that, don't you, Travis?"

"What? I'm sorry, I wasn't paying attention to what you were saying."

"You haven't quite been here all day, Travis," Tex noted. "You thinking about Lori?"

Travis nodded.

"That's it then." She wiped her hands on the apron she was wearing along with a look of mulish determination that made both Slim and Travis take notice. "We're going."

"Going where?" Travis asked.

"To Lori's. It's our Christian duty," she added, forestalling Travis's protest.

"How do you figure that?"

"You said she was going to be all alone today. We've got enough food in that kitchen to feed an army. It's our Christian duty to drop off some dinner for that hard-working girl."

"She's not a girl and she'd probably give us the boot," Travis retorted.

"No one gives *me* the boot," Tex declared.

"She's right," Slim noted with a grin. "No sense arguing with her, Travis. Once Tex gets that look on her face it's easier to wrestle bare handed with a bobcat than argue with her."

"Okay, fine. Just remember that this wasn't my idea."

"It's much too good an idea to have come from you," Tex retorted.

Lori was sitting in her oversize chair, feeling rather sorry for herself despite the cheerful clothes she was wearing. The red mohair sweater was new, a Christmas gift from her parents. It was a family tradition to wear one piece of new clothing on Christmas. The red-and-green, hunter-checked leggings she'd had for a while. Same with the green, jingle-bell earrings.

The phrase all dressed up with no place to go kept coming to mind. Not that her outfit was that elaborate by any stretch of the imagination. Demelza didn't look overly impressed by Lori's fashion sense, but then Lori had heard it was very hard to impress a cat.

The sound of a vehicle pulling into her drive surprised her. Before she could get up—Demelza was on her lap again—there was a pounding on her front door. Lori winced as Demelza took off like a shot, using all twenty claws in the process.

"I'm coming," Lori called out, realizing no one had pounded on her front door like that since Travis had come to throw a fit about her wanting a baby.

Surely it couldn't be . . . but it was. "Travis!"

He wasn't alone. Tex stood right beside him, while Slim brought up the rear.

"If Mohammed won't come to the mountain, then the mountain has to go to Mohammed," Tex said. "We brought you Christmas dinner."

Lori looked at them in surprise. "You really shouldn't have gone to all this trouble. . . ."

"I told you she wouldn't appreciate the effort," Travis said, still ticked off by the way she'd rushed off from the midnight service last night.

"I didn't say I didn't appreciate it—" Lori heatedly countered.

Putting two fingers in her mouth, Tex gave an ear-piercing whistle that shut them both up. "Time out, you two. It's Christmas Day. Time to set aside our differences." She glared first at Travis and then at Lori. "Now I want the two of you to shake hands and behave yourselves."

Lori gave Travis a sheepish grin, which he finally returned.

"Pax?" she said, holding out her hand.

"Pax," he agreed, taking her hand in his and holding it a second longer than necessary.

"Step sharply," Tex said. "We've got hot food getting cold out here."

The ice was broken as Tex organized the meal, taking over Lori's kitchen the way a field commander takes over a new camp.

Feeling she needed to contribute something to the dinner, Lori said, "I've got some cranberry Waldorf salad I made yesterday. I'll get it out of the fridge. I've got some sparkling wine in here someplace, too...ah, here it is. A patient gave this to me just a week ago."

As she held the chilled bottle up, Travis noted, "No screw top. Fancy stuff."

Lori handed him the bottle and a corkscrew. "You're good with your hands," she archly informed him. "I'm sure you can figure out how that works."

Lori got out four glasses before sitting down to the glorious feast Tex had prepared.

Never one for fancy words, Slim raised his glass and simply said, "May you get what makes you happy."

So, Lori asked herself, why had she looked at Travis as they'd clinked glasses? Travis couldn't make her happy. She had no business thinking such thoughts.

She had to keep her goals in sight. Granted, today had ended up being a nice holiday, albeit a strange one. But by next year things would be very different. By next year, she'd have a baby. That's all she needed to be happy. Not Travis.

Eight

Monday was a busy day for Lori. It was always hard to return to work after a holiday weekend. The fact that she got to tell an eager couple that they were indeed going to have a baby made it both easier and just a smidgen harder.

As she answered their many questions and asked a number of her own—about their medical history and their plans for the birth—she deliberately shoved her emotions into a back corner of her mind. Lori hated to think that she might be becoming so self-centered as to deny anyone else happiness until she had a baby.

But another look at the proud parents-to-be dispelled her worries. She was happy just looking at them. Who wouldn't be? They were so much in love, and they were going to have a baby—something they'd been wanting for some time.

Lori was patient. She could wait, knowing that she'd taken steps to get what she wanted.

Informational material from several of the country's leading sperm banks had arrived in the mail just this morning. In addition, Lori had a date with David Asher that evening. Keeping all her options open. Those were the catchwords of the day.

Lori's next patient was Sarah. "The baby's dropped," Lori noted after completing her examination. "The head is engaging in the pelvic rim."

"Isn't it early for the baby to be dropping? My due date isn't for almost three weeks."

"That's an estimated due date," Lori reminded her. "Babies do tend to have a mind of their own."

"You're not going to measure me again?"

Lori shook her head. "The measurements aren't accurate beyond this point. Up until now, when I measured the fundal height with the tape measure, the number of centimeters matched the gestational age. Clever, huh?"

"Ain't modern technology grand," Sarah mockingly agreed.

"How are the baby's movements going? Are you lying down for an hour each day and taking note of how often the baby moves?"

Sarah nodded. "I brought my notes along."

Lori looked them over. "You've got great penmanship, Sarah," she noted with a grin. "And a real way with words. 'Baby dancing around,'" she read. "'Baby trampled on my bladder again.'"

"It's kind of neat watching my tummy shifting as the baby moves. I don't know if Erica was this active in the womb and I just wasn't paying attention, or if this baby is just hyper," Sarah said. "But I value that hour the baby and I spend together. Not that we aren't together the rest of the time, too," she added with a grin.

"How are things with Tom?"

"Better since you talked to him. Thanks."

"No problem."

"But I confess that I'm starting to feel like Liz Taylor in that movie *Father's Little Dividend,* with everyone looking at me anxiously and expecting me to pop at any minute."

Lori had to smile at the analogy.

"So when do you think the baby will come?" Sarah asked.

"Not much longer now. Did your mother drive you in today?"

Sarah nodded.

"Good. And you're already preregistered at the hospital, right?"

Again she nodded. "I've even got my bags packed."

"Sounds like you're all set then. How was your Christmas?"

"Great. And yours?"

"Interesting," Lori murmured. "Very interesting."

As it turned out, Lori was running late that evening, so she didn't have a lot of time to get ready for her date with David. On top of that, Homer was still busy sanding her living room wall. Giving him a quick greeting, she immediately headed for her bedroom. Normally she would have been tempted to wear her good purple, wool-jersey dress tonight, but that was the dress she'd ended up making love with Travis in. So it was now in its dry-cleaning wrapping, relegated to the back of the closet.

She settled on a classic coatdress in a red-and-black-check design with a black velvet collar and long sleeves. She'd ordered the dress all the way from Boston, but it suited a date in Whitehorn just fine. Her short hair didn't require anything more than running a brush through it, thank heavens. She exchanged her sterling-silver turtle earrings for her best pair—a set of small pearl studs.

David arrived right on time, punctual and courteous. Lori was impressed.

He took her to the nicest restaurant in town and did his best to make her feel at ease. It worked, until Lily Mae stopped by their table.

"Why, Lori, what a surprise to see you here!" Lily Mae exclaimed. "Mr. Asher, you look very dashing this evening."

"Call me David, please," he said, standing up, which impressed Lily Mae no end.

"Nice manners, too," Lily Mae told Lori with an approving nod.

"What are you doing here, Lily Mae?" Lori asked, only afterward realizing her question might have sounded a bit rude. But she didn't feel comfortable with Whitehorn's leading gossip breathing over her shoulder.

"Oh, I have friends visiting from out of town. I'd have you two come over so I could introduce you, but I don't want to intrude. After all, you young folks probably don't want us interrupting your date."

Lori wasn't sure what she was supposed to say to that, so she kept silent. So did David.

"Well, it was nice seeing you," Lily Mae declared with a wave.

Great. The fact that she and David were out on a date would be all over town by morning. Not that Lori cared. She had nothing to hide. She was a single woman, albeit a divorced one. The fact that she'd spent Christmas Day—yesterday—with Travis didn't mean she owed him anything. It had been Tex's idea to come over, anyway.

Looking at David, Lori decided that she was doing the right thing in going out with him. It was time she got on with her life.

"I haven't been in town that long," David noted, "but it's my understanding that Lily Mae over there is a busy lady."

"She knows everything that goes on in this town. Or she likes to think so. Virgil has been giving her a run for her money lately in the gossip department though."

"Virgil?"

"The cook at the Hip Hop Café."

David nodded. "Right."

"So how do you like Whitehorn so far?"

"Seems like a nice town."

"Yes, it is." Lori nodded. "There are times when I miss certain things about Great Fall, though—like open house at Paris Gibson Square. I used to go there every year and get into trouble at the arts-and-crafts show."

David nodded. "There's not as much going on here in Whitehorn. But with the university at Bozeman, civilization isn't that far away."

By the time they'd finished their dinner, Lori had decided that she was very glad she'd met David at the bank. He was good for her. He kept her mind of off Travis. And he was a very possible candidate for her goal of having a family. He was much more down-to-earth than Travis. And when she and David had talked about family and children, Lori felt that they had been on the same wavelength.

While it was true she was soured on men, it was also true that she lived in a small town and was worried about her child having to face the comments and gossip that might occur were she to have it through a sperm bank or some other means. She was just exploring all her options—exactly as she'd told Travis she would.

Not that Lori was thinking about Travis, because she wasn't. She *was* thinking about being the center of Lily Mae's continually curious stares, however, which explained why she was nervous when David held out her chair for them to leave.

In the process, she upended her purse and spilled half its contents across the floor. Her lipstick went in one direction, her pager in another, her wallet in a third. Feeling her face turn red, Lori immediately bent down to pick them up. David gallantly retrieved her lipstick, while she reached for her pager and wallet. Only then did she realize that her pager wasn't working. Horrified, she banged it against her palm. Nothing happened.

How could that be? It had been working fine yesterday morning, when she'd had it at the hospital. Danette had made some disapproving comment about Lori setting it at the nurse's station while she changed into her elf costume.

"Excuse me, David. I've got to go check in with my service," Lori said, praying that no one had called.

Her prayers went unanswered as her service informed her that they'd been trying to reach her for the past hour. One of Lori's patients had been in a car accident along with her husband, and she was currently in the emergency room at Whitehorn County Hospital.

Her face pale, Lori returned to David, telling him she needed to get to the hospital as soon as possible.

* * *

"Glad you decided to finally join us," Dr. Straker noted sarcastically. Seeing her dress, he added, "Break up a hot date, did we?"

Telling a doctor to shut up was not only politically incorrect, it was liable to get Lori into hot water with the hospital administration. Still, she was tempted. "What's the patient's condition?" she said instead.

"The gravida was hysterical when she arrived."

Lori thought that Straker would drive anyone to that state. Referring to a pregnant patient as a gravida might be medically correct, but it was dehumanizing, and Lori hated it—which was precisely why Straker always used it.

"Her blood pressure was elevated," he added.

Whose wouldn't be? Lori thought. Straker had that affect on everyone.

"Any broken bones? Internal bleeding?" she demanded.

"I was getting to that," he leisurely replied.

Lori was tempted to grab the chart out of Straker's hands. She knew he was deliberately taking his time. But even he wouldn't risk the life of a patient, so Lori told herself that his power games had to mean her patient wasn't in any danger.

"I was about to perform an internal exam—"

"Not on your life!" Lori muttered.

"What did you say?" Dr. Straker demanded.

Knowing confrontation would get her nowhere fast, she respectfully replied, "I said that she's had enough strife, enough trauma. It might be better for the patient if I were to examine her."

By "might be" Lori meant "definitely would be," but pushing Straker wouldn't get her anywhere.

"We have a fetal monitor hooked up to her," the doctor stated. "Checked the fetal heartbeat—the strip looks good."

Lori looked at the readout strip and agreed.

"I had an ultrasound done on her. Didn't see any problems there. She's not bleeding."

Lori couldn't fault Straker's treatment. She just wished she'd been here herself for her patient, Rita Brooks, who was thirty weeks into her pregnancy. Dr. Straker finally decided to let Lori do an internal should she think one was necessary. Lori spent the next two hours reassuring her patient and the rest of the family anxiously sitting in the emergency waiting room. Luckily, the car accident had been a minor one, and Rita's condition was good—there was no sign of trauma to the baby or injury to the mother.

Once Lori had finished speaking to Rita's mother, she discovered that David was still waiting for her. "A gentleman doesn't abandon a lady on their first date," he told her with a charming smile. "How's your patient?"

"She'll be okay, thank heavens. As I just told her family, we'll keep her overnight as a safety precaution. I can't believe my beeper malfunctioned like that. I've never had any trouble with it before. And I normally make a practice of checking it every morning, but today I was rushed...."

"It worked out okay in the end," David said.

Lori nodded. She'd put in a new battery just a few weeks ago, yet it had apparently gone dead. It didn't make sense. Still, she'd replaced it with a brand-new battery and checked to make sure it was working again now.

During the short drive back to her place, she couldn't help brooding about the foul-up. She normally didn't make mistakes. What would have happened if she hadn't tipped her purse over? She could have gone another two hours without knowing that a patient needed her. And what if the car accident had been worse than it was and her patient had gone into premature labor?

Lori prided herself on being available to her patients. She felt she owed all of them that level of professionalism. And she felt she'd let Rita down by screwing up tonight.

As David pulled into her driveway, Lori said, "I'm sorry the evening didn't work out the way we'd planned."

"That's okay. We can catch the show at the Roxie any-time."

"You mean you're willing to try it again?"

He nodded. "How about New Year's Eve? I imagine you probably already have plans...."

"Actually, I don't," she replied.

"Is there anywhere special you'd like to go?"

"How about my place? I mean, I could make dinner and we could rent some videos." The entertainment choices in Whitehorn were somewhat limited. "That doesn't sound very exciting...."

"It sounds great," David declared as he accompanied her to her front door. His kiss was as charming as he was. As she watched him leave, Lori told herself that charming was better than white-hot, mindless passion. Safer, too.

On Wednesday, Travis stopped by the Hip Hop Café for his customary slice of cherry pie.

This time, Virgil waited until Travis had eaten half his pie before springing the latest gossip on him. "Lori's chasin' after some banker man," he announced with relish.

Travis glared at him.

"I'm not makin' it up, boy," Virgil insisted. "Just ask Lily Mae. She saw them at the restaurant together. The man is some bigwig from out of town. He's the new bank manager. Probably got big bucks."

"From working at the bank? I doubt it," Travis replied, wondering who the hell the guy was.

"He drives a red Corvette with custom wheels. All the women want a ride in it. I had one of them Corvettes years back. I can tell you, them cars are powerful things. Make women do wild stuff."

"Not Lori," Travis declared.

"Why not Lori? She's already got them hormones racin' through her. You add a Corvette to the mix and you got some mighty flammable goin's-on. Don't you forget how women get when they want a baby," Virgil warned.

"There's no stoppin' them. Don't ya remember me tellin' you that's how I got caught by wife number two?"

"I remember," Travis said darkly.

"You know, I saw you and Lori arguin' by them corn chips at the food market. You mighta been fightin', but there was some heavy-duty chemistry goin' on there."

The deadly look Travis gave him made Virgil gulp and hurriedly take two big steps back toward the kitchen. "Not that it's any of my business, of course. No, you're right. No concern of mine. Unlike Lily Mae, I don't believe in buttin' into other people's beeswax."

"What're you yammering on about beeswax?" Homer demanded as he joined Travis at the counter. "What does a man have to do to get a cup of coffee around here?"

"All he has to do is ask," Virgil exclaimed.

"I'm asking now. Have been for five minutes, sitting over there—" Homer jerked his thumb over his shoulder "—in that booth. But you were too busy carrying on to notice."

Virgil slammed down the white crockery with enough force to add another chip to the saucer. "Here, suck on this," he muttered, pouring the dregs of a coffeepot into the cup.

Homer drank it appreciatively. "The thicker the better," he stated. "Hi, there, Travis. How're things with you?"

Travis was so surprised to have Homer initiate a conversation with him that he temporarily forgot his anger at Virgil's nosiness. "They've been better," he muttered.

"Yeah, I know what you mean. Me, I've been busy painting the midwife's living room. She picked this weird color. Called Calypso or some such thing. Ever heard of such a dumb name for paint?"

Travis shook his head. So Lori was having Homer paint her living room, huh? Maybe he could pick the old-timer's brain and get some info on her activities. But how could he do that with Virgil the Verbose hanging around eavesdropping? "How 'bout we go sit in one of those booths over there," Travis suggested.

"Sounds fine by me," Homer agreed.

Virgil looked irritated at being left out of the conversational circle.

"Old coyote gossips like a woman," Homer said of Virgil. "Course, if I said that around the midwife, she'd probably wallop me one for insulting women or some such nonsense. She sure is a feisty thing. She don't take much guff, does she?"

"No."

Homer nodded. "Some men like that in a woman. The young fellow from the bank seems to like her just fine."

"He does? How do you know that?" Travis demanded.

"'Cause he came by the other evening to take her out to dinner. I was still sanding the wall by the fireplace, so I was there when he stopped by."

"Was she wearing a dress?"

"What?"

"Was Lori wearing a dress?"

"How the heck should I know?" Homer retorted. "She had clothes on is all I can recall for sure."

Some comfort. She didn't go out naked. Travis knew that Lori only wore dresses when she was hoping to impress someone. The last time he'd seen her in a dress had been at Hunter's wedding. And look what had happened then. Sweat broke out on his forehead. "Was the guy driving a Corvette?" he demanded.

"It was some kind of red car," Homer replied. "One of them low-slung jobs. The kind you gotta have help getting into and out of."

"Great."

"You know, now that I think on it," Homer mused, scratching his bearded chin, "seems to me she *was* wearing a dress."

"Oh, just great." Travis went on to mutter a few curses under his breath.

"You talk like that in front of a woman and you could end up in jail," Homer reminded him. "Don't forget that using foul language in front of a woman is still a misdemeanor in this town. God knows, I've nearly ended up in the slammer a time or two myself over the years. But I'm a reformed man now that my family is back here.''

"Lori was dating Kane before your daughter came back, you know," Travis said, reminding Homer of that fact about his new son-in-law.

"I heard. Not much slips by folks in this town. That's why I liked spending my time out in the open. Don't get caught up in all the goings-on here," Homer said. "I aim on heading back out come spring."

"Yeah, I know what you mean. Each time I come into town, I hear stuff that raises my blood pressure," Travis noted with a black look in Virgil's direction. "So what was your impression of this jerk from the bank, Homer?"

"What jerk from the bank?"

"The guy who picked Lori up for dinner."

"He seemed normal enough."

"Normal? What's that mean?"

"Well, heck, Travis, I didn't give the man a personality test before he left. I was just there getting the wall ready to paint."

"What did he say to her?" Travis pressed impatiently. "What did she say to him?"

"Whoa, calm down there. This was their first date. I don't think you've got cause to get riled up yet." Waiting until Travis relaxed, Homer added, "Course, that don't mean you won't have cause to worry real soon. The fellow did seem seriously smitten when he looked at her. And she did look mighty good in that dress."

"I thought you didn't notice things like that."

Homer shrugged. "She was wearing little pearls in her ears."

Great. Travis had given her a pair of pearl earrings for their first anniversary. On the top of his bureau he still had the amethyst earring that she'd worn when they'd made love. He'd hung on to it, not wanting to return something that reminded him of the passion they'd shared. After she'd stormed off when he'd kissed her on Wednesday, he'd found another one of her earrings, this time a dangly silver-feather one. It was as if she were leaving a trail of earrings behind to lead him back to her.

But he was no Red Riding Hood losing his way in the woods. Or was he getting his fairy tales mixed up here? Didn't matter. He was the wolf, and he was gonna be knocking on Lori's door real soon.

Lori was filling out paperwork, in triplicate, at the nurses' station when she heard Danette talking about her.

"She doesn't even use metal stirrups," she was telling a new nurse on the ward. "Says she doesn't approve of the lithotomy position for birth. As if she knows more than doctors who have spent years training and studying, let alone delivering healthy babies."

"Often by yanking them out with forceps because the allotted delivery time was up," Lori interjected.

Danette gasped.

"And if you're going to gossip, Danette," she continued, "the least you can do is get the story straight. What I said was that the lithotomy position was actually designed for the removal of kidney stones. *Lithotomy* literally means the operation of cutting for stone in the bladder. Look it up in any dictionary. In the nineteenth century, obstetricians borrowed the feet-in-stirrups position that surgeons had been using for lithotomies. As a midwife, I deliver babies. I don't remove stones. Stones aren't cute. Stones have rotten Apgar ratings. I don't do stones. I catch babies. Do we have that straight now?" Without waiting for an answer, she grinned at the nurse Danette had been gossiping with, who returned her grin. Then Lori left.

She arrived home that evening in time to find a mousy, bald-headed man knocking on her door. When he turned to look at her, he had the kind of helpless look that made her ask, "Can I help you?"

"I've come about..." The man paused and cleared his throat. "About the..." He paused again.

Taking pity on him, she said, "Travis didn't send you, by any chance, did he?"

The man nodded.

Lori sighed. Just what she needed. "So how much did you lose to him in the poker game?"

"Three hundred and fifty. I'm his accountant. I don't do this kind of thing as a rule, honest. But Travis can be rather persuasive."

"When he puts his mind to it, he could talk an Eskimo into buying a freezer," Lori agreed. "I just thought I'd made it clear that I no longer found his sense of humor to be amusing."

Thinking back, she couldn't remember if she'd actually laid down the law to Travis or not when she'd confronted him at his ranch a few days ago. She'd specifically told him not to send anyone else...or had she? Given the fact that he'd kissed her and distracted her, Lori couldn't remember what she'd said for sure.

It didn't matter. Clearly, Travis wasn't taking any of this seriously. Well, by God, she *was* serious. And she'd prove it to him.

Dashing off a quick note, she put it in an envelope and handed it to Travis's accountant. "Take this to him, okay?"

The man nodded, apparently glad to get off so easily.

"Tonight if possible. I'd really appreciate it," Lori added with her most persuasive smile.

"Sure thing," the accountant agreed.

Travis was in the living room, going over the ranch's books, when his accountant walked in. "Hey, great timing. I was just going over some of my tax records—"

"I didn't come about your tax records. I came to give you this." The man thrust an envelope at Travis.

"What is it?"

"It's from your ex-wife."

"Oh, yeah?" Travis sounded hopeful. That hope disappeared the instant he read Lori's familiar handwriting.

Don't bother sending any more prospects, I've found the right man for the job.

Nine

Travis tried to tap down the welling panic that tightened his throat and made the blood rush from his head to his heels. It was exactly the way he'd felt that time a steer had gone berserk and headed straight at him, breaking Travis's leg in the ensuing collision.

In the distance he heard Tex saying, "I thought I saw your accountant's car outside, but he appears to have taken off in a big hurry. I wonder who put ants in his pants? Travis, you okay? You're looking mighty pale. Was it bad news?"

Travis silently handed her Lori's note.

"Yup, I'd say this was bad news," Tex agreed.

Travis sank into his ratty recliner. "Now what do I do?"

"You remember me telling you that thinking a bad idea was a good one was a *bad* idea?"

Frowning, Travis nodded.

"Well, I wouldn't go tearing off after any more bad ideas if I was you," Tex advised.

"Don't tell me what I shouldn't do," he retorted impatiently. "Tell me what I should do."

"Answer me this first. What do you want from Lori? Aside from the obvious, I mean," she added as a ridge of red rode his high cheekbones. "I mean, are you looking to marry her again?"

"I don't know." Travis shoved his hand through his hair. "I haven't really looked that far ahead yet."

"Well, you better start looking. Lori's not the same cute teenager she was when you two fell in love. She's full grown now and has a mind of her own."

"Tell me about it," he muttered.

"If you want her, you're gonna have to court her just like any other man would."

"Like the banker is, you mean."

Tex frowned in confusion. "What banker?"

"The guy with the Corvette who she's dating now. The prospect she found for herself. Good husband material, good father material."

"How do you know that?"

"Because I had him checked out today after I heard yesterday that they'd gone out on a date Friday night."

"And what did you find out?"

"Like I said, the guy is probably good husband and good father material."

"Well, you're good husband material, you're good father material," Tex loyally maintained.

"Lori didn't think so the first time around," Travis said quietly.

Tex put a reassuring hand on his shoulder. "If Lori was over you for good, why do you think she still gets all hot and bothered around you? I saw the look on her face when she stormed outta here the other day."

"She was furious."

"That glow on her face wasn't just caused by anger, I can tell you that," Tex firmly stated.

"So what are you saying?"

"That Lori still has feelings for you. Oh, she may not be eager to admit it, in fact she might rather have her left arm cut off. But that don't change the fact that you still get to her. And I think she's using this banker man to get over you."

"Maybe I should let her go."

Tex removed her hand and gave Travis a look sharper than her favorite carving knife. "Maybe you should, if you don't know what you want," she said tartly.

"Dammit, I *do* know what I want," Travis exclaimed. "I want her! And I'm going to do whatever it takes to get her."

"Well then, all you need is a plan."

"Right. A plan. Thanks, Tex." He kissed her cheek and danced her across the living room floor.

"Hang on there," the housekeeper said breathlessly. "Don't you want to hear about the plan?"

"I think I can figure that part out for myself."

"Just remember you're courting her, Travis. You never had to do that before. When you two were in high school, you just aimed for each other like a pair of magnets."

Travis thought back and realized that Tex was right. When he had first asked Lori out, she'd said yes and that had been that. They'd started going steady shortly after that. There hadn't been any conflict in their relationship. And that had been fine with him.

"I can do courting," Travis maintained. "How hard can it be? I just get her some...what? Some flowers and candy, right?"

"I think it's gonna take more that some flowers and candy, but that's a start," Tex said. "You're gonna have to forget your anger, forget the divorce. There's no future in living in the past. You're gonna have to treat her like she's a woman you just met, a woman you're seriously attracted to."

"No problem," Travis said. After all, he still was seriously attracted to Lori. No problem there.

After ringing Lori's doorbell, Travis nervously tugged on the brim of his black Stetson and shifted his shoulders in his sheepskin coat. A huge box of candy leftover in the drugstore from Christmas rested in the crook of his arm. It was the biggest box he could find. Did chocolate get rotten? he wondered. He hadn't bought it because it was on sale, even though it had been a good buy. He'd bought it because it was the biggest. Maybe he should have gone for something fresher and more discreet. Some of those foreign chocolates he'd heard about.

Hell, he was no specialist in this field. He was a Hershey's man himself. Not very exotic. He didn't even drink imported beer.

Glancing down at his boots, he lifted one foot and rubbed it against the back of his denim-clad calf to spiff up the shine a bit. He'd put on his best boots, the gray snakeskin ones. He'd worn them when they'd made love the day of Kane's wedding.

Travis's attention shifted to the plastic-wrapped flowers in his hand. Maybe he should have gone with the red carnations instead of the roses. The carnations had been fresher. But the guy at the food market claimed you couldn't go wrong with roses. But the damn things were freezing out here. The temperature had dropped and the wind had picked up. The threat of snow was in the air.

Maybe this had been a bad idea. Maybe she wasn't home. Maybe he should leave.

She was coming to the door. Too late to panic now. What was taking her so long? Was she going to leave him standing on her front step like a lovesick moose forever?

The door opened, and she stood there in a flannel shirt and black jeans. Her shirt was checked, he noted vaguely, a pink-and-black buffalo print.

Seeing him, she said, "What's this?"

"Flowers." He shoved the bouquet at her. "And candy." The box came next.

"Your presentation needs a little work," she dryly noted.

"Meaning I'm not as smooth as the guy from the bank?" he retorted, prickly at her criticism.

"So that's what this is about." Her look told him that she suspected his motives and was disappointed in them.

Travis sighed. He wasn't doing real well here. Nothing like starting off with one foot in your mouth. A foot? Hell, make that a hoof. A moose hoof. All four of 'em.

You can do this, Travis reminded himself. "Can I come in for a minute?"

"Yes, you may," she replied.

Great time for her to be correcting his grammar now, Travis thought. Watching her, he saw that she was sniffing the roses appreciatively. The guy at the food market must have been right. Roses were a good choice. Travis wondered what the banker had brought her.

Forget the past, he told himself. Concentrate on the here and now. "Would you like me to take your coat?" she asked him.

That was further than he'd gotten last time, when she'd kept him standing in the foyer with his coat on. He was making progress.

Maybe he should have worn something fancier to come courting? Well, he *had* put on his good boots for her. And clean jeans and a clean denim shirt with a clean white T-shirt beneath it. Hell, he'd even put on clean underwear right before he left, not that he thought he'd get lucky tonight with Lori. After all, his object here was to court her, not bed her, although that prospect was damn tempting. But that wasn't the way to win her.

"I just made a fresh pot of coffee, would you like some?" she said, treating him like company.

"Sure. Fine."

"Go on in and sit down," she said, since he seemed rooted to one spot. As he moved into her living room, she tried to look at the furnishings through his eyes. After all, this was the first time he'd really seen her place. The color scheme was blue and deep rose, or would be when Homer was done painting the walls. The black-and-white photographs she'd had hung in groupings around the room were now sitting on the floor.

"I'm just about done decorating," she nervously told him. "Homer tells me he'll be done painting soon. He didn't like the color, but I think it worked out well."

She saw his gaze move over the cheerful, rose-colored walls.

"I picked up the couch and chair in Great Falls, because it wasn't wise to order a couch from a catalog without being able to test it for comfort levels. So I sat in the darn things—the chair and the couch, I mean—for about three hours at the store. They probably thought I was nuts, but I figured I was going to have this furniture for a long time and I wanted to make sure it suited me, that it was the right choice. I didn't want to make a mistake.''

You're babbling, Lori sternly reprimanded herself. Like Travis cared about her interior-decorating history? So she was nervous—who wouldn't be with her ex-husband showing up on the doorstep with candy and flowers?

Frankly, most women don't have the kind of ex-husband you do, that little, nagging voice in her head pointed out. *And they certainly don't make love with him in a church basement the day after Thanksgiving!*

So why did she have to be different? What was it about Travis that got to her? Granted, he was a very sexy man—his square-cut jaw and rugged features had caused more than one woman in Whitehorn to chase after him since their divorce. As far as Lori knew, he hadn't dated anyone seriously, though.

He'd never looked at another woman during their marriage. Well, he might have looked, she corrected herself with her innate honesty, but not for long. More like a quick glance, really, and then his gaze would return to her and he'd smile that slow smile of his—the one that said *I'm with the woman I want to be with.*

So what went wrong? she asked herself for about the twenty millionth time. Recalling what Tex had said about them being too young to stay married, Lori decided that that was the closest she'd come yet to an explanation of what had happened. It was still too vague for her peace of mind.

And it also left open the possibility that, now that she and Travis were older, they might be able to do whatever it took to keep a relationship going. But what did it take? Lori was afraid she didn't know. She wasn't sure Travis did, either. He was a man used to having his own way. Certainly not one for compromises.

He was also a man still wearing his hat. Granted, he was seldom without it, but he usually *did* take it off when visiting. He was also still standing.

"So what do you think?" she prompted. "About the room, I mean."

"It's nice. Different from the living room back at the ranch. But it looks like you. Flowery and kinda light, somehow."

She could tell by his tone of voice that Travis was as nervous as she was, and that realization startled her. Her own discomfort immediately melted as she focused on making him more comfortable.

"You know, it's silly for either of us to be so nervous," she noted ruefully.

"Who says I'm nervous?" he countered defensively.

She glanced meaningfully at his hat.

Quickly taking it off, Travis fingered it for a moment before realizing what he was doing and setting it on the Shaker coffee table, as if to remove it from temptation.

"I'm nervous, too," Lori admitted, "which is silly, considering the fact that I've known you practically half my life."

"I thought we could pretend that we'd just met," he said, the words coming out in a rush.

"Why?"

"Why?" he repeated, stalling for time. "Because if we pretended we just met, it would be easier to start over again."

"Start over again?" she repeated warily.

"I meant that we could get to know each other as if for the first time. After all, we've both changed since the divorce. Don't you think?" Hell, don't ask her, he silently berated himself. She'll only disagree with you.

Courting didn't mean riding roughshod and buffaloing her into something she didn't want, Travis reminded himself. It was more like sweet-talking a horse into thinking it was doing what it wanted, when it was actually doing what *you* wanted. Putting in those terms, Travis finally felt more comfortable with his mission here. He was great with horses.

Hell, you'd think he'd know how to court his own wife. His own ex-wife. Like she'd said, they'd known each other for ages.

Wait a second here—you just met, remember? Treat her like you would a woman you just met that you're attracted to. Trouble was, Travis hadn't ever been attracted to another woman as much as he'd been attracted to Lori. She was special that way. She was special in a lot of ways.

"It's true that I've changed a lot since the divorce," Lori belatedly acknowledged.

"I've changed, too," Travis said.

"How? How have you changed?"

"For one thing, I'm five years older than I was then."

"That's it?"

"Course not." Travis mentally scrambled to come up with something else. "I'm more mature now." That sounded good.

"In what way?"

"Dammit, I've changed. Just trust me on that, okay?" he said irritably.

"Doesn't sound to me like you've changed much," she countered.

"Well, I'll admit some things have stayed the same," Travis murmured. "Some things aren't meant to change. Like this..." He reached out to trail his index finger down her arm. Forbidden excitement shot clear to her toes.

"I thought you wanted to pretend we just met," she challenged.

"All I did was touch your arm," he innocently declared.

"It was the *way* you touched it." Flustered by what she was admitting, Lori quickly scrambled to regain lost ground. "I mean, you were deliberately trying to make me aware of you."

"That a crime?"

"What are you after, Travis?"

"You."

That's what she'd been afraid of, but hearing him admit it was like getting a shot of electricity directly in her heart.

"On the one hand you talk about starting over, about getting to know each other again, yet here you are boldly declaring that you want me," she said, just a tad shakily.

"You'd rather I lied about it?" he asked.

"You're being presumptuous. Especially with someone you supposedly just met." Lori sighed. "This isn't going to work. We can't even talk without arguing."

"We've done it before," he reminded her. "Okay, not for a while, I admit. But it can be done. I'm willing to bet on it."

"You'd bet on anything," she countered.

"I'm willing to bet a week of riding time on the mare of your choice out at the ranch."

Bull's-eye! He was offering the one thing that would tempt her to agree, and she could tell by the look in his blue eyes that he knew it. The truth was that she'd missed riding since leaving the ranch. Not that winter was the best time for it, but spring would be coming eventually. And she did love to ride—to feel the wind in her face, the sound of it rushing in her ears as she became one with the horse.

"What if you lose?" she said. "You have to give up something important to you."

Something important—hell, he'd given *her* up when he'd agreed to their divorce. What else did she want from him?

"Your boots," she said, as if answering his unspoken question.

"What?"

"Your dress boots." She pointed to them. "You've got to hand them over for a month, maybe two."

"Why? What the hell would you do with my boots?"

"I wouldn't do anything with them. That's not the point."

"What *is* the point?"

"That you wouldn't be able to wear them. They're your one vanity."

"Fine. If I lose the bet, you can have my boots for a month."

"Two."

"Sure, both boots for a month."

"Two months. Unless you think you're going to lose this bet?"

"Of course not." Geez! At this point, he had a hard time remembering what the bet was even about! To talk without arguing—that was it. Lori had a way of tying his thoughts in knots.

"Then you agree to the terms?" she asked.

"Sure. I argue, I lose my boots for two months. What are you giving up if you lose? Seems to me you're getting the better side of the deal here."

"If neither one of us argues, then I get to ride your horse at my convenience. And you get to keep your boots."

The sparkle in her eyes made him agree to this nonsense. Anything to see that expression on her face. "Okay. Deal."

They shook hands on it. Then there was an awkward moment of silence as they both sought to come up with some topic of conversation that would be innocuous.

"Nice weather," Lori ended up saying lamely.

"No fair talking about the weather," Travis declared.

"You didn't say I couldn't talk about the weather when we made the bet. You're trying to welsh," she said accusingly.

"Are you arguing?" he countered.

"No. There must be some things we agree on."

"Tex's chili," Travis answered with a grin.

"Out of this world," Lori agreed with a smile.

"Chunky peanut butter," Travis said.

"Chocolate-chip-cookie dough," she added.

"Have you noticed that we've done nothing but talk about food?" Travis dryly inquired.

"Probably because I'm starved," Lori admitted. "The truth is I was just about to eat when you got here." She paused and looked at him almost shyly. "Would you like to join me?"

"I didn't come over to mooch food off of you," he protested.

"It's just a casserole, nothing fancy, but there's plenty for two. Come on, join me. Have some dinner to go with that cup of coffee I promised you awhile ago."

"Okay. You got a deal."

"Good."

As Travis followed her into the dining room, which was empty except for a table and four matching chairs, he noted that her furniture was much fancier than that out at his ranch. They didn't even have a dining room. And Lori's furniture all matched. The armchair in her living room was in much better shape than his ratty recliner at home.

Thinking about her furniture kept Travis from thinking about how good Lori looked in those black jeans she was wearing. They cupped her bottom the way he longed to. He was trying to be good. On his best behavior, in fact.

And it must have worked; after all she *had* invited him to stay for dinner. Didn't matter that he'd eaten before he'd left the ranch. He wasn't about to let an opportunity like this pass him by.

Lori handed him plates with pretty flowers around the rim and told him to set the table. A second later she gave him silverware. It took him a minute to remember on which side of the plate the fork went.

The hash-brown-ham casserole was served in a fancy serving dish that matched the plates. In a separate bowl was a salad with lettuce, shredded carrots and red cabbage.

After sampling a bite, Travis noted, "This is good."

"Maris gave me the recipe," Lori said.

"How are she, Luke and the baby doing?"

"Fine. I haven't talked to her a lot lately."

"Why not? She's your oldest friend. You two have a fight or something?" Travis asked.

"No, nothing like that. I've just been busy." And she hadn't wanted to hear Maris's opinion on Lori's decision to have a baby. Maris wasn't exactly the most subtle person on the face of the earth. It was only a matter of time before she heard the rumors about Lori wanting a baby. And when she did, she was liable to be disapproving.

Lori also didn't want her friend to know how much she envied the fact that Maris had a baby. A year ago, being a godmother had been enough for her. It no longer was. She wanted what Maris had—stability, happiness and a child.

But did she want a husband, too? Lori wasn't sure on that score yet. It was one of many things she was still trying to work out.

"I didn't make anything for dessert," she confessed.

"You've got the chocolate I brought," Travis said. Bringing the box from the living room, he opened it and he held it out for her to study. "Pick a flavor, any flavor. There's a chart here that says what those squiggly designs on top mean. Or you can just take your chances."

Lori looked at the chart and selected a dark, chocolate-covered cherry with liquid filling.

Travis made an absentminded selection, distracted by the sight of Lori delicately licking cherry filling from her lips.

Her eyes met his. She felt the fire in his gaze as surely as if she'd been touched by a flame. His attention returned to her mouth, which was now dry with nervous anticipation. Her lips tingled at the raw hunger of his look, a visual kiss that was unexpectedly arousing.

The special moment was interrupted by Demelza, who came into the room, only to take off like a shot after seeing Travis.

"What was the black streak that flew through here?" Travis inquired dryly.

"My cat, Demelza."

"She looks scrawny compared to the barn cats."

"Most of your barn cats are the size of mountain lions. At least they were."

"Still are. What on earth made you take in a stray?"

"The look in her eyes."

Travis wondered what kind of look that might be and how he could adapt it. Maybe it would work for him.

Not that he wanted to live here in town with Lori. It was too crowded in Whitehorn for him. He needed to live where you could stretch out both arms and not run into someone. Whitehorn wasn't Denver or New York City, but it was big enough. His heart was with his ranch. And with Lori? a little voice in his head questioned.

Looking at him, Lori wondered what Travis was thinking about. She could deal with him when he was being impossible, but this Travis—the one who awkwardly brought her flowers and chocolate— she was finding hard to resist. She'd never been courted by him before. In high school, he'd asked her out, she'd said yes and that had been that. There'd been no need for wooing, no need for romancing.

Now there was. At least Travis thought so. Lori couldn't help wondering how much of this sudden impulse on his part was due to the fact that he felt he had competition in the form of David Asher.

Granted, she'd dated Kane, but for some reason Travis hadn't seemed to think he was competition. Probably because he hadn't been, Lori admitted to herself now. But in those days she'd still been looking for Mr. Right. Now she was willing to settle for...what? Mr. Close Enough?

Perhaps "settle for" was the wrong term to use. The truth was that Lori had stopped looking for perfection. Now she just wanted to build a life for herself and that baby she wanted so desperately.

And while there were many options available to single women these days, Lori was living in a relatively small town in Montana. Not the most liberal of locations. She was torn.

On the one hand was the traditional life of a wife and mother. She loved her career, but believed strongly in family values, too. She didn't really want to raise her baby alone. A child needed both parents, as each had a unique contribution to make in a child's development.

On the other hand, Lori didn't want to live a lie, marrying any man just to satisfy someone else's idea of what was right.

The mutual silence was interrupted by the sound of her beeper going off. She hadn't had any trouble with it since the incident a few days ago, when the battery had mysteriously gone dead. Still, she was spooked and checked it several times a night.

"Excuse me, I've got to call in," Lori told Travis.

The call was from Sarah. "It's time," she gasped, before handing the phone to her husband, Tom, who gave Lori the particulars about the contractions—time apart, intensity.

"Yep, sounds like it's time, all right," Lori agreed. "I'll meet you both at the hospital."

"Drive safely. It's snowing pretty heavily out there," Tom said.

Lori knew that Tom had recently put studded snow tires on his four-wheel-drive truck so that nothing would stop him from getting Sarah to the hospital. "I'll be careful," she said.

Returning to the dining room, she told Travis, "Duty calls. I've got a patient in labor."

As she and Travis stepped outside a few moments later, the snow was swirling. Lori had heard the weather report earlier that afternoon. The prediction was for one to four inches of snow, nothing her trusty Toyota couldn't handle.

But when she went to start it, the engine was dead. She panicked. This had never happened to her before!

Lori's clinical studies had included advanced obstetrics/ gynecology for normal women, family planning and newborn care. She knew little about combustion engines, though. Which is why she always had her car regularly maintained by the best mechanic in Whitehorn.

Travis lifted the hood for her but couldn't immediately fix whatever was wrong. "I have a feeling it's the alternator," he told her. "But I can't do anything about it right now. I better give you a lift to the hospital. It's on my way home, anyway."

"Okay. Thanks."

As she got into the pickup truck, Lori had a feeling she was crossing a threshold and there was no going back.

Lori hopped out of the truck at the hospital's front entrance, vaguely hearing Travis say something about wanting to wait for her. Her thoughts were already on her patient as she took the two flights to the maternity floor rather than wait for the elevator. It was just her luck that the first person she met upstairs was Dr. Straker.

"So you decided to be on time today," he noted mockingly. "I'm sure your nervous patient appreciates that. It's been a little hit-and-miss lately, hasn't it?"

"Not really."

"Let me give you a little friendly advice. If I were you, I'd watch my step."

"You're no friend of mine, Straker," Lori murmured under her breath. Louder, she said, "If you'll excuse me, I've got a patient to see."

Dr. Straker watched Lori go, wondering who she thought she was to dismiss him that way. She was nothing but a lowly little midwife. Not fit to scrape his boots.

He had plans to take care of her. Things were moving along. If he had his way, and he planned to, Lori Bains wouldn't be practicing her folklore at this hospital much longer.

"Oh, you're still here, Dr. Straker," Danette noted with a smile. "I thought you'd go before this snowstorm gets any worse."

"I was just leaving," Dr. Straker replied. "I was waiting for Mary Jo."

"Mary Jo Kincaid?" Not only did she volunteer for the children's story hour in town, Mary Jo was also the wife of Dugin Kincaid, only surviving son of Whitehorn's wealthiest family, and therefore someone for whom Danette had the utmost respect.

"That's right. I saw her downstairs earlier. She said she was visiting a sick friend, and she was worried about driving home in the snowstorm, so I offered to give her a lift."

"You're such a Good Samaritan," Danette said in admiration.

"Well, I do what I can," Dr. Straker said. "See you tomorrow."

Mary Jo was waiting for him in the small lobby near the hospital entrance. Courteously taking her arm, he led her through the wind-driven snow toward his white, customized Cadillac.

Once they were both inside, Mary Jo turned to look at him. "You're sure we're not taking a risk by leaving my car here in the parking lot?" she asked in an uncertain voice that matched her dainty and delicate appearance.

Errol Straker patted her on the shoulder reassuringly before sliding his hand down to cup her breast beneath her coat. "Stop worrying."

Mary Jo's gasp was one of pleasure, not outrage. She liked the feel of Dr. Errol Straker's caresses. She liked the way she could play her well-thought-out games with him. He, more than anyone else in town, understood her. For he was a complicated man himself. Not like the rest of the men in Whitehorn, including her husband.

Mary Jo didn't speak again until they were out of town. "I don't want you to get into any trouble because of me," she told Errol, leaning closer and put her hand on his thigh.

"You let me be the judge of that," he muttered, pulling his car over to the side of the road.

"What if someone sees us?" she asked, even as she was undoing his jacket.

"A little danger is a turn-on, don't you think?" he said as he lowered her to the velvet-covered seat.

Mary Jo just smiled.

"You're doing fine, Sarah," Lori commented after completing her exam. "Dilated five centimeters."

She had already talked to Sarah and her husband about what analgesics could be used and under what circumstances, about Sarah's preferences in her care during labor.

"Can I get up and do some walking?" Sarah asked.

"I don't see why not. You're not near the pushing stage yet."

Ten minutes later Lori and Sarah were walking up and down the hallway outside her room. Whitehorn County Hospital wasn't big enough to have birthing suites like the hospital Lori had worked at in Great Falls. But Lori knew that it didn't take nice wallpaper and furnishings to make a birthing suite—it took continuity of care, and having both labor and birth take place in the same room rather than shuttling the pregnant moms back and forth.

That continuity of care was what Lori provided. It might not be the norm in other rooms on this floor, with other patients, but it was with hers. And it drove Danette, self-proclaimed queen bee of the ward, nuts.

"She's not supposed to be out here." Danette bristled, pointing at Sarah as if she were an escapee from prison.

"Cool it, Danette," Lori retorted. "You know there are times when I promote patients walking a bit. The activity spurs labor."

As if on cue, Sarah tightened her hold on Lori's hand and puffed her way through another labor pain.

"She's going to have the baby right out here!" Danette exclaimed.

"She is not," Lori declared. "Breathe, Sarah. Inhale. Deep breathe." She didn't wince as Sarah squeezed her hand hard before letting up. "Good girl." Turning to Danette, she said, "Don't you have some forms to fill out?"

Sniffing, Danette headed for the nurse's station.

"Ready to go lie down again?" Lori asked Sarah.

"Naw," Sarah replied. "I thought we'd go toilet paper the nurse's station."

Lori grinned. "I'm game. Probably wouldn't be the adult thing to do, though."

"Spoilsport. Okay, then head me back to the room, my husband and that comfy-looking rocker."

"You just want that handsome husband of yours to massage your tummy during your contractions again."

"You bet," Sarah agreed. "I've gotta get some perks out of this deal."

"Easy. Easy now," Lori told Sarah as labor progressed to the final stage. Tom was helping Sarah sit up, providing his physical support for the pushing stage. "That's it, Sarah. Beautiful. You're doing great. Perfect."

Sarah pushed again and the baby's head crowned.

"I can see the baby's head now," Lori told her.

"Is it a girl?"

"I can't tell from this end, Sarah," Lori noted with a grin. Meeting her patient's exhausted but excited eyes, Lori said, "You're doing great! Fantastic. Just a few more seconds and we'll know whether you have a daughter or son."

Sarah was panting now as she pushed again. The baby's head shifted. "I can see the forehead now, and a great pair of eyebrows. Ah, gotcha," Lori exclaimed as, with a final push, the baby came sliding out. "Welcome to the world, little one," she whispered. "You've got a daughter," she told Sarah, holding the infant up for her to see.

Setting the baby on Sarah's stomach for her and Tom to touch and hold, Lori efficiently clamped and cut the umbilical cord. The infant's arms and legs were wiggling as Lori wrapped her in a receiving blanket and placed her in Sarah's arms. The afterbirth was taken care of a short while later.

Once the baby had been cleaned up and the newborn exam completed, Sarah, who had by then recovered a bit of her energy, said, "Winona was right. She told me I'd have a girl." Looking at Lori, she added, "We want to name her Lori, if that's okay with you."

Tears filled Lori's eyes. She didn't know what to say, so she just nodded. The emotion was so intense it could only be broken by laughter. Fittingly, at that very moment the newborn surprised Sarah by rooting around and latching onto her breast, and the three adults burst out laughing.

The baby would be rooming with her mother. Leaving the new family alone together, Lori took care of some arrangements and started the required paperwork. There were forms for everything: Apgar ratings for heartbeat, respiration, muscle tone, color; details of everything from the newborn's fingernails to its reflexes, in addition to its weight and length.

Two hours after the delivery Lori completed her last exam for the time being and said good-night to the new family. She'd return to the hospital tomorrow to check on Sarah and the baby again. In the hospital locker room, she changed out of her soiled lavendar scrubs into her own clothes, recalling as she did so that Danette only wore pristine white uniforms, as crisp and unbending as their wearer.

Only when Lori was about to use the pay phone in the lobby to call a cab for herself did she see Travis pacing the circumference of the waiting room.

"I'm sorry," she murmured. "No one told me you were waiting for me. You didn't have to do that."

"I wanted to."

Lori remembered David waiting for her when her patient had been in the car accident. Her feelings that night compared to finding Travis here were like comparing a Little League game to the World Series. Lori was too tired to chide herself for her reaction.

"I'll drive you home," he said.

Only when they were almost outside did they realize that the snowstorm was full-blown and had been for some time. The security guard at the exit told them that the radio was reporting snow falling at the rate of an inch an hour.

Lori checked her watch. She and Travis had been at the hospital almost ten hours. The short trek across the parking lot felt like a marathon. The snow had drifted as high as the door handles on some of the vehicles they passed. Set off by 45-mile-an-hour winds, the ensuing whiteout made visibility almost nil.

Particles of snow hit Lori's face like tiny needles, and the wind whistled right through her clothing. When a gust almost knocked her off her feet, Travis put his arm around her and led her to the snow-covered mound that was his truck. He'd wanted to pick her up at the door, but she'd refused.

Once they were finally inside the vehicle, Travis turned the heat on high and switched on the radio. A winter-storm warning had been posted, with over a foot of snow expected. The report also stated that parts of Route 191 were closed due to drifting snow. The east-west roads were the worst, as the wind blew the snow right over them. The state police were telling motorists to stay home.

Even the short distance to her house the driving was treacherous. Putting his arm around her again, Travis helped her fight the gale and stinging snow to her front door.

There was no getting around it. Lori knew what she had to do. "You'd better stay with me tonight," she murmured.

Ten

"Stay with you?" Travis repeated with a raised eyebrow.

"I meant on the couch," Lori clarified.

"Oh."

"The weather is too bad for you to be out driving," she added.

Travis didn't argue with her.

"I'll go get some sheets."

"Does the couch make up into one of those hide-a-bed things?" Travis asked upon her return.

"No, I'm afraid it doesn't. But it is pretty comfortable. I've slept on it a time or two myself. Fell asleep while watching TV."

Travis didn't point out that her slight frame was a might bit shorter than his brawny six-foot-three-inch build. He wasn't about to say anything that might make her reconsider her decision to let him spend the night.

"You look tired and excited all at the same time," he noted, taking the top sheet from her and finishing the job of making up the couch.

"Probably because that's how I feel."

"You know, I've had experience with calving," Travis noted, "but tonight was different. Tell me something, why do women want a baby? Do they know what it will be like?"

"*I* know what it will be like," Lori replied.

"And you want a baby anyway?"

"God, yes," she whispered fervently.

Seeing the look on her face, Travis was ready to admit that he'd made a mistake in underestimating how much Lori really wanted a child. Wanting to understand her reasons, he asked, "Why?"

"For so many reasons ... I can't explain."

"Try."

"It's more than just *wanting* a baby. It's deeper than that. It's as if I'm missing a part of myself. I dream about a baby of my own, imagine holding it and not having to give it back to the mother because *I'm* the mother and that baby is *mine*—mine to love, to care for, protect, cuddle, watch grow up. I feel such yearning, I can't even describe it."

She didn't have to. Travis knew all about yearning. He'd been yearning for Lori for as long as he could remember and, certainly since Kane's wedding, that yearning had only gotten stronger.

Yes, Travis could understand yearning, all right. And now he understood how Lori felt—the only problem was she felt that way about the prospect of having a baby, not about being with him.

"I just ache to have a baby," Lori whispered.

Travis ached, too. Ached to have Lori back in his life and in his bed.

But she was so wrapped up in this baby thing that she couldn't see straight. And he was so wrapped up in her that his vision wasn't much better.

He wanted to talk to her about having a baby with him, but the shadows of exhaustion on her face stopped him. This wasn't the time. Not yet. But soon.

Travis wondered if he could do what Sarah's husband had done tonight. Would he be able to see Lori in pain and not panic? Sure, he'd seen hundreds of calves born, but he'd never seen a human baby born. "Birth is a messy thing," he muttered, half under his breath.

"So is life," Lori retorted.

He saw the grit and determination in her eyes. She was set on having a baby with or without him. Well, okay, so she wasn't set on having a baby *with* him, yet. But she would.

Seeing his expression, Lori thought Travis might still be brooding about the birth, so she decided to reassure him as best as she could. "Sarah's labor actually wasn't that long. It was just under eight hours. I've had some patients whose labor lasted almost twenty-four hours."

His face grew pale. "Doesn't the idea of being in pain for that length of time scare you?" It sure scared the hell out of him.

Lori shook her head. "I'm more afraid of things unknown than things I know. I know about pregnancy and labor. It's my specialty. And the pain isn't at the same level throughout labor. It varies a lot."

"Can't you use drugs or something to stop the pain?"

"I have authority to do that, yes. If that's what a patient wants."

"Who wouldn't want that?"

"Medicating the mother can slow down the birth process, and it means that the baby also feels the effects of the medication. But I do medicate patients if it's necessary. I talk about options with my patients ahead of time, so we're all on the same wavelength."

"I would think that talking about it and going *through* it are two different things," Travis noted wryly.

"Patients have the right to change their minds, and I talk about that, too. Being involved in the decision-making process is the important thing for most of them. But it's amazing what preparation and coaching can do for pain management."

"All that huffing and puffing Sarah's husband was doing?" At her curious look, he added, "I met the guy down by the vending machine in the lobby. We talked a little."

"Breathing exercises do help," Lori said. "And the end result was a perfect little baby girl."

"I heard they're going to name her after you."

Lori nodded, too moved for a moment to speak.

Travis cupped her face in his hands, and gently brushed her tears away. "I was so proud of you tonight," he whispered.

"You were?"

He nodded.

"Why?" she had to ask.

"Because."

Lori smiled slightly in acknowledgment of one of his favorite words. Years ago, when she'd asked him why he loved her, he'd said, "Because." When she'd asked him why he wanted to marry her, he'd said, "Because." There was something about the way he said it, the way he imbued the word with a wealth of meaning, that instead of a brush-off it became a verbal shorthand, a code word that only the two of them knew.

"It's late. You should get some sleep," he said.

"Actually, it's early." She held out her easy-to-read watch to show him that it was just going on three a.m. "But you're right. I'm beat. I'll see you in the morning."

Lori took a quick shower, realizing as she did so that when she and Travis were married, they'd never talked the way they had tonight. Never discussed labor pains or pregnancy. Never talked about him being proud of her.

By the time Lori went to her room and closed the door, tiredly slipping out of her robe and tumbling into bed, she was wondering *why* she and Travis hadn't talked like that while they'd been married. Maybe because they'd been too busy talking about bills and schedules—or not talking at all. Some of those moments of silence had been filled with the greatest passion she'd ever known, others with the deepest anger.

Those were her last thoughts before slumber and exhaustion claimed her.

Lori woke to the sun shining in her eyes. Blinking sleepily, she realized she hadn't drawn the drapes last night. It was early yet, just a little after seven. When she got up to pull the drapes closed, she noticed the winter wonderland outside. Only four hours of sleep and here she was, tempted to go outside and play in the snow.

Maybe she'd have a cup of coffee first to see if this childish urge would pass. She might as well tug on some clothes while she was at it. She put on a pair of pink sweatpants and a matching sweatshirt. To get to the kitchen, she had to pass Travis, who was still sleeping on her couch. He looked uncomfortable, with his long legs sticking out over the arm. Golden stubble shadowed his face.

Looking down at him, Lori was struck by memories of waking with him in bed beside her, of the two of them nuzzling together under the covers. The good times came to mind. And there had been plenty of them—in the beginning.

Outside of bed, she and Travis had never played, even though they'd been young. The responsibilities had weighed heavily on them both.

"Let's go out and make snow angels." The suggestion popped out of her mouth.

Travis lifted one lid, to stare at her bleary-eyed.

"Come on, it'll be fun." She was already heading for the front door and the coat stand there. She had a mohair cardigan hanging alongside her coat. After tugging on her thermal boots, she added a thick down parka on top of the cardigan she'd just put on.

"You're crazy," Travis muttered.

"You're right. Go back to bed."

"It's a couch, not a bed. Unless you want to call it a bed of nails."

But she wasn't listening to him. "Wait a second," he commanded, getting up cautiously, like a man who had a few vertebrae out of place. Reaching to the ceiling, he got the kinks out.

Lori tried not to stare. Lord, he was a sexy man! From the tip of his bare feet to the top of his tousled golden hair, he exuded sensual heat. Wide, powerful shoulders tapered to a narrow waist and lean hips. His long legs were showcased to perfection in worn-and-wrinkled denim.

"Wait a second," he repeated. "You can't go outside like that. It's still blowing like crazy out there. You need a hat." He plucked one from the top hook and tugged it onto her head, almost lowering the knit cap clear down over her eyes in the process.

Then he grabbed his sheepskin coat and stuck his feet in his good boots.

Lori eyed them doubtfully. "Won't the snow ruin them?"

"My boots are made of sterner stuff than that," he retorted, although truth to tell, he'd never worn them into a snowbank before.

"If I need to be bundled up, so do you," she told him, taking a hot-pink-and-black-checked scarf from a hook and wrapping it around his neck and ears several times. "There." She stood back to admire her handiwork. "It goes very nicely with your black Stetson," she noted approvingly, as he placed his hat on his head. "Last one outside is a rotten egg!" she added, racing for the front door.

Using a snow shovel she kept on her front porch, Travis cleared a narrow path for them. Everything facing west was splattered with the windblown snow—the blue spruce in her front yard, the trunk of the cottonwood, the shutters on her house. Beneath the blanket of snow, familiar things were either transformed into mysterious mounds or disappeared altogether.

Lori hadn't gone but a few feet from her front porch when she became stuck in a snowdrift up to her thighs.

"I see you might be in need of a tow truck, ma'am," Travis mockingly noted with a tip of his hat. "I heard a young heifer got in over her head hereabouts."

"What's your fee?" she countered.

Too late she realized she'd given him the perfect opening. "A kiss," he replied solemnly.

"Do you take plastic?"

"Plastic kisses? No, ma'am. I only accept the real thing."

She shifted again in a vain attempt to free herself. "It's highway robbery!"

"Take it or leave it."

"Okay, pull me out."

He did—right into his arms. "Time to pay up," he murmured, his warm breath ricocheting off her cold lips.

She kissed him—on his cheek.

"Welsher," he called after her as she skipped away, avoiding any more snowdrifts.

"Watch who you're calling a welsher," she said, picking up a handful of snow and packing it into a ball. "Are you gonna take that back?" she asked, weighing the snowball in her hand threateningly.

Travis shook his head. "You couldn't hit the broadside of a barn from twelve inches away," he taunted.

Lori aimed and threw, knocking his black Stetson clear off his head.

"No one messes with a cowboy's hat," Travis growled, replacing his Stetson before grabbing a handful of snow himself. "You're in trouble, lady! Big trouble!"

"Put that down right now," Lori said in her sternest nurse's voice. "I mean it, Travis. Don't even think about throwing it—" *Whoff!* She ended up with a mouthful of snow.

"You've done it now," she growled. "This is war!"

The ensuing snowball fight had plenty of fire power but little accuracy. Lori was too busy gathering snowballs and ducking to take much time to aim. She was pleased to note that Travis was having a similar problem. She ended up laughing so hard she couldn't see straight.

"Time out," she yelled, breathless. Leaning backward, she let herself fall into the soft snow.

"You okay?" Travis asked in concern, dropping his snowy weapon and immediately coming to her.

"Fine. I'm just making a snow angel," she said, smiling up at him. "Surely you made them when you were a kid?"

At his blank look, she realized that he didn't know what she was talking about.

"Okay, here's what you do, Travis. Stand over there, about three feet away from me. Perfect. Now fall back onto the snow."

"No way! I'd look like a beached turtle."

"Who cares? There's no one here to see you but me. Come on," she coaxed with her best smile. "It'll be fun."

Looking around to make sure no one else was out and about this early, Travis finally flopped backward, albeit cautiously. His Stetson slid down to his nose before he shifted it to a better angle.

"Okay, now move your arms and legs like this." She showed him the sweeping movement that created the angel's wings and gown in the snow.

The sudden scraping sound of a snowplow was accompanied by a shout as Virgil yelled, "Hey, are you two loco drunk or what?"

"Good morning to you, too, Virgil," Lori called out with a cheerful wave, getting up with care so as not to ruin her angel impression in the snow.

Travis jumped to his feet again with male awkwardness before shooting a black look at the departing snowplow... and Virgil along with it.

Lori recalled wondering if Travis had ever been as young as Tommy, the cowboy with the nervous stutter and the inability to let go of his hat. Only now was Lori starting to realize that she'd *never* seen Travis act that young, even when they were in high school. His dad's health had never been the best, and Travis had consequently taken on more than his share of work at the ranch. She'd rarely seem him as lighthearted or playful as he was this morning.

And that was a shame. Because Travis was really adorable in this mood. It was a side of him she found irresistible.

"Forget Virgil," she told him, reaching on tiptoes to carefully straighten his battered hat.

He caught her gloved hands in his. Lori forgot what else she was going to say. His look had the ability to wipe her mind clean, like a slate. Meanwhile her heart took up the slack, filling with wonder and fear. There were no words to describe how she felt. He was able to take her to a special place, to a certain level of happiness, without saying a word.

The moment was interrupted by the bark of the rambunctious Irish setter, Salty, that lived three doors down. Salty came bounding over, or tried to. The snow was almost up to her neck and that slowed her progress some, which made her bark more.

As Lori and Travis watched, Salty got mad and took mouthfuls of snow, biting at it as if to get the white wet stuff out of her way. Seconds later the Irish setter ran up to Lori. In her doggy enthusiasm, she knocked Lori right into Travis.

As the two humans fell into the snow once more, Salty gave them a canine grin before taking off.

"Who was that masked dog?" Travis demanded, mimicking the "Lone Ranger."

Giggling and wiggling, Lori was trying to lift herself off Travis's chest. All she ended up doing was twisting, so that she was now face-to-face with him. His hat had fallen off in the scuffle. So had her knit cap. Somehow he got a hand in her hair, a warm hand unprotected by a glove. His palm cupped her nape as he slowly guided her down so he could kiss her.

She felt the warmth of his mouth as he seductively consumed her protests before she could even decide whether or not to make them. In keeping with the winter wonderland, his kiss was magical. It started slowly and progressed quickly as he played an elaborate and erotic game of hide-and-seek with his tongue.

Pleasure buffeted her as surely as the wind had buffeted them last night. Was buffeting them still...

"It's freezing out here," Travis muttered in between kisses.

"I know," Lori agreed with a shiver. "Let's go in and have some hot cocoa to warm up."

Travis could think of other, better ways to get warmed up. "You know what tonight is?" he asked once they were inside and had removed their wet coats. "New Year's Eve. Perfect night for new beginnings. Now that the roads are plowed, I could pick up a thick juicy steak, maybe even get some champagne—"

"I can't."

"Why not? Are you working? Your car still isn't fixed—"

"I know. I'm going to go call the garage right now." Lori turned to leave, but his hand on her arm stopped her.

"Not until you tell me why we can't spend New Year's Eve together." Travis could tell by the look on her face that he wasn't going to like her answer.

"I've already got plans," Lori admitted.

"With that banker?"

She didn't see much point in equivocating. "That's right."

"Cancel," Travis ordered.

His tone of voice irked her. "No."

"What do you mean, no?"

"What does no usually mean?" she countered.

"That you're out of your mind," he angrily retorted.

"That's not the dictionary definition of the word, as I recall," Lori snapped back.

"Stop being cute. You're out of your mind if you think I'm going to let you—"

"*Let* me?" she said dangerously.

"Okay, not the best choice of words, maybe," Travis admitted. "What do you want from me? You want me to sit here like a wimp while you go around dating other men?"

"Certainly not. I don't expect you to sit anywhere. I had expected you to be reasonable about this, but that was clearly a mistake."

"You bet it was," he said.

"I don't know what made me think you'd be mature about this—"

"Mature?" he interrupted. "Hah!"

"I rest my case."

"Fine. While you and your banker beau are toasting in the New Year, you just think about this." Grabbing her around the waist, he hauled her into his arms and kissed her. What started in anger soon melted into passion. In direct contrast to their earlier kiss, this one was elemental in its raw hunger. It wasn't fancy and it wasn't tender, but in its own way it was as devastatingly effective.

Travis spared her one last burning glare, his blue eyes like the heart of a flame, before jamming his hat on his head and taking off.

Listening to his pickup truck roaring out of her driveway, Lori suddenly remembered their bet from last night, about them not arguing. Checking her watch, she muttered to herself, "We lasted all of what, maybe twelve hours."

What happened to their bet now that they'd argued? Lori had a sinking feeling she and Travis might both be losers. They had a snowball's chance in Hades of making a go of things again.

Lori didn't see or hear from Travis for the next twelve days. As things turned out, she rang in the New Year alone, because David came down with the flu that was going around. They had dinner a few days later instead. David was a nice man. Lori didn't go boneless when he kissed her. She tried to imagine what kind of child she'd have if the two of them were to... And that was part of the problem. Deep down, she couldn't imagine the two of them being intimate. She just didn't feel that way about David. Yet.

Lori told herself she was setting her standards too high, reminding herself that nothing was perfect. The important thing was the baby. The rest would work itself out. In time.

Meanwhile, Homer had finally finished his painting job and was going to hold off building the bookshelves she needed until February. Lori was pleased with his work. She'd rehung her black-and-white framed landscape photographs, wondering as she did so why life couldn't be equally black-and-white instead of infinite shades of gray.

Work kept her busy most of the time. For some reason she had a number of patients coming in for pap tests. She suspected it was because word had finally spread that she was trained to do more than deliver babies.

The first thing she'd done after Travis stormed out was call the mechanic, who fixed her car despite the holiday. The second thing she'd done was to shed a tear or two over the fight she'd had with Travis. Okay, so she'd used up almost half a box of facial tissues, but during that time she'd gotten the alternator in her car fixed and obtained a clean automotive bill of health. Her own mental health was another thing.

Determined not to dwell on Travis, she completed a foot-high stack of paperwork at the office, mostly insurance-claim forms, and in the evenings even managed to watch three more episodes of *Poldark*.

Despite the fact that the hero of the BBC-TV series was a dark-haired and brooding Englishman from Cornwall, he reminded her of Travis. She'd decided that male arrogance apparently knew no physical boundaries. Actually, there were similarities between Travis and Ross Poldark; she saw it in their smoldering looks and the low patience level they had with the women in their lives. Maybe it was a testosterone thing, Lori considered darkly.

Demelza had settled down to being a house cat as if to the manor born. One of her favorite spots was still on top of the TV set, where she could warm her tummy while perusing the room at large. She was still skittish of strangers.

To Lori's surprise, the next time she went out to visit Winona, her friend already knew about Demelza. "So how's that cat of yours?" she asked.

"How did you know I have a cat now?" Lori queried.

"I sent her your way. I couldn't get her to trust me, but I knew she'd trust you."

"But this is miles from my house."

"I get out some, you know," Winona declared. "I saw her in town. She's a town cat, not a country one. She's got class under that dirty exterior."

"I named her Demelza."

"Big name for a witch cat," Winona noted.

"Witch cat?"

"Black cat with green eyes. Witch cat."

"Well, I call her Dem for short. And if she's a witch cat, then maybe she can give me a few clues about putting a hex on Straker."

"What's he done now?"

"Just been his own obnoxious self."

"The man is a pain in the behind."

"You won't get any argument from me there," Lori agreed, remembering the way Straker had taunted her when she'd arrived for Sarah's delivery.

"I've gotten some strange vibes from him over the years," Winona murmured. "Nothing I can put my finger on, but it's something . . . some kind of trouble. Definitely negative energy."

"I know what you mean." Lori sipped appreciatively at the tea Winona had prepared.

"Well, I'm glad you took that lovely black cat in. Some folks are still so stupidly superstitious."

"She's brought me *good* luck, not bad," Lori replied. "In fact, I met someone new. David Asher. He's only been in town a few months. He's originally from Great Falls."

"A big-city type."

"Most wouldn't consider Great Falls to be a big city," Lori countered. "We're not talking New York or Chicago here."

"We'll get back to this David in a minute, but first tell me—Sarah had a girl, didn't she."

Lori nodded.

"I told her last summer her baby would be a girl. My success rate on those premonitions is 100%, you know. Some other things are fuzzy in my visions, but the sex of a pregnant mom's baby is one of my strong suits," Winona said proudly.

"That and harvesting the best honey in the county."

Winona nodded her head modestly before saying, "Thanks, but complimenting me isn't going to distract me from the subject, you know. Tell me more about this David you're seeing."

"He's the new branch manager at the bank."

"Nice brown eyes, dark hair?" Winona inserted.

Lori nodded.

"I've met him. He's a good man."

"I'm glad you think so. You haven't picked up any bad vibes from him, have you?" Lori asked.

"Only when I bounced that seventy-two dollar check, not that it was my fault. I explained that I gave the bank a check to deposit—"

"I was asking if you'd sensed anything about him *personally,*" Lori clarified.

"Not at all," Winona replied.

"Good."

"He's not the man for *you,* of course," she added.

"Excuse me?"

"Travis is the man for you," Winona firmly declared.

"Travis and I already tried making a go of things. We got married and it didn't work."

Winona waved her hand, as if shooing away a pesky fly. "You were too young then."

"Is this a premonition we're talking about?"

"Heck no, common sense would tell you that."

"So what makes you think that Travis and I are meant for each other even though we're divorced?" Lori demanded.

"The fact that Virgil saw the two of you rolling around in the snow in front of your house the other morning."

"We weren't rolling around in the snow, we were making snow angels."

"At the crack of dawn, practically."

"He was stranded by the blizzard," Lori said defensively.

"What other man would you want to make snow angels with?"

Lori was silent.

"See?" Winona looked smug. "I told you."

"You really think Travis and I have changed enough to make a go of things now?

"Only *you* can answer that question."

"We still argue a lot. In fact, we're not even speaking at the moment." Lori sighed. "Why can't you just get a premonition, Winona, and makes things a little easier here?"

"It's not supposed to be easy."

"No kidding," Lori muttered.

"How does Travis feel?" Winona asked her.

"He said he wants me."

"What about the baby you want?"

"He was at the hospital when Sarah delivered. He looked shook by the concept. Afterward we talked about a lot of things, but in more general terms. Not specifically how he'd feel about my having a baby."

"Maybe you should talk to him specifically," Winona suggested.

Lori shook her head. "I told you, we're not speaking at the moment. I'd be better off with David."

Winona ended up having the last word. "Who are you trying to convince? Me or you?"

"Smells good," Travis told Tex as he sat down with the others to a dinner of chicken-fried steak, mashed potatoes and mixed vegetables. "Looks like the weather is finally going to clear up tomorrow." The snowstorm that had kept him at Lori's had hit twelve days ago. Travis hadn't seen Lori since. They'd had another four inches of snow in the interim and he'd been kept busy with work at the ranch. Thank God he hadn't lost any cattle in the blizzard. Even though he moved his herd down to the hay meadow for winter, the storm had packed one hell of a wallop.

The dinnertime conversation centered on the ranch for the rest of the meal, with Slim and the ranch hands contributing every now and again. Afterward, Travis headed for the big oak desk in the living room.

First he completed the necessary information on the five bulls he planned on selling in March—three two-year-olds in an auction and two yearlings in a private-treaty sale. Then Travis returned to the job of working on tax records, putting things in enough order so that his accountant, who kept bugging him to get a computer, would be able to manage from there. Numbers weren't Travis's favorite thing. He preferred being outdoors, to feel the big sky over his head—and in Montana, the sky was bigger than just about any-place else in the world. Not that Travis had done a lot of traveling, but he'd seen pictures. And no place compared to his home state. He was mighty proud to be a Montanan.

It was one of the few states in the lower forty-eight that had enough room for a man to spread out. Travis hated be-ing hemmed in, or even feeling that way. For some reason his marriage came to mind, and he recalled the long hours he'd spent out on the range. When calving season started, in March, he'd barely have time to grab a few hours sleep before he'd be in the saddle again. Every day newborn calves would be hitting the ground, while Travis and his hands kept an eye on things. Danger was all around, from predators to late-spring snowstorms.

Six or seven weeks later, his work shifted into a different, slightly less hectic gear as he moved the herd to higher ground and began branding. Haying was his least-favorite season, for the work was monotonous. After five or six weeks of that, he welcomed the chance to get back to cattle work again—rounding up, weaning, shipping.

Now it was winter, the slowest season on the ranch. Travis, Slim and Tommy were done with feeding the herd by eleven-thirty in the morning, and Travis had the rest of the day to himself. Plenty of time to brood over Lori.

"I can tell by that strange look on your face that you're thinking about Lori again," Tex declared as she plunked a cup of coffee on the corner of his desk. "You haven't talked about her since you stayed overnight at her place during the blizzard. I think I'll be able to save your good boots, by the way."

"Thanks."

"So what about Lori?"

"We had a fight," Travis reluctantly acknowledged.

"Surprise, surprise," Tex drawled.

He gave her a dark look, to which she paid no attention.

"And what did you two fight about this time?" Tex demanded.

He glared at her. "Don't you have something to watch on TV?" Three years ago he and Slim had gone in together to get a satellite dish so that Tex could watch her favorite soaps, as well as CNN and "American Movie Classics," of which she was a faithful devotee; Travis and Slim enjoyed the sports channels. Cable TV hadn't come to Whitehorn yet and it was doubtful it would in this century. Besides, the nearby mountains made normal reception in their area fuzzy at best.

For years Travis had thought the number on John Elway's chest was nine, not seven. Now he got to watch the Broncos as clearly as if he were right in Mile High Stadium. The satellite dish, their one extravagance, was actually a fairly common sight in that part of the country.

"Slim's watching some sports thing," Tex told Travis. "He knew I wanted to talk to you."

"Lecture is more like it," Travis muttered.

"Why would I lecture you? There's no talking to a horse with stones in its ears."

"I haven't heard that one before," Travis noted.

"That's because I just made it up. But don't go changing the subject. Last I heard you were on your way to go courting Lori. That was your plan and it appeared to be successful, since you didn't even come home that night."

"I stayed in town because of the blizzard."

"I happen to know that your truck can make it through three times that amount of snow."

"You might know that, but Lori doesn't. She offered to let me stay the night at her place, so I did."

"And?" Tex prompted.

"And the next morning we fought."

"Did you two...?"

"Not that it's any of your business," Travis growled, "but no, we didn't."

Tex nodded sagaciously. "Ah, that explains a lot."

"What's that supposed to mean?"

"I mean it explains why you've been ornerier than a seven-hundred-pound heifer with the bloat for the past two weeks almost."

Travis glared once again, his expression darkening.

"So you and Lori fought because the two of you didn't—"

"No," Travis growled. "We fought about the fact that she had a date for New Year's Eve with her banker boyfriend and she wouldn't break it for me."

"You egged her on again."

"Oh, so now this is all my fault?"

"I didn't say that. Knowing Lori as I do, I suspect she played her part in the fireworks between you two. But I can't control her. Can't control you, either," Tex noted in exasperation. "But I can at least try to make you see the error of your ways. What happened to the idea of starting over with Lori? I thought you were going to pretend you'd just met her."

"I tried that."

"And?"

"And it worked for a while."

"'Til you ordered her to break her plans with that banker, I'll bet," Tex observed.

Tired of taking one step forward and two back with Lori, Travis snapped, "What else was I supposed to do?"

"Talk *to* her instead of yell *at* her."

"I could talk till I'm blue in the face, but it wouldn't make any difference. She's gonna do what she's gonna do, anyway."

"That's my point."

"Fine. If she wants that banker so damn much, she can have him!" Travis shouted.

"Now don't you go saying things like that, lest they come true." With another dire look, Tex left him to stew in his own juices.

"How is a convention of midwives like a granola bar?" Dr. Straker was asking Danette as Lori approached the nurses' station.

"I give up," Danette said with a simpering smile.

"They're both filled with nuts and flakes," Dr. Straker replied.

Danette and Straker laughed, while the new nurse on the floor stared at Lori as if uncertain what to do.

Seeing her, Dr. Straker laughed all the harder. "Come on, Lori, don't be a bad sport," he chided. "Can't you take a joke?" Grinning like a Cheshire cat, he headed off, slapping the back of one of his physician colleagues as he went.

With his departure, Lori silently brooded that there were times when it was like pulling teeth to get some respect. For the most part, she had the respect of the staff here, with the exception of a few folks—Straker and Danette most notably. Being a midwife meant being good *wasn't* good enough. Lori had to be flawless, or as close to it as humanly possible. She couldn't create the slightest opportunity for her techniques or skills to be questioned or criticized. She had to have grace under pressure.

Lori liked to think she had that—professionally, at least. And to date, she'd never been the least bit lax with her patients. Almost never... That incident with her beeper malfunctioning still bothered her. What if she hadn't tipped over her purse when she had? What if the car accident had been more serious and her patient's condition more critical? Lori was only too well aware that with that incident, she'd given Dr. Straker his first opportunity for real criticism.

She didn't know what she could do about it, except continue to ignore his provoking ways and do her job, including the paperwork she needed to complete this evening. Rita Brooks, the patient who'd been in the minor car accident at thirty weeks, had delivered a healthy baby boy tonight, nine pounds nine ounces.

But before hitting the paperwork, Lori needed something to fortify herself with first—a candy bar with coconut inside and dark chocolate outside. Unfortunately, the only vending machine that carried that particular brand was downstairs near the emergency room. Still, it was worth the trip.

Lori used the stairs instead of the elevator and told herself she was burning the calories she was about to consume.

As she passed the emergency area, out of the corner of her eye she saw a familiar-looking black Stetson on a head bowed with dread. Her heart stopped. It was Travis, sitting in a neon orange plastic chair in the waiting room, his elbows resting on his knees, hands gripped together as if in prayer. And in that instant, Lori knew something was wrong—*very* wrong.

Eleven

"Travis?" Hurrying to his side, Lori gently touched him on his shoulder, and he instantly leapt to his feet. "What's wrong?" she asked. At first she'd thought he might be in the emergency area because he was injured, but she was reassured on that point. He didn't appear to be physically hurt, through there was a world of pain in his blue eyes. "What are you doing here?"

"I brought Tex in." His voice sounded harsh and dried up, as if seared by emotion.

"Tex? What happened?"

"There was an accident. She was in the kitchen... there was a slick spot on the floor... she fell and hit her head on the linoleum. I thought at first she was dead. She was lying there so still." His gaze shifted from Lori to an empty place in the distance. "I walked in and found her like that."

"Did she regain consciousness?"

Travis shook his head. "Slim is with her... I haven't heard anything since I brought her in. It's been almost an hour...."

"I'll go see what I can found out," Lori promised. "Take it easy, it'll be all right."

She hurried off before Travis could tell her that it *wouldn't* be all right, that the reason Tex had gone stomping into the kitchen in such a high temper was because of the confrontation they'd had. Travis had shouted at her. And when he'd gone into the kitchen a few minutes later to apologize, he'd found her lying there as still as snow.

Travis had expected his father's death. Had seen it coming. After all, his dad had been in poor health for some time. But Tex had never been sick a day in her life. She'd always been there for him. Sturdy as a western fence.

Lori returned and Travis leapt to his feet again. "How is she?"

"She's going to be all right. She's finally recovered consciousness."

"Thank God." Travis sank back into the uncomfortable orange chair and ran a shaky hand through his already tousled hair.

"They want to keep her overnight for observation. She's got a concussion, but the tests didn't indicate any bone fractures."

"Concussion?" Travis repeated in dismay.

Lori nodded. Seeing the panic on his face, she sat beside him and took his cold hand in hers. "Travis, you've had concussions. Three of them, as I recall. Once when you were making that winning touchdown in high school. Once when you fell off your horse—"

"I was thrown, I didn't fall off," he said, automatically correcting her. "Besides, I was a hell of a lot younger than Tex when I had those concussions." Turning to face her, he said, "You're not lying to me? Are you sure she'll be okay?"

"Well, she'll have a heck of a headache, but she'll be just fine. They'll keep a close eye on her."

Travis nodded. "You bet. I'll make sure of that. I'm staying the night."

"What would be the point of doing that? She'll be well taken care of here. In fact, they're getting a room ready for her now, and as soon as she's settled you can go up and see her. She's not alone. Slim is still with her. Or you can go back and see her now, if you'd rather," Lori added, sensing that Travis needed to reassure himself that his surrogate mother was okay. For that's what Tex was to him, much more than just a housekeeper.

"I'd rather see her now," Travis said.

"I'll take you on back," Lori replied, leading him through the mazelike emergency area to the curtained cubicle where Tex and Slim were. Sensing that the three of them needed time alone, Lori told Travis, "I've got some paperwork to finish upstairs, but I'll be back later."

Travis nodded and, taking a deep breath, entered the cubicle.

"Why, Travis, I do believe you're looking a little green around the gills," Tex noted as he came closer. "Just about the color of my split-pea soup, wouldn't you say, Slim?"

"This is a heck of a way to get some time off," Travis retorted in kind, his voice gruff with unspoken emotion.

"That's what I told her," Slim agreed.

"Oh, get off with the two of you," Tex said. "No fair ganging up on an injured old woman!"

"I thought you hated to be called old," Travis countered.

"You were supposed to correct me," Tex told him. "A bit slow on the uptake, you two. Who's got the concussion here, me or you?"

Joking though she was, Travis could see the pain in her eyes, and it ate at him.

"Now you go on back to the ranch," she told him after they'd talked a few minutes. "I'll be fine. Be back home in the morning. Meanwhile, you and the ranch hands stay out of my kitchen. No messing with my stove if you know what's good for you."

"Yes, ma'am."

"I raised him right," Tex told Slim.

But as he left, Travis didn't agree that he'd been raised right. If so, he would never have yelled at her the way he had earlier that evening. Guilt settled like a boulder on his shoulders.

Travis returned to the waiting room, where he stayed, his face grim, until Slim stopped by. "She's upstairs, settled in her room. I just signed her admission papers. Tex has got a hard head, so don't you go worrying about her," he told Travis.

"Yeah, right. She hasn't been in a hospital in over thirty years, Slim."

"I know that, but you can't stay here all night," Slim answered.

"That's what I told him earlier," Lori said, having just rejoined them after completing her paperwork upstairs.

"I'm not leaving yet," Travis stubbornly maintained.

"Then come with me down to the hospital cafeteria for some coffee," Lori invited, taking hold of Travis's arm and practically hauling him after her.

At that time of night there weren't many people in the cafeteria, which was closed except for basics like hot drinks. The place smelled like disinfectant and microwave food. Once they were seated at a table for two, with a cup of hot black coffee in front of Travis, Lori made conversation that required no participation on his part while she periodically fussed at him to drink his coffee before it got cold. "It's bearable when it's hot," she noted, "but undrinkable once it cools down. Cafeteria coffee is meant to be strong, not tasty."

"Why aren't you drinking any?"

"Are you kidding?" she retorted with a grin. "I know better. That's why I drink tea. Earl Grey with milk and sugar. Want a taste?" She held out her cup.

He made a face and shook his head.

Lori let silence fill the space between them. But that silence was laced with something more. Travis was clearly brooding about something.

"Tex is going to be all right, really," she reassured him yet again. "I know it must have been a shock to find her unconscious like that—"

"You don't understand," he curtly interrupted. "It's my fault that she fell. She was upset because we'd been arguing earlier."

"You and Tex?" Lori said in disbelief. "You two never argue."

"I shouted at her." Travis's voice was filled with regret.

"I'm sure she shouted back."

Travis shook his head. "No, she didn't."

"What were you arguing about?" Travis didn't reply, but Lori could read the answer on his face. "It was me, wasn't it?" she guessed. "Then maybe I should feel guilty for starting everything."

"It's not your fault."

"It's not yours, either," she stated. "Tex's injury was caused by an accident. It's fine for you to feel regret or fear, but guilt is pointless."

"Don't tell me how to feel!" Travis practically shouted, before bending his head and running his fingers through his hair. "I'm sorry," he muttered. "It's been a hell of a night."

"What do you think Tex would say if she saw you sitting here racked with guilt?"

His smile was a long time coming, but it slowly appeared, starting at the right outer corner of his mouth. "She'd probably kick my butt across the cafeteria," he ruefully acknowledged.

Lori nodded in agreement. "I rest my case."

He reached his hand over the Formica table to twine his fingers through hers. "Thanks for being here tonight."

"I work here."

"You know what I mean."

"Yeah, I know," she replied. "Feel better now?"

Travis nodded.

There was a meaningful moment of silence as their eyes met and said what words couldn't.

"What are we going to do?" Travis finally asked.

"Do?" she repeated, her gaze sliding away from his.

"About us." Gently cupping her cheek with his hand, he used his thumb to tip her chin up until she met his look head-on. His gaze was direct as he said, "I don't know

about you, but I'm tired of all this fighting you and I have
been doing."

"So am I," she softly admitted.

"I don't want to give up on us." His hand fell to the table once more. "But I need to know something." Taking her
fingers in his, he fiddled with them, running his thumb over
the back of her knuckles. "No lies, okay?"

"Okay."

"Are you in love with this banker guy?" Travis asked.

Lori shook her head.

"Are you in love with me?" he continued.

"I don't know," she whispered.

"Fair enough." His gruff voice reflected his acceptance
of her reply, acknowledging that it wasn't what he wanted
to hear, while admitting it wasn't as bad as he feared.

Lori wanted to ask him if he was in love with her, but she
was afraid of what his answer might be. What if he said no?
What if he said yes?

Instead he said, "Here's what I think. I think that when
Tex is better, we need to get away from all this, even if it's
just for a day. Go someplace neutral. Not the ranch. Not
here in town, either. We need some time together. Because
I know that what's between us is worth fighting for. What
do you say? Will you think about it?"

Lori nodded.

"Good." He gave her hand a squeeze.

At that moment Lori felt as if more connected them than
just their fingers. It was as if a bridge had been formed,
binding them together. For the first time in a long time, she
and Travis weren't burning bridges, they were building
them.

Errol Straker looked down at Mary Jo, who was lying in
his bed. "Won't your husband miss you?"

"I told him I'd be staying late in town because of the li-
brary-board meeting," she whispered. "I think he believed
me."

"I'm sure he did. I can't believe you married such a wimp."

"He's no wimp," she said with just the right amount of bitterness. "That's just an act." Mary Jo had always considered herself to be a good actress, and the role she'd come up with this time was a doozie. She could use Errol's help with the next step in her grand plan. To do that, she needed to bring out what few protective instincts the man might have. "Dugin wants people to think he's easily swayed. But beneath that mild-mannered exterior he's really a monster." Closing her eyes, she shuddered delicately, and prepared to deliver her carefully calculated lies about her husband. "I think his older brother's death in Vietnam all those years ago affected him deeply. Compared to Wayne, who was a hero and a perfect son, Dugin never measured up in his father's eyes. Things have gotten even worse since his father's fatal heart attack awhile back. Now it's too late for Dugin to ever get his father's respect, and that eats away at him inside. He can't win, so he takes it out on me," Mary Jo admitted, her voice edged with a sob.

Errol gathered her close, muttering, "The bastard!"

Two tears rolled down her cheeks as she whispered, "I know some people might say that I married him for his money, but it's not true." Shifting away so that she could look Errol in the eye, she earnestly added, "I really thought I loved him. But then..."

"Then?"

"Then I met you and discovered what love is all about," she huskily confessed. "What a *real* man is like." Mary Jo observed the way Errol preened with male pride. Men were so predictable.

"I hate the fact that you have to go back to him," Errol murmured.

"I'd be afraid to leave." Mary Jo knew she'd played the part of abused victim well. After all, she'd been slapped around plenty in her life—once so badly she'd ended up in the hospital, where her life had changed forever. Putting her fingers on Errol's lips, Mary Jo said, "Don't let's talk about Dugin anymore. Let's enjoy the time we have." Her kiss put a halt to further conversation.

Step one complete, Mary Jo told herself. *You deserve an Oscar for that performance!*

The next morning, Molly and Lori had a few minutes before patients started arriving at the family practice. With Molly catching the flu right after the holidays, Lori hadn't had a chance to talk to her much lately. And she was bursting to talk to someone about the transition that had taken place last night with Travis.

So when Molly asked, "What's new?" Lori spilled the beans.

"Travis has asked me to go away with him for a day," she confessed.

"He did?" Molly was clearly surprised by this bit of news. "What did you say?"

"I said I'd think about it."

"Last I heard you and Travis weren't on speaking terms."

"I know. But Tex was hurt in a fall out at the ranch last night, and Travis and I got to talking...." Lori's voice trailed off. "All we did was talk, and not even about us, really. But it made me feel closer to him than I have in years."

"What about David?" Molly asked.

"Maybe I have to put my past to rest before I can move forward."

"And maybe you'll be getting into deeper trouble instead," Molly said.

"It's just for a day. What can happen in a day?" Remembering what had happened on Kane Hunter's wedding day, Lori amended her previous comment. "Okay, so I'll be careful."

"You do that."

It seemed to be Lori's day for receiving friendly advice, for later that evening Maris unexpectedly dropped by her house for a visit.

"Come on in. Where's that adorable godson of mine?" Lori asked.

"I left him back at the ranch with Luke for some male-bonding time together. I figured it's Luke's turn to change a few diapers. Actually, I wanted to talk to you."

"You could have called me. You didn't have to drive all the way into town."

"I was afraid you'd put me off on the phone," Maris declared.

"Well, can I get you some coffee or something to drink?"

"No, thanks."

"What was it you wanted to talk to me about?" Lori asked as the two of them sat on her denim-covered couch.

"You've been acting strange the past few weeks," Maris said bluntly. "Since Thanksgiving, in fact. And then I hear from Lily Mae that there's talk of you wanting a baby. Is this true?"

Lori nodded.

"Why didn't you talk to me about it?" Maris's voice reflected both anger and pain. "I'm your oldest friend, yet I had to find out from the town gossip!"

"I couldn't talk to you."

"Why not?"

"Because I didn't think you'd understand. Molly already—"

"You talked to Molly about this and you didn't talk to me?" Maris interrupted her to demand. "I've known you ten times longer than she has."

"Sometimes it's easier to talk to new friends than old ones about some things. I didn't want you telling me I was being ridiculous."

"I wouldn't have told you that," Maris exclaimed.

"Sure, you say that now—"

"Listen, I understand more than you could know. When I first met Luke, I tried to trick him into getting me pregnant," Maris confessed.

Lori didn't know what to say. She had a hard time imagining her friend tricking anyone. Maris wasn't the devious type. Far from it. "Things worked out between you and Luke, though."

"That's right. The reason I'm telling you this is because I *can* sympathize with wanting a baby so much you'd go to extremes to do it."

"I had no idea...."

"You weren't supposed to," Maris said.

"Unlike my situation, where everyone in town seems to know," Lori muttered.

"How did that happen?" Maris asked.

"Danette at the hospital overheard me talking to Molly on my birthday. You know how this town is. By the time the story made the rounds, it got exaggerated."

"Is that when Travis came pounding on your door?" At Lori's astonished look, Maris said, "Yes, I heard about that from Lily Mae, too."

"She doesn't miss much, does she?"

"Nope. So what's going on with you and Travis?" Maris demanded. "When I saw both of you singing in the Christmas choir, I couldn't believe it."

"It wasn't planned. As far as I knew, Travis only sang in the shower."

"And when was the last time you saw him in the shower?" Maris mockingly inquired, with the directness of a long-time friend.

"Not since the divorce."

"So there's nothing going on with you and Travis now?" Maris asked.

Lori's blush gave her away.

"Come on," Maris prompted. "What's happening here?"

"I don't know. It doesn't make sense. I've been back in Whitehorn for almost three years and I managed to handle Travis just fine."

"*Handle?*" Maris asked with a raised eyebrow.

Lori tossed a floral throw pillow at her. "You know what I mean."

"So what happened to change things?"

"Kane's wedding."

"Ah." Maris nodded.

"It's not that I was brokenhearted when he married Moriah. Okay, maybe my heart was a little dented. But Kane wasn't the grand passion of my life."

"No. Travis was that."

Lori nodded. "And that didn't work out, either. So I've had grand passion and I've had mutual respect and friendship. Neither lasted. Maybe I'm not meant to sustain a relationship," she noted glumly. "Maybe I don't have what it takes."

"That's ridiculous. Of course you have what it takes. You're a warm and loving person, Lori. Everyone likes you."

"Be that as it may, things just haven't worked out for me, and the years are marching on. It's time I considered other options for becoming a parent. But then I tell myself that this is Montana, not California or the East Coast. Values are very traditional here, and that's good, that's why I like it here. But still...it would mean that if I decided to go the single-parent route, my child might suffer for it. Aside from not having a father, he or she would have to contend with gossip, with talk from the other kids. I don't want my child to have to face that."

"I heard you were dating the new bank manager, David something-or-other."

Lori nodded. "We went out on two dates together. He's a really nice guy."

"But he's not special?"

Lori shook her head. "I thought I didn't want special."

"And now?"

"Now I don't know. Travis says he wants me back. He actually came courting with candy and flowers."

Maris grinned. "I would have loved to have seen that."

"Some of the best times of my life have been spent with Travis. Some of the worst times, too. And that's my dilemma, or part of it, anyway. Travis and I weren't able to make a go of it in the past. It would be foolish of us to try again. You were married before. You know what I mean."

"Ray was very different from Travis."

"I know. You're right. Travis is a good man. He was still a good man, albeit an impossible one, when we got divorced. Just a good, impossible man I didn't love anymore, and who didn't love me."

"I'm not sure about that last part. Seems to me that Travis never really got over you."

"Part of me never got over him, either," Lori whispered. "But I'm scared. Travis says we're different people now. That we've grown and matured. We still fight, though."

"Nothing wrong with fighting. Luke and I do it on occasion," Maris said. Then she added, "The making up is the good part."

Her friend's grin made Lori smile. The two of them laughed before Lori admitted, "Winona keeps telling me that Travis is the man for me."

"Winona's not always right."

"Yeah, but she's been right about a lot of things. Anyway, the bottom line is that I've agreed to spend a day with Travis, away from Whitehorn. We need to find someplace neutral to talk some things out. I called him right before you came over."

"Where are you going?"

"Not far. Just down to West Yellowstone."

"I hope things work out."

"Thanks. And thanks for stopping by, Maris. I'm glad we cleared the air. And I'm sorry for not confiding in you earlier."

"That's okay. Just see that it doesn't happen again."

Lori nodded and gave her friend a big hug.

By the time Lori had made the necessary arrangements for her to be able to leave Whitehorn for the day, it was a Saturday near the end of January. This time of year darkness fell during business hours, and long underwear became *de rigueur*, as temperatures often plummeted below zero and wind chills became outrageous. As Tex, who was recovering nicely from her concussion, had often said in winters past, "Fifty below zero feels the same as thirty below. After a point, the numbers don't matter."

Although the sky was overcast today, the temperature felt positively balmy—but then, after a week of below-zero weather, twenty degrees would seem that way. There was a fifty-percent chance of snow later in the afternoon. Lori sat in Travis's pickup truck as they sped down the highway, and tried not to show her nervousness.

She couldn't even remember the last time she'd left town just for the fun of it. In her line of work, she had to be available. She'd only gotten away today because a window of opportunity had presented itself, a break where none of her patients was due to deliver. Travis had a cellular phone in his pickup so she could call in to her service should her beeper go off. West Yellowstone wasn't that far away—she could be back in Whitehorn in a little more than an hour, if need be. Meanwhile, one of the family-practice physicians was on call.

Lori's attention returned to the passing countryside. Winter cloaked the land like a fresh coat of paint, whitening and reflecting the diffused January light. The recent bout of subzero temperatures had created ice crystals atop the snow, Mother Nature's own sparkling gems. Looking out the truck-cab window, Lori noticed the road sign for the tiny town of Wisdom. Beyond that lay the Crazy Mountains—the Crazies, as they were fondly called.

So there she was, driving with her ex-husband some-where between Wisdom and the Crazies—figuratively speaking, as well as literally. For going away with him was either the craziest or the wisest thing she'd ever done.

"So who's bright idea was this, anyway?" Lori muttered as she braced her poles in the snow and leaned over her skis to catch her breath.

"Yours," Travis retorted from beside her.

"Cross-country skiing has been proved to be the best aerobic exercise," she said, as if trying to remind herself why she'd chosen this particular activity for their day together.

"What about making love? Where does that rate on the aerobic-exercise scale?"

A perfect ten. The thought came to Lori's mind in a flash. So did the memories of the last time they'd made love. It had been almost two months ago now. Two months of cold, lonely nights and hot memories.

So what was she doing cross-country skiing and not snuggling in bed with Travis? The renegade thought crossed her mind and was instantly chased out. Despite her verbal complaint, she *was* having a good time. West Yellowstone proudly claimed it was the snowmobiling capital of the world, but Lori preferred the silence of skiing. She had no intention of slinging her leg over the equivalent of a Harley on skis, hanging on to Travis for dear life as they roared around Yellowstone Park. He'd be in the driver's seat and she didn't want him there. She wanted him on equal ground with her.

And beautiful ground it was. But then it was hard not to find something beautiful to look at in this part of the state. Lori was grateful that her forebears had had the foresight to protect some of Montana's best scenery—in Glacier National Park to the north and Yellowstone to the south.

Actually, most of Yellowstone was located in Wyoming, but Montana was only too proud to claim a small part of it as its own. The combination of mountains and valleys cut out of the landscape, adorned with waterfalls and steamy geysers, was a powerful one. Once it got hold of your soul it never let go.

Lori could still remember the first time her parents had taken her to Yellowstone. She'd probably been five at the time. Old Faithful had looked gigantic to her then, almost frightening in its power. In fact, the park was filled with boiling mud cauldrons, and it had seemed to her childish imagination to be the perfect place for witches to live.

It was only later, as she got older and her parents took her again and again, that Lori learned to love the land's eccentric beauty. And to cherish all the out-of-the-way places beyond Old Faithful—from the pastel-colored terraces at Mammoth Hot Springs, to the petrified trees on Specimen Ridge, to the deep-cut gorge of Yellowstone's Grand Canyon, to her dad's favorite secluded campground at Indian Creek.

All these things and more Lori remembered and loved about this park. It had been too many years since she'd been back to the area.

Travis interrupted her thoughts to say, "When are we going to eat? I'm starving!"

"We've almost completed this ski trail."

"Clever of them to have it start and end behind a restaurant," Travis noted.

"Good planning," she agreed.

As far as he was concerned, good planning described his decision to ski behind Lori, which allowed him to watch her. And there was plenty to keep him occupied. The long length of her legs encased in woolen leggings. The way her fanny moved as she kicked with her skis. The curve of her hips. Yes, Travis was definitely enjoying the view.

He wasn't sure about the skiing. He was just glad none of his rancher friends could see him. Skiing wasn't exactly a cowboy activity. At the rental place, he'd had to trade his jeans for woolen pants, along with the rest of the paraphernalia required. Still, he had to admit that cross-country ski-ing did prove useful for getting around at this time of year, which is why he'd learned it in the first place. The weather played havoc on machinery, often times forcing ranchers to rely on the old-fashioned, tried-and-true way of doing things.

Last week, during the frigid cold spell, Travis had had to hitch up his two shire workhorses to the flatbed wagon in order to get the feed out to the herd. His tractor had frozen up. So had the fast-moving stream that provided drinking water for the livestock, requiring him to chop a fresh hole in it every morning while Tommy and Granger dumped seventy-pound bales of hay off the wagon for the hungry cattle.

Now Travis was the one who was hungry, and it wasn't just for food. He was hungry for Lori. The day was almost half over and they still hadn't talked. As soon as they'd ar-rived in West Yellowstone and she'd caught sight of a sign advertising cross-country-ski rentals, she'd taken hold of that idea like a barn cat pouncing on a mouse. He was hop-ing that when they stopped to eat, they'd get back on track.

Not that Travis knew what to say. He didn't have a clue. By the time they reached the restaurant, a Swiss-chalet style place, and had turned in their rental gear, he got cold feet. Lori was having fun; he could see it in her face. Did he re-ally want to risk breaking that mood by dredging up their past, asking her why she'd divorced him?

Maybe the wisest move would be to fall back on plan A—to pretend they'd recently met and that he was fiercely at-tracted to her. Yes, Travis liked that idea. After ordering lunch—sirloin steak for him, beef stew for her—he talked to her. About her work, about the goings-on at the ranch, about anything and everything. So long as she kept that glow on her face, he was a happy camper.

They talked for a couple hours in the practically deserted restaurant, while outside the weather was taking a turn for the worse. They left the warmth inside to face a blast of wind-driven snow, not falling downward but flying sideways.

Call her crazy, but Lori had secretly always loved snow. Loved looking at it fall, dark against the white, cloudy sky, and only turning white as it came closer to her upturned face. She got a kick out of tasting snowflakes on her tongue and was still amazed at the idea of no two snowflakes being exactly alike. But the white stuff did make getting around a nightmare.

Lori and Travis both listened to the weather report on the radio of his pickup truck. It didn't sound good, at least not for the next fourteen hours or so.

Lori felt a definite sense of déjà vu here. The last time a blizzard had hit, Travis had ended up spending the night, which was what was going to happen this time as well.

Only now, Travis gave her another option. "We can try and drive back if you're needed at the hospital," he said. "My truck should be able to make it. But to my way of thinking, there's no sense doing that if we don't have to."

Seeing the weather conditions, Lori agreed. It made sense to stay where they were until the storm blew over. Using his cellular phone, she called in to her service and checked to make sure no one had been trying to reach her. Explaining what had happened, she promised to call back with a forwarding phone number once they were settled for the night. The forecasters, who hadn't even seen this one coming, were now saying this latest storm would be over by morning.

The snowmobile and ski fanatics in the area were delighted with the promise of more snow. They'd already filled most of the hotel rooms in the small town. After three attempts, Travis was finally able to get them a room.

"A room?" Lori repeated. "As in *one?*"

"That's all they had left. At this point I wasn't about to argue."

Lori didn't really feel like arguing, either. The truth was that the physical activity of the afternoon was starting to make itself felt. She was dying for a hot bath, but first called her answering service again and gave them the motel's phone number should she need to be reached in an emergency. Travis took a hot shower while she made her call, and emerged from the bathroom wearing his jeans and white T-shirt.

She ended up spending almost half an hour in the tub, an old-fashioned one like the one she had at home. It wasn't until she got out of the tub that she realized she didn't have anything to put on other than the thick bath towel provided by the motel.

She wrapped it sarong style, tucking the end of the towel between her breasts before gingerly leaving the bathroom. Despite the bath, she still felt stiff.

Travis took one look at her and ordered her onto the bed.

"You sweet-talker, you," she retorted. "You've got such a way with words."

"What did you think I had in mind?"

"Why don't you tell me?" she countered.

"I thought you could use a massage to help loosen you up."

Lori wasn't sure that was such a good idea. Any of it. Sharing this room—and its one queen-size bed—with him. Having him give her a massage. Loosening her up.

But, true to form, Travis didn't really give her a choice. Murmuring soft reassurances, as if she were a skittish colt, he guided her toward the bed, and next thing she knew, she was groaning in pleasure as he kneaded the muscles at the back of her legs.

Laying there, Lori found her thoughts focusing on his hands, rugged hands that had gentled a horse, that had been scratched by barbed wire despite leather gloves, that had coaxed so many newborn calves into the world. And then she thought about her own hands, capable hands that had calmed a patient, or guided a newborn infant into the world.

As if sensing her thoughts, Travis moved his fingers down her arm to her left hand. She was silent as he pressed his palm to hers, as if studying the differences in size and texture.

"You've got such a delicate hand," he murmured. "Did you ever think about how similar we are in some ways—both of us bringing new life into the world? Yet look how different our hands are."

"Yours are strong hands. Work roughened."

"Callused. They're big and awkward," he said dismissively. "But your hands are—"

"Chafed and dry," she wryly inserted. "From too much soap and not enough hand lotion. A drawback of the profession, I'm afraid."

"You should take care of these hands," he told her.

"Hands are one of the most important tools a midwife has," she noted, trying to sound professional, when inside she was melting.

"Tools? These hands are magic." Travis placed them on his chest, forcing her to turn around and face him in the process. "Feel what they can do," he whispered.

She felt the thrum of his heartbeat beneath her palms. She lay neither on her back nor on her stomach, but poised on her side in anticipation. Cupping his hands around her shoulders, Travis gently eased Lori onto her back, all the while maintaining their eye contact. She felt herself falling into the blue depths of his gaze, the intense blue of a Montana sky.

Silently he was asking questions, reading her answer in her gaze as he shifted his right hand from her shoulder to slide it back down her arm. His touch was slow, his hand skimming her skin for the sheer pleasure of touching her. Somehow, the towel came undone without her even knowing it.

Travis stroked her body first with his palm, the roughness of his calluses adding an erotic texture to the caress. He tested the creamy softness of her breast before comparing it to the skin near her navel, and then the even-softer flesh of her inner thigh.

He was taking his time, the way one might trail one's hand in the water while meandering downstream in a boat. And Travis was meandering, all right. Dallying at the back of her knee, cupping her calf, sliding his palm beneath the arch of her foot, hopping to the other foot and retracing his route on that leg, until her nerve endings were shivering in delight. Thousands of them. She tingled in places she'd only studied in anatomy classes.

Her entire body, from head to toe, was humming with the memory of where he'd touched her. And he'd touched her everywhere, covering her with dedicated thoroughness, as if his palm were the wide brush and she the canvas he was priming.

Lori thought surely that now Travis had completed his tactile seduction, he'd kiss her. But he didn't. Instead he started all over again, this time with just one fingertip. Now his caress was the brilliant stroke of the finest artist's brush, creatively delineating the form, pausing over the strokes of color around the naked tips of her breasts. There he paused for countless moments, to silently admire and adore, his thumb providing assistance as he brushed the underside of her nipple, creating a friction that was undeniably arousing.

Lori gasped, unable to stay quiet a second longer. The pleasure was too intense. Murmuring her name, he lowered his head to take her into his mouth, his tongue darting out to swirl around the rosy peaks with avid care.

Lori felt the forbidden excitement within her growing. She was both hot and cold, shivering and steaming inside. A secret hot spring of desire was coming to life, the tugging of his mouth creating tiny quakes of sheer bliss.

As Travis shifted and lavished her other breast with identical care, he brought his hand over her ribs, over the indentation of her waist to her pelvic bone, where he rode the ridge down to the juncture of her thighs. There he boldly cupped her, pressing against her with the heel of his hand.

Lori felt as if she were about to explode. And when he intimately brushed the tiny nub hidden in the thatch of curls, she did explode. Into a million pieces. Not just once, but a number of times as he continued his erotic movements—bringing her to the peak, waiting until she'd slid down the other side of the mountain, only to take her higher next time.

A boneless mass of satisfaction, Lori could only lie there and stare at him in amazement. Lifting his head from her breast, Travis gazed down at her with the naughtiest of smiles. He looked like a man who'd successfully completed a mission.

When she was able to, she told him so.

"I did have something to prove," he huskily admitted.

"That you could drive me out of my mind?" she inquired with sultry satisfaction.

"That this chemistry between us isn't a fluke. That it isn't something that will burn out. It's not something that will go away. It's long and enduring."

"But what about you? You're still—"

"Hungry for you. Starving in, fact," he noted ruefully.

"Then why didn't you . . . ?"

"Because the last time we made love it was fast and furious. I wanted to show you something more."

"I'd love to see something more, cowboy," Lori huskily whispered, even as she reached out to undo the metallic snap on his jeans. "Why don't you come on down here and show me?"

Travis paused, momentarily at war with himself. On the one hand, he didn't want Lori to later regret what they were about to do. On the other hand, this might be the best way to get her back, to tighten the bonds between them.

"Are you really sure about wanting a baby?" he asked, staring into her eyes with expressive intentness.

Lori nodded.

"Then have mine," Travis murmured.

Twelve

"I don't know," Lori whispered. "That would be too complicated—"

Travis put his hand on her lips, stopping her words. "Not complicated at all. Let me show you how simple it would be," he murmured huskily.

Finally he kissed her. His mouth brushed hers with slow, reverent strokes that soon escalated into hungry craving. With rough gentleness he caught her bottom lip between his teeth, drawing it into his mouth to alternately suck and nibble until Lori was shivering with excitement.

Determined not to remain a passive participant, she did some nibbling and sucking of her own. Delighted with his growl of pleasure, she widened her explorations, nibbling on his earlobe, tracing the cordoned tendons along his neck with her tongue.

She wanted him to know that this was a two-way street, that the chemistry went both ways and that if she was addicted to it, so was he. Powerless and powerful. They both were.

The ensuing dalliance was a soaring combination of sultry taste and touch as she made her way over his body, removing his clothing with eager abandon. Their fingers frequently collided as they both attempted to get rid of his shirt and jeans with reckless haste. The snaps on his shirt popping as they came undone sounded like gunshots over the panting pace of their heavy breathing.

Meanwhile their kisses were covering the entire spectrum, from red-hot passion to indigo tenderness. Each time

Travis broke off one kiss, he started the next one a heartbeat later. Lori liked it that way. She adored the way he delicately tickled the roof of her mouth with his tongue. She
melted at the way he carried his kisses to the underside of her
chin, the corner of her eye, the tip of her nose, her left tem-
ple and then her right, moving on to her ear. Ah, her ear. He
remembered exactly how to drive her up a wall by rever-
ently probing the inward swirl with the wet tip of his tongue.

Shivering, she tightened her hold on his shoulders and
brought him down so that he rested upon her like a blanket, a heavy, throbbing blanket. Pushing him onto his back,
she hovered over him, brushing her breasts against his bare
chest. Cupping his big hand around the back of her head,
he speared his fingers through her hair and tugged her down
so he could kiss her.

Now the thrust of his tongue was elemental in its mim-
icry of the joining that was yet to come. Straddling his hips,
she shifted against him, loving the feel of him bucking beneath her.

Gripping her hips, he placed her where he needed her to
be and verbally encouraged her to guide him home. She did,
taking him in her capable hands and stroking him even as
she led him to her. Lifting up, she positioned herself just
right and then came down ever so slowly.

An avalanche of pure ecstasy rushed over her, tingling,
humming, rippling, contracting—so intensely powerful that
she was poised on the knife edge between pleasure and pain.

"Slow down, darlin'" Travis growled, his blue eyes
glowing. "Or this is gonna be over before it begins." His big
hands tightened their hold on her hips at her next provocatively lingering move. "That's it. Like that . . ."

Satisfaction loomed just out of reach as he paced their
progress, scaling the blissful mountain plateau by plateau,
until reaching the towering peak. Once there Lori was momentarily suspended in a nirvana of the senses before becoming consumed by the undulating pulses of raw pleasure.
They peaked through her until she heard his shout of com-

pletion and he stiffened beneath her. She felt the warm flow as he spilled his seed deep within her. As she collapsed in dizzy delight, the thought hit her that this was perfection.

Lori woke in the middle of the night, not knowing exactly what it was that had disturbed her. The weight of Travis's arm around her rib cage was both achingly familiar and excitingly new. Once awake, she couldn't get back to sleep, so she carefully slid from the bed and wrapped Travis's denim shirt around herself. The hem almost reached her knees.

She padded on bare feet across the polished hardwood floor to the window. Pushing aside the drape, she saw that it was still snowing out, although lightly now and without the fierceness of the wind. The sound of a coyote barking in the distance brought to mind the memory of another winter night illuminated by snow.

The autumn after they were married, the first snowfall had come early, and Lori had gotten up in the night to look outside, much as she was doing now. She'd heard the call of a coyote then, too. She'd thought it had sounded lonely and had been ridiculously tempted to invite it in next to the warmth of the fire. She'd confessed as much to Travis when he'd gotten up and joined her at the window.

Lori smiled at the memory. Travis, in that practical way of his, had reminded her that coyotes were not a rancher's best friend. Most considered them to be nothing more than varmints, and now that wolves had been driven from the state, the number-one-enemy position had fallen onto the coyote's wily shoulders. Travis had told her all the reasons why ranchers and coyotes didn't mix. She'd known already, of course. Lori might have grown up in town, but she'd lived in Montana her entire life. She knew all about the ranchers' grievances.

But it didn't change what was in her heart. The coyote had been there first. So had the wolf, for that matter. The Native Americans had managed to live in peace with both for hundreds of years. Yet in the span of two generations, the white settlers had eradicated several species in their quest to tame the land.

Buffalo were a good example. At one point their numbers had dwindled until only a few hundred survived instead of millions. Conservation efforts at Yellowstone at the beginning of the century had brought them back to the park. But it had been a close call. Other species hadn't been as lucky.

Call her foolishly naive and optimistic, but Lori longed for a policy of live and let live. It would probably never happen. Conservationists versus ranchers; the debate raged all the way to Washington, D.C. It was something Lori and Travis had talked about. Argued about. In the end, Travis had respected her hopes and perhaps even shared a few of them, although he'd never admit that. But he couldn't afford to lose calves to coyotes or hay to elk. He had a hard enough time staying one step ahead of the bank as it was.

Lori knew Travis loved the land and respected it. Loved it too much, she'd often thought. Broke his back working on it.

But there was no taking Travis from his roots. And she didn't want to. She just wanted the grip those roots had on him to loosen enough to allow some room for her.

Looking at Travis as he slept, a shaft of light from the window softening the rugged lines of his face, Lori wondered if that would ever happen.

Travis opened his eyes the next morning to find Lori sitting in the chair by the window, fully dressed. "You're up early," he murmured.

"I thought I'd better get ready to go."

"Mmm," he answered, getting out of bed to stretch with the laziness of a mountain cat. A sleek, naked mountain cat. Lori's gaze slid down her ex-husband's body, from his wide, muscled shoulders and powerful torso to his lean hips, until she reached the part of him that was heavy and quickly becoming aroused. "I'm ready to go, too," he huskily drawled.

"Where do you think you're going, undressed that way?" she inquired, her primness caused by nerves.

"To heaven and back," he told her with the dark smile of a maverick. "With you."

He hunkered down in front of her, reaching out and snaring her head with his work-roughened, magic-creating hand and pulling her into his kiss—a kiss that was waiting for her, eliminating the preliminaries and going straight to the heart of the matter. His tongue lazily curled around hers in an erotic greeting that set her heart pumping wildly.

Murmuring her name, Travis broke off that kiss and began the next—a short seductive raid that was there and gone and there again—slanting his head one way, then the other.

"What are you doing?" she asked breathlessly.

"Trying to decide if I like kissing you from the left or the right best."

"And?"

"I can't decide."

Lori decided that his kisses were driving her mad. They were deliberately tantalizing, promising without delivering.

"Aren't you warm, darlin'?" he drawled seductively. "You feel mighty hot to me." He slid his hand from her knee up her thigh to the throbbing juncture in between her legs. "Mighty hot."

Lori gasped. The friction of his hand rubbing against her almost paralyzed her with pleasure.

"Let me help," he whispered, using his free hand to undo a few buttons on her red flannel shirt with admirable dexterity. "After all, there's no need to be in such a hurry," he told her as he undid another button. "It's still early and we've got some time yet, right?"

"Right," she whispered.

"There..." He pushed her shirt aside and leaned forward to kiss her collarbone above the ribbed neckline of her thermal, fishnet undershirt. "Is that better? No? Then let's go on a little trip through these layers of clothing...."

He slowly peeled her shirt off. Beneath her fishnet underwear was a lacy bra in rose-colored satin. Since she'd only been wearing a towel after her bath last night, he hadn't had a chance to see her underwear. "When we were skiing yesterday, I kept imagining what you were wearing under all these clothes. Now I see." He slid an index finger through the open fishnet weave to caress her bare skin just above the lacy cup of her bra. "Nice. Real nice."

"You've suddenly gotten awfully talkative, cowboy," Lori noted.

"That may be, but I'm at a loss for words to describe how beautiful you are."

"I wasn't complaining," she said softly.

"I should hope not," he drawled. "I'm the one who should be complaining at the way all these clothes are covering you up." Abandoning his caresses near her breast, he reached for her foot and tugged her boots off. "Layers." He pulled her woolen socks off. "I like layers." Her next pair of socks were removed more slowly. Propping her foot on his bare knee, he kissed her high instep before tossing her sock over his shoulder.

Lori was already working on the fastening of her woolen leggings, then started shimmying out of them. Travis ducked as they went sailing over his head. She was now seated in the chair in her fishnet long johns and undershirt, panties and bra. The panties matched the rose-colored bra and tempted Travis to explore the lacy edges. Sliding a finger through the fishnet weave, he hooked the elastic and pulled it away from her moist heat. "Ah, darlin'" he whispered. "You're gettin' me all bothered. I'm tryin' to go slow here...."

She yanked her undershirt off and tugged him to her, cradling him at her breast as he tongued her nipple through the satin material. Working blindly, he reached around her to undo her bra. The moment the piece of lingerie slid away, he cupped her in both palms. "Look," he whispered. "Look how perfectly you fit into my hands."

Lori gazed down to see him holding her, her skin pale in contrast to his tanned hands. It was wildly exhilarating to watch him caressing her this way. Excitement shot through her. Her bra still dangled by the strap on one arm as she speared her fingers through his golden hair, kissing every inch of his face she could reach. His skin was like velvet sandpaper, with the sandy shadow of a day-and-night's growth of beard.

He slid his hands around to her back, down her spine, beneath the elastic waistband of her long johns, his fingertip teasing the crevice at the top of her derriere.

His mouth covered her sighs of pleasure, incorporating them into a kiss that was tender and rough. Moments later, they both struggled to remove her long johns and panties with as much speed as possible.

When she was as naked as he, Travis pulled her onto his lap as he knelt before her. Lori wrapped her arms and legs around him, holding on tightly as he came to her in one smooth move. She burrowed her face in the hollow of his shoulder, overcome by the incredible feel of him lodged deep within her. His large hands cupped her derriere as he lifted up. She gasped as ripples of ecstasy shot through her. They made love with primordial energy, the hunger elemental and raw, as was the pleasure. His face etched with iron intent, Travis made sure of her satisfaction before allowing his own. When Lori climaxed it was as if she'd died and been born again. Travis shuddered and reached his own climax an instant later.

"Oh, darlin'." Still intimately joined with her, he bracketed her face with his callused hands and kissed the tears of joy from her face. "Even when we go slow we're still fire."

Lori nodded her agreement. The movement set her silver, teardrop earrings swinging.

Watching them, Travis was reminded of the intricate Zuni earrings he'd bought for her for Christmas, but hadn't had the nerve to give her. Brushing her earring with his thumb, he thought of the two single earrings—one amethyst, the other a silver feather—that he still had on top of his dresser.

He wasn't ready to give them back to her yet. Not that he really needed a physical reminder of Lori. She was in his blood. Embedded there. Always had been. Always would be... and there was no getting around it.

"Where do we go from here?" Travis asked later. As he tucked his shirt into his jeans, he wondered if he was imagining her floral scent on the denim material.

"Back to Whitehorn."

"That's not what I meant and you know it."

"I know," she said. "I'm sorry, I didn't mean to be glib. I don't honestly know where we go from here."

His expression darkened. "Is this supposed to be a one-night stand or what?"

"It meant more than that to me."

"To me, too."

In the ensuing silence he saw from the look on her face that, despite the magic they'd shared, Lori was still hesitant. She hadn't made love that way. Not at all. Then she knew what she wanted. It was only when she was fully clothed and in complete control of her faculties that the doubts set in again.

Travis supposed he couldn't blame her. He'd promised to court her slowly, saying they'd talk and spend a day together, and instead they'd ended up in bed again. Only this time there was no going back. No fighting and pretending it hadn't happened.

"Maybe we should go back to my plan to court you," he suggested.

"Why? You already got what you wanted." The words slipped out, revealing one of her fears.

"No, I didn't," he growled. His ragged voice contrasted sharply with his tender touch as he cupped her face with his large hand. "I want you back in my life. I might not have really realized exactly how special what we have was while we were married, but I sure as hell realize it now.''

Lori didn't know what to say.

Travis sighed. ''We'll go back to Whitehorn after we grab some breakfast and take care of some business.''

''Business?'' Lori wondered what kind of business Travis would have in West Yellowstone. Was he checking into livestock or feed? Was that why he'd suggested they come down here? Because he really wanted to take care of ranch business? She was as jealous of that land of his as if it were another woman. It wasn't healthy for their relationship. Never had been; she knew that. So she made no comment as they ate breakfast at the café attached to the motel.

Lori wondered how Travis had registered them last night. As husband and wife? Her name was still Lori Parker Bains. Why was that? she asked herself. Why hadn't she returned to her maiden name after the divorce? The truth was becoming painfully clear. Because she hadn't wanted to give up all her ties to Travis.

''What are you thinking about?'' he asked her as she stared into the milky swirls of her coffee, as if looking for the answers to life's questions.

''Nothing,'' she murmured.

He knew it wasn't the truth, but didn't press her. Instead he said, ''Are you going to eat that piece of toast?''

''You've already eaten four pieces.''

''I've got a mighty big appetite, ma'am,'' Travis drawled.

''I noticed that,'' she retorted in kind, her grin wicked.

''I was hoping you might.''

Their eyes met and time lost all meaning. As if she were gazing through the wrong end of a telescope, Lori felt the world filter down to encompass his eyes and nothing else. His face was slightly sunburned from their skiing yesterday. The added color made his eyes seem even bluer, a soft color in such a hard man. The color of washed jeans. But it was the warmth of his gaze, the intimate messages being relayed to her through his visual shorthand that left her breathless and forced her to finally look away.

"So tell me more about this business of yours," she said.

"It's a surprise." When she was about to protest, he leaned across the table and kissed her. "You'll see soon enough."

She did see and couldn't believe her eyes. "A sleigh ride?"

Travis nodded. "I promised you one years ago and never got around to it."

Lori knew how much this gesture meant. Not only had he remembered his failure to make good on his long-standing promise, but he'd done so despite the fact that he'd thought it a silly request for her to have made in the first place. After all, he had horses on the ranch, and the flatbed wagon he used in the winter to feed the herd had sleigh runners on it. So what if it didn't have seats and rattled like a death trap. How different could a sleigh be?

They'd had the discussion many times. In the end, he'd finally promised to someday take her on a sleigh ride. But someday had never come. Until now.

"How did you arrange this?" Lori asked in delighted disbelief.

Travis just shrugged. "A buddy of mine runs this stable for tourists in season. I called him last night while you were taking your bath and he happened to have a sleigh he offered to let me borrow for an hour or so."

Noting the small size of the sleigh, which looked like something on a Christmas card, Lori said, "Just the two of us?"

"That's right, ma'am. Do you trust me to take you for a spin?"

He'd already sent her heart into a spin, the slow smile on his face an irresistible inducement. Giving him her gloved hand, she allowed him to help her up into the sleigh. He tucked a wool blanket and sheepskins around her before agilely hopping onto the seat beside her.

With a nod to the stable hand, Travis slapped the reins and they were off. The sound of sleigh bells on the horses' leather harnesses filled the air. The day was bright and sunny, yesterday's snow already melting from the branches and falling with wet plops as the sleigh smoothly glided through the woods.

Snuggling together beneath the blanket as Travis drove the team made Lori feel like a homesteader, as if she'd stepped back in time a hundred years. Travis stopped twice along the trail, once to show her a herd of elk foraging for food and once to point out a bald eagle.

"My dad used to say that Yellowstone had three seasons—July, August and winter," Travis noted dryly.

"I like winter best," Lori murmured, her breath white in the chilly air.

"I remember."

His look made her wonder what else he remembered. The pain of her asking him for a divorce; the last fight they'd had before she'd moved out? Could they really put all that behind them and start again?

In these beautiful surroundings, Lori was hopeful that they could. It was hard not to be hopeful in the midst of such a magical setting. The icy glory of a frozen waterfall or the grandeur of a snow-covered mountain peak etched against the brilliant blue sky made Lori's problems seem small.

After a sleigh ride that was everything she'd imagined it would be, they finally headed back home. Lori was sorry to leave what had been an enchanted place for her. She was afraid that, like the legendary Shangri-La, once she and Travis left this mythical valley and returned to the reality of their lives in Whitehorn, things would be very different. This interlude would be over and the magic would die.

Thirteen

The closer they got to Whitehorn, the more uncertain Lori became. Travis, who was never one to talk up a storm, was equally quiet.

He liked the silence between them. He'd never been a man of many words. Having Lori beside him, with the open road ahead of him, heading home, was all a man could ask for.

Well, almost all. He could ask her to move in with him on the ranch, and was damned tempted to do so, but had to keep reminding himself that he had to tread carefully here. It wouldn't do him any good trying to buffalo Lori. She was as stubborn as a bison.

No, he couldn't push her. She had to be coaxed and convinced, the way he got yearlings used to the saddle blanket first…before tossing on the saddle. That was it. Travis had to start slowly.

Hard to do, considering the incredible way they'd made love last night and this morning. Travis didn't even want to acknowledge his hidden fear that she'd only wanted him for her stud-sperm search. That he'd been a necessary requirement to her goal of having a baby. He told himself it didn't matter what her reasons were, that if she got pregnant, she'd be tied to him with a bond that couldn't be broken.

Still, he'd give his gray snakeskin boots to know what she was thinking.

Lori wondered what Travis was thinking. She'd noticed the possessive looks he'd cast her way. She hoped he wasn't going to ask her to move in with him. Because she wasn't ready for that. She hadn't been ready for them to have made love again, but it had happened anyway. Which just went to show that she couldn't be trusted to be wise and sensible around Travis.

She winced as she recalled how confidently she'd assured Molly she'd be careful. Her hand hovered over her stomach as she considered the possibility of her being pregnant as a result of their recent lovemaking. Travis had promised to show her how simple her having his baby would be, but she wasn't fool enough to think that the road wasn't filled with problematic chuckholes. For one thing, Travis was a very old-fashioned kind of guy. He had very definite ideas about things, including single moms and a father's responsibilities. And Lori was torn about wanting the best for her baby, which meant having two parents.

When they were almost at Whitehorn, Lori's beeper went off. Using Travis's cellular phone, she called in to her service. One of her patients needed her. Lori's day off was over.

In the next two weeks they got so much snow that even Lori was tired of seeing it. The radio and newspaper heralded the fact that this part of the state had seen more snow in the past month than they often got in an entire winter. Travis was tied up at the ranch, trying to get feed to all his animals. The snow made everything take longer.

Lori checked in on Winona by phone to make sure she was okay. She also continued her weekly visits to the clinic at the reservation, adding chains to her tires when the road was particularly bad.

Travis called her often, usually right before bedtime. "I miss you," he'd say in his rough and sexy voice.

"You sound lonesome, cowboy," Lori noted huskily.

"Damn right. Miss me?"

"Mmm."

"You yawning or saying you miss me?"

"Both," she replied, her grin reflected in her tone.

"So how many babies did you birth today?"

"*I* didn't birth any. The patient does the birthing. I just catch the babies when they come out."

"Yeah, right. And I just ship the cattle off when the truck comes," he countered mockingly. "You work too hard."

"And you don't?"

"I'm a man...."

"Don't even say it," she warned him.

"What?" he demanded innocently.

"You were about to make some ridiculous chauvinist comment, but luckily I saved you from yourself."

"And who's gonna save me from this hungry need inside of me?"

"What kind of need might that be?" Lori countered, twining her finger around the twisted cord of the phone and wishing she could twine her hands through his golden hair instead.

"A physical ache."

"Hmm. I've had some medical training, perhaps I can be of some assistance."

"I'm sure you could be, but you're too damn far away."

"Perhaps you'd better describe this ache to me. Is there any...swelling...involved?"

"Yeah," he growled. "Throbbing, too."

"This sounds serious. Perhaps you should feel the afflicted area and see if it's hard."

Travis groaned. "You're wicked. And the only one I want feeling the afflicted area is you. I'm sure you'd find it hard enough to suit you."

"I'm sure I would. If I were there, I'd have to size up the situation. Examine you thoroughly. My stethoscope can be cold. But my hands are usually warm."

"One more word," he warned, his voice gritty with arousal, "and I'm coming over. As it is, I'm on the verge of coming."

"Only on the verge?" she murmured. "I'm falling down on the job here." She went on to whisper what she'd do to him if she were there beside him.

Travis retorted by telling Lori exactly what he'd do to her if she were in bed with him, his erotic description direct and exciting.

"Now neither one of us will be able to sleep," she noted shakily.

"Not without taking a cold shower." Travis got in the last word by describing how he'd take her in the shower, while she was slippery with soap. The sound of her breathless gasp made him smile. "Sleep tight, darlin'," he drawled, before hanging up.

Lori would have called him back, but she had to be at work early in the morning and it was already nearing midnight. Plus she was on call tonight, which meant that any time the phone rang, she had to be prepared for it to be a patient and to answer whatever questions and deal with whatever situations might arise. But dealing with Travis was something else again.

What had gotten into her to verbally seduce him that way? She'd never acted like that the entire time they were married. She wasn't sure he'd wanted her to. Western men respected their women, cherished them. Cowboy lore had it that a painted horse was better than a painted woman. Lori wondered if Travis still felt that way, especially after tonight's conversation. Somehow, she doubted it. With that thought in mind, she fell asleep with a smile on her lips.

The next night when Travis called her he said, "Is this the same wild woman who drove me crazy last night?"

"Could be," Lori murmured.

"I've got plans for you."

"I can imagine," she retorted impishly. "You told me about some of them last night."

"Oh, I plan on doing more than just *telling* you. I plan on showing you. In person. Valentine's Day."

"In that case perhaps we should meet somewhere private," she suggested. "Like my place."

"Just what I had in mind."

"I know exactly what you have in mind."

"Not yet," Travis murmured huskily, "but you will."

A chinook finally blew in the day before Valentine's Day. Lori woke to the *thunk* of icicles falling from the eave-spouts, done in by their own weight.

She had to visit a patient at the hospital before getting to the family practice. Her day got off to a rocky start when she spotted Dr. Straker being fawned over by Danette. It appeared the doctor had brought in a box of Valentine's chocolates a day early for "his girls."

Biting her tongue and minding her own business, Lori saw to her patient and then returned to the nurses' station to fill out some of the never-ending paperwork surrounding patient care and health services. She only vaguely noted the sound of someone clearing his throat behind her as she diligently continued writing.

"Nurse Bains."

Lori looked up to find Dr. Straker staring at her disapprovingly. "Yes?"

"You're in my seat."

"Excuse me?"

"I need that chair. I've got patients' records to write."

Oh, and I don't? Lori thought to herself. The chair wasn't his, of course. It was an extra chair at the nurses' station, meant for whomever got to it first. Unless you had M.D. after your name. Then, clearly, nurses were expected to jump out of their chairs for the almighty doctor.

"I'll be done in a minute," Lori politely said, refusing to give up her chair.

"You'll be done sooner than that." Straker's voice had taken on a menacing tone that Lori didn't appreciate one bit.

"Here." The new nurse on the floor bounced out of her chair. "Sit here, Dr. Straker."

With a final glare at Lori, one that promised retribution, Dr. Straker smiled warmly at the new nurse and kibitzed with her while writing out his report.

Lori had a feeling there would be an additional report written out on her and her insubordinate behavior. Not that Straker had a leg to stand on. There was nothing written in the personnel book about nurses having to give up their chairs for doctors. No, it was one of those unwritten rules of authority that drove Lori nuts. The pecking order.

She was still unsettled fifteen minutes later when she met a bunch of her co-workers down in the cafeteria for a coffee break. Actually, Lori opted for apple juice instead of tea. She hadn't been feeling quite herself this morning, and she hadn't eaten breakfast yet. It was just going on nine. She had her first appointment at the family practice in an hour.

"Hey, Lori, I heard you hung on to your chair," Nancy from Pediatrics said as Lori joined them. "Good for you!"

"It was no big deal," Lori muttered as she sipped her juice.

"I'm sure Straker the Streaker thought it was big news," Nancy maintained.

"How did he get that nickname, anyway?" the secretary from Admissions asked.

"He used to make a point of using the shower in the locker room and walking naked to his locker," Nancy replied.

Lori made a face, wondering if the sudden nausea she was feeling was at the idea of seeing Straker naked. Seconds later the nausea grew to alarming proportions. "Excuse me," she muttered, jumping from the table and rushing to the women's room, which thankfully was located nearby.

She barely made it there in time to throw up.

When she returned to the cafeteria, looking pale, Danette had joined the others at her table. "I heard you in the ladies' room. Sounds like someone's pregnant to me."

"Lay off, Danette," Nancy said. "The food in this cafeteria would make anyone sick."

By that afternoon, there was a hospital pool going as to whether or not Lori was pregnant, and a separate pool on who the father might be. The secretary in Admissions called Lori at the family practice right before five to warn her. "I didn't want you to walk in tomorrow and hear about it."

Lori knew it wouldn't do any good to confront Danette, who would just deny any knowledge.

Besides, her first concern was whether or not she really was pregnant. Her period would normally be due tomorrow, and she'd always been regular. That night exhaustion overcame excitement and Lori fell asleep as soon as her head hit the pillow. First thing the next morning she took a home pregnancy test. Afterward she sat on the closed toilet seat, staring at the test's plus sign in awe. A baby. She really was going to have a baby!

Lori noticed that her breasts had seemed a bit more tender and the nipples a little enlarged. It could just have been her imagination...but it wasn't. She was pregnant. Tears came to her eyes and spilled over her cheeks as she hugged herself, hugged Demelza, and danced from room to room before collapsing breathless onto the bed. She was going to be a mom. Wow! Lori wondered if her patients felt this same sense of awed excitement when she told them they were pregnant.

Then she wondered what Travis would say when he found out. What would his reaction be? Would he be thrilled at the prospect of being a father? Or dismayed?

Today was Valentine's Day, she'd agreed to spend the evening with Travis. She had to tell him tonight.

That night, after she'd changed from her work clothes into a pink mohair sweater and black leggings, Lori found herself practicing in front of the bathroom mirror. Practicing her speech to Travis, practicing ways to tell him about the baby. As she did so, the irony of the fact that she'd told hundreds of women that they were pregnant, yet couldn't think how to tell her ex-husband about her own pregnancy, didn't escape her.

"Travis. Guess what? I'm pregnant." *Too direct. Needs more buildup.*

She tried again, smiling at her reflection in the mirror. "I'm expecting." She shook her head. *Too subtle.*

"I'm in a family way? I have a bun in the oven? The rabbit died? You're about to become a daddy?" She wasn't sure about that last one. She was going to be a mommy, but would Travis be a daddy? He'd never actually said he wanted to become a father.

She panicked, before calming herself with the reminder that *she'd* wanted this baby, and was capable of raising it herself if need be. Before she'd made the commitment to have a child, she'd gone over her financial records and planned everything out. It wasn't an ideal situation, but it could be done without harm to the child.

And having only one parent wouldn't harm the child? a little voice inside taunted. Lori didn't want to have to raise her child alone. She'd just have to wait and see how Travis reacted.

He arrived promptly at seven, a good sign for a man who rarely wore a watch. "Doesn't matter what time it is in my line of work," he used to tell her. "I can judge close enough by the sun."

He was wearing his Western suit and a simple bola tie, the clip in engraved silver. He handed her flowers and a heart-shaped box of chocolate with a little less awkwardness than he had the first time he'd come courting, before New Year's. The kiss he gave her had no awkwardness at all. Instead it had plenty of fire and intensity, passion and hunger.

Only when they were both breathless did he rest his forehead against hers. "I missed you," he whispered against her mouth.

"Me, too," she whispered back.

She stayed in the loose circle of his arms a moment longer before moving away and helping him off with his coat. "I've got something to tell you," she said as he hung the sheepskin coat and his slightly battered black hat on her coat rack.

"Is it something I'm going to want to hear?" he asked cautiously.

Lori didn't know the answer to that one. She only knew that she couldn't wade through dinner without first telling him she was pregnant. The anticipation was too much for her already unsettled stomach to take.

"Would you like a drink?" she asked, stalling for time. *Tell him!*

"A beer would be great."

She went into the kitchen to get him one and almost ran into him in the dining room. "Here." She handed him the chilled bottle with fingers that trembled slightly. Travis never drank beer out of a glass if he could help it.

"You said you had something to tell me?" he reminded her after taking a swig.

"Umm, that's right. Why don't we go sit on the couch?" she suggested in her best hostess voice.

"You're making me nervous here, darlin'," Travis told her. "What's going on?"

Lori sat perched on the couch, waiting for Travis to settle beside her before she blurted out, "I'm pregnant."

Her eyes were glued to his face, eagerly searching for his reaction. She wasn't sure if she was reading it right, she was so wound up. Was that excitement or nervousness she saw in his blue eyes? Or both? Did he look stunned or was she imagining that?

For some reason, she heard herself saying, "The baby is yours—"

Travis put his fingers on her lips, silencing her. "I know that," he whispered.

In that moment, Lori knew she loved him. Knew it to the bottom of her soul. She'd always loved him, and now knew she always would.

That didn't mean that loving him would make it any easier to live with him. But for that moment, she let the realization wash over her like a warm summer rain. She loved Travis. The question was, did he love her?

She knew he wanted her; he'd told her and shown her that much. But wanting and loving were two different things. And he'd never spoken of wanting or loving a baby. He'd only asked her if *she* had wanted a baby, had never said what *he'd* wanted.

"Aren't you going to say anything?" she asked.

"Wow," he murmured softly. "A baby." He seemed a little overwhelmed by the concept. "How do you feel? Shouldn't you be lying down or something?"

"I'm fine. Some nausea now and then, but that's to be expected."

"Are you happy?"

Lori nodded, wishing she had the nerve to ask if he was happy, too.

"This is great. I just didn't expect it to happen so fast. I thought maybe we'd have to practice a bit more," he noted with a maverick grin.

He looked happy, she decided. And rather cocky about the entire matter. As if he'd just won a bronc-riding contest. As if he'd just passed a masculinity test.

And what did that make her? His fertility proving ground? Nerves got the better of her. Lori saw the chocolate box sitting on the end table, and next thing she knew she was ripping open the cellophane covering and grabbing a handful of chocolates.

Seconds later, Travis yanked the box away from her. "Too many sweets aren't good for you when you're pregnant."

"How do you know?" Her voice reflected her resentment at his high-handed attitude.

"I've been reading up on it. Just in case... A baby. Wow." He shook his head, running his hands through his hair. "So when will it be here?"

"It's here now." She patted her stomach.

"I meant a due date."

"Toward the end of November."

"We'll have a baby for next Christmas. That'll be great!" His blue eyes gleamed with excitement. "We'll get the tree at the ranch all decorated and take lots of pictures. Boots. How old does a baby have to be to wear cowboy boots?"

"It could be a girl," she reminded him.

"She can wear boots."

"I think we're getting ahead of ourselves here," Lori said.

"You're right. Babies wear booties first, right? And a pony. We'll have to get the kid a pony. And a Denver Broncos sleeper. I saw them in a magazine. They've got them for babies. You'll be moving back to the ranch, naturally, and you'll have to get rid of the cat. I read someplace that pregnant women can get sick from cats.''

"It's from cleaning cat boxes, which is why I've hired the kid next door to do it. And I had Demelza thoroughly checked out at the vet when I had her spayed last month.''

"Well, I suppose you could keep the cat. Not much place for a house cat on a ranch, though.''

"That's fine, since neither Demelza nor I are moving to your ranch.''

"You're pregnant with my child. Of course you'll come to the ranch.''

"Why should I?'' she countered.

"Because I can take care of you there.''

"I don't need taking care of. Besides, the ranch is too far from the hospital.''

"I'd make sure you'd get to the hospital in time to have the baby,'' he said.

"I meant too far for me to drive to work every day.''

"Work?''

"Right. You know, the place you go to do your job?''

"There's no need for you to work while you're pregnant.''

"Women do it every day.''

"Not my woman.''

"Do you hear yourself? You sound like a throwback to the fifties. The 1850s. And who says I'm your woman?''

"I do.''

"I don't.''

"Lori, think about this. You're pregnant with my baby. It only makes sense that we get married. A kid needs two parents.''

"I'm aware of that.''

"Then what's your problem?''

"I'm not the one with a problem!'' she declared. "You're the one ordering me around.''

"We're going to be parents and we're going to do it together," Travis stated. "No more walking out or running
away when we fight."

"I'm not going to spend the next nine months fighting
with you, Travis," she said wearily.

"Damn right you're not. It wouldn't be good for you or
the baby."

"Where are you going?" she demanded as he got up and
started walking away.

"To the kitchen. To put dinner on the table. You look
beat."

"Gee, thanks," she muttered, stealing another chocolate
to console herself.

"You're welcome."

Dinner didn't turn out at all the way she'd originally
planned. There was no way to anticipate the sight of a cowboy like Travis wearing an apron—his jacket discarded, his
white shirtsleeves rolled up as he dished out dinner. Lori's
heart melted as he fussed over her like a mother hen.

Feeling herself weakening, she repeated, "I'm not moving out to the ranch."

"We'll talk about it later," he said, adding a dollop of
sour cream to her perfectly baked potato, placed alongside
a tender-looking steak. "Eat."

"What are you looking at?" Errol asked Mary Jo as he
entered his bedroom.

Mary Jo started guiltily. She couldn't afford to have Errol
see the map she'd been studying. Errol had his place in her
plans, but he certainly wasn't privy to them. He was just a
minor cog in the bigger wheel. A wheel that would bring
Mary Jo wealth and independence. No more relying on a
man. She'd wasted enough of her life being dependent on
male handouts, having to be satisfied with the crumbs. Now
she was after the brass ring . . . or in her case, the sapphires.
With them, she'd finally be free. "What am I looking at?"
she repeated. "Nothing. Library information. I didn't hear
you come in."

"I'm glad you're here. It's been a hell of a day."

Mary Jo hastily stuffed the map into her purse before directing all her attention to Errol. "You poor baby." She sat him on the bed. Kneeling in front of him, she rubbed the furrows from his forehead. "Tell me all about it."

"It's that damn midwife."

"Lori Parker Bains?"

"We have only one midwife in this town, but I think I've finally found a way to get rid of her. Have you heard the news about her carrying her ex-husband's baby?"

"I try not to listen to gossip," Mary Jo murmured. Unless it helped her cause or fit into her plans.

"Well, she's single and knocked up—not the best example of professional stability."

Mary Jo knew all about being single and pregnant. It stunk. A dead-end road. A trap. She'd done well to get out of it the way she had.

"I brought the matter up with the hospital administration over lunch today. I thought I'd fixed that damned midwife's wagon when she messed up and couldn't be reached when a patient needed her. It was a good plan," he murmured. "Replace a good battery in her beeper with a bad one. Simple enough to do. That was step one."

"Why, Errol, are you saying you sabotaged her beeper?"

Errol didn't reply, and Mary Jo started looking at him with new eyes, eyes that were approving.

There might be hope for this guy after all, Mary Jo thought to herself. He was willing to break some rules to get what he wanted. That could prove to be very useful.

"I can see why you'd do such a thing," Mary Jo reassured him. "It's for the good of the hospital."

"Damn right. And then there was the matter of Marilee Taylor dying out at the Walker place earlier this year when the midwife was attending, so I made sure to bring that up again."

"I thought that Marilee was in a car accident and went into labor suddenly. Lori was just driving by—"

"The details don't matter," Errol exclaimed. "It's merely one of a long line of foul-ups. She provided the final nail to her coffin herself with this baby thing. Anyway, after talking to the hospital administrator today, I convinced him that it's time to have a hearing about the suitability of keeping the midwife on staff at the hospital." Errol absently stroked Mary Jo's arm. "What about your husband?"

"I told him I was meeting some friends after work and would be late."

"No, I meant how do you think he'd vote on this midwife issue? After all, Kincaid is on the hospital board of directors, although he doesn't do much more than sit there like a limp dishrag."

"That's all he ever does in bed," Mary Jo murmured, seductively running her hand up Errol's leg to the juncture of his thighs. "Forget about the hospital. Forget about the damned midwife. Just think about me—your very own Valentine."

As Lori headed for the hospital Monday morning, she brooded over the fact that she and Travis still hadn't settled things. He was still blithely acting as if she'd be moving in with him once she got over this bout of independence. As if she were suffering from the flu, or temporary insanity. That's how he'd been treating her the past few days. As if she were delicate and might break.

She'd finally gotten the upper hand last night when he'd stopped by her place. He'd been giving her a long lecture on the importance of drinking enough milk when she had walked right up to him and kissed him speechless. The stunned look in his eyes had made her feel great.

The official-looking document Lori discovered in her box in the hospital mail room did not make her feel great, however. Opening it, she read the formally typed sentences with stunned incredulity. Certain words jumped off the page at her: *...formal hearing has been scheduled to reevaluate your position on staff at the hospital...you are requested to ap-*

pear in front of the hospital board on Monday, April 10.
Seven weeks away.

Lori sat on a nearby stool and reread the letter. She'd had a bad feeling in the pit of her stomach ever since Straker had given her the evil eye for not giving up her chair a few days ago. She'd written the feeling off as morning sickness and had taken to sucking watermelon lollipops—she had one in her mouth now, in fact. But seeing this official notice made her realize that she'd had a premonition that trouble was brewing.

A formal hearing? A witch-hunt, more likely! What was she going to do? The answer came immediately: she'd show up at the damn hearing and do her best to clear her name.

Lori refused to let Straker drive her off. But she was getting tired of constantly having to defend herself against his attacks. Maybe it would be better for her to take a position elsewhere. Of course, there wasn't an "elsewhere" here in Whitehorn, which left her where—returning to Great Falls to practice?

It was tempting. A few years ago Lori would have done just that. But now she was pregnant. She had no idea how she was going to break the news to her parents. Travis was right; they'd never been wild about him, although they hadn't disliked him as much as he thought. But they wouldn't understand how she'd gotten pregnant by her ex-husband, whom she had no immediate plans to marry. No, they wouldn't understand that at all. Half of Whitehorn didn't understand. Lori wasn't sure the hospital board would, either.

Looking at her other hand, Lori realized she'd gotten another letter in today's mail, this one from Anne, the midwife who'd been her mentor in Great Falls. As she ripped the envelope open, she wondered if she should have stayed in Great Falls, where she wouldn't have to fight boneheads like Dr. Straker. The atmosphere at the birthing center had been much more congenial and accepting and supportive.

Had she stayed in Great Falls, she wouldn't have fallen in love with her ex-husband again and become pregnant with his child. There was no going back. She was staying where she was and fighting for her position.

Travis was sitting on a lumpy swivel stool at the counter of the Hip Hop Café, nursing a cup of coffee and eating a slice of pie. Since he'd gotten bad news the last two times he'd eaten cherry pie, he'd chosen apple this time.

As he ate, he brooded over the situation with Lori and his fear that she didn't need him anymore. She had what she'd wanted—a baby. And now that his "job" was done, she obviously was having doubts about the wisdom of keeping up her relationship with him. She certainly wasn't willing to move back to the ranch yet. Not by a long shot. He hadn't even seriously proposed to her yet, although that was certainly on his mind.

Virgil took a break from the kitchen to come out and refill Travis's coffee cup. "That Dr. Straker stopped by earlier. In my book doctors rate right up there with lawyers, two rungs beneath rattlesnakes on the ladder of life. But I heard him talkin', hospital gossip. About Lori. You know what they're sayin'?"

"I know what *I'm* saying. And that is that Lori and I are engaged," Travis declared in a dangerous voice, deliberately loud enough for everyone in the café to hear. "We plan on remarrying. And the first man who says anything bad about my fiancée will be the first to lose his front teeth."

"I just got these dentures to fit. I'm not about to get them knocked out," Virgil hastily assured him.

Lori was just preparing to leave the family practice that evening when she almost ran into Lily Mae bustling in the front door.

"What exciting news," the woman exclaimed, giving Lori a hug. "I'm so glad for you!"

"What news?" she asked in confusion.

"I just came from the Hip Hop Café. I'd no sooner set one foot in the door than I heard Travis declaring to one and all that you two are engaged!"

Fourteen

"Engaged?" Lori repeated in disbelief.

"Ah, I can tell by the look on your face that it was meant to be a surprise. Well, the cat's out of the bag now, I'm afraid," Lily Mae stated. "I told you, I just came from the café, where I heard Travis making the announcement myself. So when is the happy date?"

"What?" Lori's mind scrambled to decipher what Lily Mae was telling her. Surely the woman couldn't have heard Travis correctly?

"The happy date," Lily Mae prompted. "When are you and Travis planning on tying the knot again?"

"I don't know. I mean, we're not."

"I see." The older woman nodded understandingly. "You two haven't had time to set a date yet."

"No. That's not it. Travis and I aren't engaged."

"It's a little late to be trying to keep this news a secret now," Lily Mae declared.

"I'm not trying to keep it secret and there is no news. We're not engaged."

Lily Mae frowned in confusion. "But what about the baby? And why did Travis say you were engaged?"

"I have no idea why Travis does half the things he does," Lori muttered. "And the baby is just fine, thank you."

"But if you're not going to marry Travis, who are you going to marry?"

"No one."

Lily's Mae's penciled eyebrows rose two inches. "No one?"

"I mean, my plans aren't certain yet."

"You don't mean to be thinking of having a baby—" Lily Mae looked around to make sure the coast was clear "—out of wedlock?"

"I don't mean to be forced into a marriage until I'm sure it's the right thing to do," Lori replied.

"Did you and Travis have another fight?" Lily Mae asked, as if this were the only explanation that made sense.

"Not yet, but we're about to," Lori muttered.

Lori found Travis drinking coffee at the counter of the Hip Hop Café. Walking up to him, she tapped him on the shoulder. "We need to talk," she declared.

"Sure thing, honey," Travis said, reaching into his pocket to pay for his coffee. "See you later, Virgil. And don't you forget what I said."

Lori heard the warning tone in Travis's voice.

Virgil, surprisingly silent for once, merely waved his spatula through the doorway to the kitchen.

Once outside, Travis draped his arm around Lori's shoulders as he said, "You should be wearing a scarf. It's colder than you think out here."

"I'm fine."

"What did you want to talk to me about?"

"Not here," she curtly replied, well aware of the stares being directed at them from those still inside the café. "At my place."

"Is it the baby?" Travis asked in concern. "Has something happened to the baby?"

"The baby is fine. The mother is not."

"Oh, God. It's something serious, isn't it?"

"It's something serious, but not about my health. I'm as healthy as a horse."

"You looked flushed." He gently guided her to his pickup, which was parked nearby. "Don't you worry about a thing. I'll get you right home."

He did, exceeding the speed limit by a good fifteen miles an hour. Wrapping his arm around her, he led her inside and directly to the couch. "Here, lie down. I'll go get you some water or something."

"I don't need water," Lori said. "I need to talk to you."

"Okay, fine." Travis sat on the couch beside her. "I'm right here. What did you want to say?"

"Lily Mae came over to the family practice as I was leaving a short while ago. She said the strangest thing."

"Lily Mae has been known to do that," he replied.

"She claimed she heard you telling Virgil and the rest of the Hip Hop Café that we were engaged."

"And?"

"And I told her she must have been mistaken, that you and I aren't engaged."

Travis frowned. "Why did you tell her that?"

"Because it's the truth."

"That's no reason. You'll just have to tell her that you were confused or upset or something and made a mistake."

"*I* made a mistake?" Lori repeated in disbelief.

"It can happen to anyone," Travis said, patting her hand to keep her calm.

Lori snatched her hand away and glared at him. "I didn't make any mistakes, Travis, but it appears you made a big one."

"How's that?"

"By telling half the town that we're engaged. Without mentioning a thing to me about it beforehand."

"So that's why you're so mad. Because I didn't talk to you first. Honey, I didn't plan it like that. Believe me, this isn't the way I imagined our engagement starting off."

"It's not starting off. We are *not* engaged."

"You were expecting something romantic...."

"I wasn't expecting you to revert back to your old tricks of taking charge of things without bothering to consult with me first."

"Whoa, hold on there a minute. I told you I didn't plan this. But I wasn't about to stand by and let folks talk about you and my baby disrespectfully."

"You've made no secret of the fact that you want us to be together again. Ever since I told you I was pregnant, you've done nothing but badger me to move back to the ranch with you."

The accusation stung. "You don't know the meaning of the word *badger*. You're acting like I've tried to buffalo you into something, when the truth of the matter is that I've been patient as a saint with all your hemming and hawing—"

"Hemming and hawing!" she repeated in disbelief.

"The bottom line here is that no child of mine is going to be born into this world a bastard!" he growled.

To Lori's dismay, she burst into tears.

Travis stared at her in equal dismay. "Aw, honey, don't cry. Things will be fine, you'll see." Sliding his arms around her, he tucked her into his comforting embrace, rocking her as if she were a child.

"It's hormones," she told him in between sniffs. "It's natural at this point for pregnant women to feel weepy and cry at the drop of a hat."

"I'm still wearing my hat," Travis noted dryly. "I'll try not to drop it around you." His attempt at levity was accompanied by soothing strokes through her short blond hair. As he absently circled his thumb over her silver snowflake earring, he murmured, "You know, I've got one of your earrings." Truth was, he had two, but he wasn't ready to give both up just yet. Not until he had a firmer hold on Lori. "The silver feather one. You left it behind that time you came out to the ranch and fought with me in the barn."

Lori recalled only too well that they'd done more than fight. He'd kissed her senseless that day. And she hadn't regained her senses yet. Talk about senseless—she'd left her car in front of the Hip Hop Café. That realization just hit her. "I need my car."

Travis leaned away from her to say, "I'll get someone to drive it over for you." Once that call had been made, he returned to her side. "Did something else happen today to set you off?"

"Being told I'm engaged isn't enough?" she countered.

Travis shrugged. "Could be. But I got the impression there's something else."

The hearing. Lori had almost forgotten about the hearing. She briefly filled Travis in.

"Can they do that?" he demanded. "Call you in front of the hospital board?"

Lori nodded.

"Why?" he asked.

"It's simple. Dr. Straker doesn't want me practicing in what he thinks of as *his* hospital."

"Want me to punch the guy's lights out?"

"No. But thank you for offering."

"How about I just hog-tie him and drag him around the corral by his heels for a while?"

"Don't think I'm not tempted," she muttered.

"I know you're tempted," Travis said softly, and she knew he was no longer referring to punishing Straker. "But you're still skittish. Why is that? Think you can tell me why you don't want to get married?"

"I'm scared," Lori admitted before putting some distance between herself and Travis on the couch. "When we were married, sometimes I'd find myself wondering if it was possible to love someone too much. I wanted so badly to please you. So I did things I thought would make you happy. I made sacrifices. Little at first, then bigger as time went on. And I ended up getting mad at you in the process."

"What kind of sacrifices?" Travis demanded.

"Lots of them, going all the way back to when we first met. Do you know why I became a cheerleader when we were in high school?"

"Because you liked it?"

"Wrong. Because of you."

"Me?"

"That's right. You were a star on the football team and I wanted to spend time with you, to have you be proud of me.

So I worked darn hard to get on that cheerleading squad, was the only freshman to make it."

"You didn't want to be a cheerleader?"

"Let's just say my heart wasn't with my pom-poms," she noted mockingly.

"Then you should have quit," he said bluntly. "I never told you to become a cheerleader. I never had feelings about it one way or the other, except that I thought you looked cute in that cheerleading outfit. As for making sacrifices, I know that it was a step down for you to be moving from your parent's nice house here in town out to the ranch. Your parents never let me forget it. They never approved of me. They always wanted something better for their little girl. Some*one* better."

"I didn't divorce you to please my parents," she replied. "As a future parent, I'm sick and tired of parents getting the blame for everything."

"I don't blame your parents. I blame *you.*"

"You don't pull your punches, do you?" she said shakily.

"I can't afford to. I've tried everything to get you back, from yelling at you to courting you. Maybe it's time for some plain honesty."

"I agree. But that doesn't mean I'm going to take the blame for our divorce just because I was the one who wanted it," she said.

"I don't blame you for the divorce—we were both in that marriage and we both made mistakes."

"That's the first time you've ever admitted that," she quietly noted.

"Like I said, I think it's time for some honesty here. On both our parts."

"If you don't blame me for the divorce, then what were you talking about before?"

"I blame you for trying to please your parents, for trying to please me—only to be furious about it afterward. For making assumptions about what would make me happy. For not talking to me then the way you are now."

"I refuse to take the rap for that last one," she protested. "There's no way you would have listened had I talked to you back then. You gave me ten-minute segments of your time. After eighteen hours out on the range, you weren't exactly ready to come home and have a heart-to-heart discussion with your teenage wife."

"You regret being a cheerleader and I regret there not being enough hours in the day. I know you felt I wasn't there for you when we were married," he said stiffly.

"I regret marrying so young," Lori replied. "It wasn't just you. We weren't ready to face the things we had to face."

"We're not that young anymore."

"That's right," she agreed. "Which is why I'm going to please myself this time around, selfish though that may sound. I don't mean it that way. It's just that I'm not going do something I'm not sure of simply to satisfy someone else's idea of what is right. It has to feel right to me."

"And what about the baby?" Travis demanded, his voice revealing his impatience.

"I love this baby."

"And you think I won't?"

"I think you're using this situation to get me back," she accused.

Her words angered him, probably because she was right. But hell, that was no crime. She had no cause to go looking at him as if he were the enemy. It hurt. Like being thrown by a horse and then kicked in the ribs. "You used me to get the baby you wanted so damn much," Travis retorted. "So we're even."

"I won't be rushed into a decision," she informed him.

His expression became grim. "Listen, as the baby's father, I've got certain rights. Just think about that while you're making all these grand plans of yours." His voice was as icy as a February night. "I've got to get back to the ranch. But don't think this is over, because it's not. You're not the only one involved here. There's that baby of ours. My son or daughter."

"I realize that. Which is why I was thinking about joint custody—"

"You should be thinking about marriage. To me. Especially in light of this hospital hearing. Being a single mother isn't going to endear you to the conservative hospital board."

"I am not about to get married to please the hospital board," she declared.

"No, as you already bragged, you're hell-bent on pleasing yourself and to hell with the rest of us. Well, I'm just as hell-bent on being here for my child, whether you like it or not. You can count on it!"

The news of Travis's and Lori's spat spread through Whitehorn faster than a summer brushfire. While most folks were sensitive enough to mind their own business, some were determined to give advice during the next two weeks. Lily Mae fussed, handing Lori articles about the troubles single moms faced each time she walked into the Hip Hop Café. As a result, Lori had taken to bringing her own lunch to work.

That worked, for a while. Then Molly at the family practice baked Lori a loaf of wheat bread and asked her about David. "It wasn't serious between you two, was it?" she inquired.

Preoccupied, Lori shook her head. This morning her black jeans had felt tight, so she'd had to put on a pair of gray wool slacks to go with the pink cashmere pullover. Her earrings were pink ice. She hadn't lost any since Travis had returned the silvery feather one she'd left behind in his barn in December.

It seemed so long ago now. He'd kissed her senseless, she'd gotten mad, they'd fought, she'd stormed out. It had happened often enough. But this last fight had been different somehow. It felt temporary. And it seemed to have less anger.

She'd received her missing silver earring yesterday. Travis had sent it to her in a small protected mailing bag, along with an article about the importance of family. He wasn't telling her anything she didn't already know. Lori had to admit that the statistics were pretty scary. One said that as many as half of the 12 million infants and toddlers in this country confronted at least one risk factor regarding their healthy development—factors that included things like lack of medical care, poverty, violence and disintegrating families.

The first three weren't a problem for Lori, but the last one hit her big time. Disintegrating families. She had an image of something solid just crumbling away.

Lori knew how that felt. She'd been there. She didn't want to make the same mistake twice. Then she recalled one of Tex's familiar sayings: "Don't throw the baby out with the bath water."

Had she given up on her marriage too easily? Leaving Travis hadn't been easy at all. But maybe she had left too soon and had expected too much—expected him to know what she wanted, what she needed, as if reading her mind.

She no longer had those expectations. Now she didn't know what to expect.

"Lori, you didn't answer my question." The sound of Molly's puzzled voice brought her back to her surroundings—the staff room at the family practice, where scales and a blood-pressure machine shared the space with cupboards filled with either medicine or junk food. Doctors were notorious noshers, and nurses weren't far behind. There never seemed to be time to eat a real meal.

But Lori was now making the time. She knew how important it was to her baby. So she was drinking the eight eight-ounce glasses of water a day, and visiting the bathroom accordingly. She made sure to include two vegetable and two fruit portions....

"Lori?" Molly repeated.

"I'm sorry." Blinking, Lori deliberately refocused her attention on her friend, wondering as she did so if prolonged daydreaming was a side effect of pregnancy. "I was thinking...."

"You've got your plate full," Molly acknowledged.

"You can say that again," Lori noted with a grin at the paper plate stacked with healthy food.

"I know you've had a lot on your mind lately, what with the hospital hearing and your pregnancy...."

Lori heard the strain in her friend's voice. "What's wrong, Molly?"

"Would it upset you to hear that David and I are...seeing each other?" she asked hesitantly.

"Not at all," Lori replied. "David is a nice guy. And we all know that you're exceptional," she added with a grin.

"You're the one who is exceptional," Molly declared. "I don't think I'd have the courage to do what you've done."

"And what is it that I've done?"

Molly's reply was simple. "Gone after what you wanted."

Molly might think Lori was exceptional, but at the hospital, Danette and Dr. Straker were having a field day. Although neither said anything to her face, Lori knew they were talking about her plenty behind her back. But she also knew that she had lots of support from the others on the hospital staff, including Kane.

"We haven't had much time to talk since I got married," Kane said, after having tracked her down the next morning in a quiet corner of the cafeteria.

Carefully sipping her peppermint tea, and patting the pocket of her lavender lab coat to make sure she had a day's supply of watermelon lollipops with her, Lori replied, "A lot has happened since then."

"So I've heard. If there's anything I can do to help, you only have to ask."

"Thanks."

"I want you to know that I think this hospital hearing is an insult," Kane said. "And I intend to testify on your behalf. I've already told the board that, as well as Winona."

Lori frowned in confusion. "Winona?"

"Haven't you heard? She's organizing public support for your cause. She's got half the town signed up already. I took one of her petitions out to the clinic on the res and got two pages of signatures already. Just remember, we've taken on the IHS and won. We can beat this hospital board, too."

Lori knew of Kane's low opinion of the Indian Health Services, and of his frustration at the bureaucratic snafus. "I appreciate your support. And the work Winona is doing. I didn't realize."

"I hope you're taking care of yourself during this critical time," Kane said, his voice layered with concern.

"I'm fine. Honestly. A little queasy in the mornings. But excited."

"I know how much you wanted children."

Lori nodded.

"I hope you find your happiness with Travis," Kane quietly told her. "I know I found mine with Moriah. If I could just add a word of advice..."

"You might as well," she said wryly. "Everyone else in town has."

"Don't let past hurts get in the way of your future. I've been there, and it doesn't pay. Dump the excess baggage before it weighs you down so much that you can't move forward."

Lori remembered Kane's words long after he'd left. Excess baggage. There was still some of that left over from her divorce, although she had indeed dumped a lot of it when she'd gotten angry with Travis and finally admitted some of her feelings. He hadn't let her off easy, holding her responsible for this need she had to please other people. It was a need she was still trying to get over.

The news that Winona was organizing public support had been a surprise. Winona hadn't said anything about it when she had met her at the post office the other day. It had been a springlike day, and Lori had been in a hurry, so she hadn't done up her coat. Winona had stopped to chat a few moments and then had put her hand on Lori's stomach. "A girl," she stated with a firm nod a second later. "You and Travis are going to have a daughter. I told you you two would have a baby, remember?"

With a cheerful wave of her hand, she'd been off, claiming she had lots to do.

"Thanks for coming, folks. We'll meet again on Friday. Remember, we've still got lots to do, so get as many signatures on those petitions as you can. The hospital hearing is only a few weeks away," Winona told the small group gathered at the Stop 'N' Swap "storage facility," otherwise known as a barn, which housed a lot of her stock in bad weather. Some things improved by a few seasons of getting covered in snow, others didn't.

People, most of them women and most in their twenties and early thirties with an armful of kids, tramped out to their cars, leaving the drafty barn empty of humans—aside from Winona and Homer.

"How 'bout a nice cup of tea to take the edge off?" Winona suggested.

"Sounds mighty tempting." At one point, Homer would have taken that tea with a hefty dose of whiskey, but since his daughter and granddaughter had come back into his life, he was a reformed man. In that respect, anyway.

Homer followed Winona into her comfy home, gently nudging aside a cat to sit on the couch.

"Is it just me or are these young folks looking younger all the time?" Winona mused as she turned the gas flame on under her whistling kettle. "Have you noticed how they start treating you funny after a certain age?"

"Yeah, as if you're half-deaf and have lost what little brains you might have had," Homer retorted.

She nodded emphatically. "You got it."

"You know, sometimes I kinda get the feeling that my daughter wants to put me out to pasture, have me settle down in front of the TV, but I ain't ready for that yet. Not by a long shot. There's plenty of life left in this old body yet!"

"You reach a certain age and folks start treating you like you've got one foot in the retirement home and one in the grave."

"That's why come spring, I'm heading back up into the mountains again," Homer stated. "A man needs his freedom."

"I can understand that. And I know you don't participate much in town goings-on, Homer, so I appreciate you pitching in to help Lori."

Homer shrugged. "The midwife is getting a bum rap. I remember when I found Ethan Walker's sister in that snowstorm and took her to his ranch. She and the baby both would have been goners for sure if the midwife hadn't shown up when she did. And now they're acting like she did something wrong. It ain't right, I tell you."

"I agree. We've got to stick up for what's right," Winona maintained.

The whistling of the teakettle seemed to emphasize her statement, and Winona took it as a good sign. Poor Lori could use a few good signs about now.

Lori could hardly believe it was already the first week in March. Stubborn islands of snow were still firmly entrenched in places the sun hadn't reached and areas with northern exposures, the same places where people rested in the dusty heat of summer. Montana was a land of extremes, and Lori's emotions over the past few months had been equally extreme. From fury at Travis...to passion...to pain...to pleasure.

Lori, who'd finished visiting the patients she had scheduled for home visits today, was on her way to the No Bull Ranch to talk to Maris. She'd already called her old friend—the day after Valentine's day, in fact—so Maris wouldn't hear about her pregnancy from anyone else first. Lori didn't want Maris hearing the news via Whitehorn's grapevine the way she'd heard about her wanting to have a baby.

Lori spent the first ten minutes of her visit cuddling her godson, Clay, and imagining what it would feel like once her own baby was born. She knew that at this point in her first trimester, five weeks along, it was much too soon for her to feel her baby moving. Clinically, she knew her baby was only a quarter of an inch long, or about the size of a raisin.

She was looking forward to the end of her first trimester—the third month, when her baby's heartbeat could be heard. The fifth month, June, when she'd start feeling her baby moving for the first time. Would Travis be there with her? Would he be at her side to hear the heartbeat, to feel the quickening, the movement of their child?

So far, in the advice department, Lily Mae had handed out articles, Molly had confessed she was dating David and Winona had told Lori she was going to have a girl. But Maris...Maris was the one who said nothing at all. She just listened as Lori poured her heart out, confiding her fears, listing her past mistakes, listing Travis's faults, listing his strengths, listing hers as well, confessing her love for Travis and confiding her hopes for the future.

"So what do you think?" Lori finally said.

"I think you should be talking to Travis, not me," Maris answered with customary bluntness. "So when are you going to get your behind over there?"

Fifteen

Travis didn't need a calendar to tell him it was March. Calving season was coming into full swing and that was calendar enough. He'd been checking on the herd, cutting a few more pregnant cows and leading them into the holding pen near the barn. Actually, his horse, Tar Baby, had done the leading. Travis had just supervised the operation.

Birthing difficulties were relatively rare with cows, but they didn't always give birth easily and he needed each calf. Travis was only too well aware of all the potential calamities out there waiting to derail a rancher—blizzards, blight, locusts, fickle markets, sick livestock, drought, hail. Those possibilities and others crouched at the edge of his consciousness and played a part in his nightmares, because it was a rare year that didn't have at least one major misfortune and a bunch of minor crises. The trick was to survive. Travis prided himself on being a survivor.

Now he'd taken a break to just sit in his saddle and breathe the sharp spring air. He loosely held the reins in his right hand while stroking Tar Baby's mane with his left. Tar Baby wasn't a fancy thoroughbred. She was just a sturdy cow pony, but she had heart and a smooth gallop, the most important requirements for an animal that was his main means of transportation. She was also smarter than any cow he'd run across. Which wasn't hard, since cows weren't known for their intelligence. But they sure could be stubborn critters.

That naturally got him to thinking of Lori. Talk about stubborn! She could give cows lessons. She wouldn't be rushed into a decision, she'd informed him. In his opinion, rushed was getting married in Reno. The same day.

Now the whole town was probably talking. Are they engaged or aren't they? Not that he'd been back to town since his argument with Lori two weeks ago. Virgil had taken pleasure in calling him and telling him he'd just baked a blackberry pie, Travis's all-time favorite. The old coyote was trying to bait him into coming into town, but Travis wasn't biting. He could do without getting tons of unwanted advice.

Not that he'd gotten off altogether. Tex had given him an earful, telling him how pregnant moms had to be treated with kid gloves because they tended to fly off the handle faster—not that he wouldn't cause any woman to fly off the handle, she'd tartly added. Travis wondered what it was about women that made them stick together in times like this.

To his surprise, Slim had been the one to offer a homespun saying, not Tex. He hadn't given Travis any advice, for which he'd been grateful. All his foreman had said was, "Remember, son, a woman's heart is like a campfire. If you don't tend to it regular like, you'll lose it."

So what kind of choice did Travis have—lose the woman he loved or the ranch he loved? Both demanded a lot of his time. Both held a huge chunk of his heart.

Travis was only too well aware that, like the family farmer, the family rancher was fast becoming an endangered species. Their numbers were dwindling. Huge corporations had taken over. So had real-estate speculators with their condo rentals and vacation homes for folks who only visited a few weeks out of the year. Talk about wasted land use. And then there were the precious mineral and water rights, not to mention gas and oil. Everybody seemed to want a piece of the action, chasing the almighty buck and not giving a damn about the land.

Travis's ties to the land ran deep. He was a third-generation rancher, but he wasn't sure his son or daughter would feel the same way—or would be able to.

His thoughts were interrupted by the sound of Slim's voice shouting his name. Travis recognized the motion his

foreman made with his hat. They had another calf ready to
drop and the mama was in trouble.

Lori approached Travis's ranch with some trepidation.
She hadn't been out here since he'd kissed her in his barn.
She found him in the barn again, this time performing duties as a cow's midwife. Lori listened to the rough magic of
his voice as he clucked and soothed, consoling the agitated
cow. Lori knew enough about ranch work to know that the
cow had been brought into the barn because it was having
trouble pushing.

She watched Travis work, not wanting to distract him at
this point. She also enjoyed the sheer pleasure of looking at
him without having to hide her feelings. If he knew she loved
him, he'd have her back here in an instant. Was it such a
crime to want to make sure things were right first? And with
this upcoming hospital hearing hanging over her head . . .

Lori's attention returned to the man she loved. Through
his lifetime of experience, Travis had attained an athlete's
grace around ranch work. He moved with confidence,
making the simplest or earthiest job appear almost poetic,
even though his actions were streamlined for efficiency.

In assessing the situation, Lori realized that all that could
be seen of the calf were its tiny, pearl-colored hooves,
around which Slim had already tied a rope. The rope was
attached to a contraption Lori recognized as a calf puller—
a long pole with two bars at one end, wedged against the
cow's hind end, and a hand crank at the other. Travis was
slowly cranking the rope up, pulling the calf into the world.

From a midwife's perspective, Lori watched as more of
the legs and then the pink calf nose appeared. The head
squeezed out, but the shoulders got stuck briefly before
slipping out in turn. The cow moaned and suddenly the calf
slithered out in a wet, slippery clump.

An instant later Travis was on his knees, peeling away bits
of mucous and membrane from the newborn's mouth and
nostrils. The cow showed little interest in her baby, moving
away as if she had played no part in its being there. Travis

blew in the calf's face, and the little animal started before taking a breath.

Grabbing some of the mucous, Slim took it to the mama cow and rubbed it on her face, giving her a scent of her baby.

Travis helped the newborn calf to its wobbly feet before picking it up and taking it over to its mother, who finally started licking it.

The scene brought tears to Lori's eyes. She'd seen calves born before, had even helped out herself on many occasions. But the miracle of birth never failed to get to her. Especially now that she was pregnant herself.

After a certain point in their marriage, calving had just been another chore that kept Travis away from her. The pregnant cows were checked at dawn, noon and every two hours afterward. Invariably, they gave birth at night; same as human babies, there seemed to be something about the middle of the night that triggered birth.

"Lori!" Travis turned to find her standing at the entrance to the stall, tears in her eyes. "You okay? Is something wrong?"

Lori shook her head. "Nothing's wrong. I was in the area and thought I'd stop by."

"Why the tears?"

She pointed to the picture-perfect scene of mama and baby.

"You always were a sucker for babies," he noted softly.

She shrugged self-consciously. "I cry at births and weddings."

Her words brought to mind Kane's wedding...which got her to thinking about the last time she and Travis had made love—in West Yellowstone at the end of January. Lori knew her own eyes had to be reflecting the same memories his were—the creative passion, the shared freedom, the soaring satisfaction.

Her face flushed. Seeing that, Travis tilted his head toward the barn door. "Let's talk outside. It's warm in here.

I'll just clean up first.'' He used the hose in the barn to wash up.

Lori cheated a little and stood in the doorway, watching him rather than waiting outside. He scrubbed down his arms and hands with soap before rinsing off, leaving the long sleeves on his shirt rolled up. He was wearing one of his "calving" shirts, the checked ones he wasn't that fond of. It had pearl snaps like all his work shirts. He discarded the soiled shirt for a new one, affording her a glimpse of his bare torso in the process.

Flustered, Lori looked away from the temptation of powerful muscles to a less-provocative area. She noted that his black Stetson looked a little more battered than usual. There was a plain black leather, braided band around the crown of his hat—nothing fancy, just enduring. That was Travis in a nutshell.

Straightening, he stared at her from beneath the low-riding brim of his hat, his gaze measuring.

Lori wished she had the courage to take a leap of faith and let herself just drown in his Montana-sky blue eyes. But she couldn't. There was too much as stake.

Turning, she waited for him outside, hoping the brisk air would help clear her thoughts. When he joined her, she said, "I came to the ranch to tell you that I'll be out of town for the weekend. I didn't want you to worry if you couldn't reach me.''

"Where are you going?'' he demanded.

"Great Falls.''

"I don't think that's a good idea, to go traipsing off to Great Falls while you're pregnant. Why are you going?''

"For a prenatal checkup.''

"What's wrong with the doctors in Whitehorn?''

"I prefer seeing a midwife in Great Falls,'' Lori replied. "She was my mentor when I worked there.''

"I'm coming with you,'' Travis stated.

She looked at him in surprise. "It's calving season. You can't leave.''

"Watch me. How long is this trip going to take?''

"Overnight."

"No problem. I'm coming."

"You might try asking," she muttered.

"If I did, you might say no," he countered.

Despite that rocky start, Travis was on his best behavior on the trip. They opted to drive the hour or so to Billings and then catch a commuter flight from there to Great Falls. Luckily, the airline was running a special discounted fare, although it did require them to stay over Saturday night and return on Sunday.

Once in Great Falls, it was strange for Lori to have Travis accompany her around a city where she'd had her other life, a life without him. He was doing his best to be supportive, until he heard the news upon accompanying her to her appointment that Lori wanted to have her baby at home instead of at the hospital.

"That's the stupidest idea I've heard yet," he bluntly declared.

"You'll have to excuse Travis," Lori told Anne with a glare in his direction. "He's not exactly the most diplomatic man in the world."

"Damn right," he stated.

Anne didn't look intimidated. "Well, Travis, I can assure you that Lori is in the best of health, and that home birth isn't as strange as you seem to think. Many of our patients prefer to stay in familiar surroundings and have the midwife come to them, instead of the other way around."

"And what if something goes wrong? Can you guarantee that Lori won't die?" Travis demanded.

"Of course she can't," Lori answered on the midwife's behalf. "There's also no guarantee that *you* won't die, Travis. And at this point the chances of that are higher, because I'm tempted to strangle you myself," she muttered in exasperation.

"Why don't I leave you two alone to talk this over for a few minutes," Anne suggested.

Once she'd left, Lori quietly told Travis, "I would like your support in this, but I'll do without it if I have to."

Travis knew she was also saying that she'd do without him if she had to. And it ate at him like a cancer.

"Why can't you have your baby at Whitehorn County Hospital like everyone else does?" he demanded.

"Because I *work* there. I don't want to have my baby there, if I can help it. I certainly wouldn't want Kane delivering it, not that he isn't a great doctor."

Travis agreed that he didn't want Kane Hunter doing anything as intimate as delivering Lori's baby.

"Aside from Kane, *I'm* the only other person I'd trust and feel totally comfortable with and I'll be busy in labor myself."

"Do you trust this woman?" He nodded toward the door the midwife had closed behind her.

"She has a name, Travis. It's Anne, and yes, I trust her completely."

"This is too far for you to travel."

"I agree. Which is why it's great that Anne has decided to take a sabbatical from her partnership at the birthing center here and come to Whitehorn by early summer. That way, she'll be able to take over the care of some of my patients when I go on maternity leave, as well as take me on as a patient."

"You two seem to have everything all figured out."

"Not quite everything."

"I want to know what's going on every step of the way. Like I told you before, I might know about birthing calves, but not about human babies. I want to learn. I need to learn to feel okay about this. I don't intend to lose you." His voice was gritty.

Lori's expression softened as she assured him, "Nothing is going to happen to me, Travis. Women have babies all the time and an overwhelming majority of the deliveries are normal."

"It's the others I'm worried about."

"You know, ranching isn't the safest line of work, either. There's more chance of you getting hurt than me."

"Does that bother you?"

Lori nodded. "It always did."

The look in her blue eyes surprised him as much as her admission did. "You never told me."

She shrugged and looked away. "I figured you'd tell me I was being stupid."

"There you go again," he said irritably, "putting words in my mouth."

"Well, you did just declare that having a home birth was the stupidest thing you'd ever heard," she dryly reminded him.

"That's because you sprang the news on me. You've got a habit of doing that, you know. Not talking about things ahead of time, just keeping quiet, stewing, making up your own mind come hell or high water. Then springing the news on me. 'Travis, I want a divorce,'" he quoted. "'Travis, I'm having a baby and don't need you anymore. Travis, I'm having my baby at home and don't give a damn what you think.'"

"That's not what I said," Lori protested, upset that he would think that.

"It's what I heard," he retorted. "How do you think that makes me feel? Do you even care?"

"Of course I care. More than you know," she whispered.

"Then why are you refusing to marry me?"

"I didn't refuse," she corrected. "I said I wouldn't be rushed into a decision."

"Yeah, well, you can't wait around forever. The baby is going to be here."

"And you don't want any child of yours to be born a bastard," she said wearily. "I know. It's noble of you to want to marry me to give this baby a name, but don't you see? That's not the best reason for a marriage."

"And what is the best reason?"

Love. The answer came to Lori in a heartbeat. But she'd loved Travis before. And he'd loved her. So what would be different this time around?

"I need more time," she repeated. "Once the hospital hearing is over I'll be able to think more clearly. Until then, I just want to keep things as stress-free as possible, okay?"

Travis reluctantly nodded.

"And please stop worrying. Heck, half the ranchers you know have delivered their own kids. Well, maybe not half, but a fair number. Billy's wife calved out last night." Lori mimicked the twang of a long-time rancher they both knew.

Travis smiled at her accurate portrayal. "I don't aim to be using a calf puller on you."

"That's why we have Anne. So you won't have to use one."

Anne returned to the room. "So, have you two settled things?"

"Not completely," Travis admitted. "But if Lori wants to have the baby at home, I guess that's okay by me."

"He's great with a calf puller," Lori proudly told Anne. "You should see him with the pregnant cows."

A line of red showed on his high cheekbones. "Cut it out, Lori," he muttered. "You're not a pregnant cow."

"I should hope not," Anne stated with a smile. "Now, we've got lots of ground to cover on this visit, so let's get started...."

By the time Travis and Lori checked into a nearby hotel for the night, Lori was beat down to her socks. She felt as if she hadn't slept in a week. She didn't protest when Travis signed them up for one room. Instead she took a bath, careful not to make the water too hot, as that could be very harmful to the baby at this stage. Then, with her knit-cotton sleepshirt on, she crawled under the bed covers.

When Travis came out of the shower and joined her a short time later, she stiffened, dreading having to tell him that she wasn't in the mood tonight.

"Travis, I can't—"

"Shh," he murmured. "I'm just going to hold you."

He could tell by her body language that she didn't believe him. He sighed and supposed he couldn't blame her.

His track record where self-restraint was concerned wasn't exactly the best. But what he felt now went beyond sex.

So he just held her, tucking her into his embrace, so that she was pressed against his side while he lay on his back. Then he used his hand to soothe and calm her, brushing his fingers through her hair, across her nape, massaging her taut spine.

Gradually, as Lori realized he didn't intend to go beyond comforting, she relaxed and then drifted off to sleep.

Looking down as she slept, Travis slowed his movements but didn't stop them. He'd read a book on pregnancy Tex had dug up for him. And today Lori had bought him a book written especially for prospective fathers. That had made him feel good. Made him feel hopeful.

He wished that he could keep Lori at his side this way all the time. It was a pipe dream. He was beginning to realize that now. For one thing, the only time she was this quiet was when she was asleep. She wasn't the same acquiescent girl he'd married the first time around.

Travis recalled something Tex had said before he'd first considered courting Lori—that there's no future in living in the past. He had let go of the pain and the anger, but he was still trying to recapture what they'd had, forcing Lori to conform to his memories of what a wife should be.

For all his self-assurances that he wouldn't rush her, the truth was that behind his every move was the intention that she come back to him, that he could somehow maneuver her into a corral, the way you maneuver a wild mustang.

He would love to tie Lori to him with bonds so strong they couldn't be broken. But tying Lori was like trying to rope the wind, Travis decided. A frustrating experience and ultimately a useless one.

Because the wind was meant to be free. So was Lori. Free to come to him if she wanted. But it had to be *her* choice. He saw that now.

All the bonds and ties in the world wouldn't keep her if she didn't want to be with him. Hell, their divorce proved that. Simply tying her to him with marriage vows hadn't been enough. As Slim had told him, a woman's heart took constant tending. Travis wanted to do that with Lori, but didn't know how successful he'd be. Was his best good enough?

All he knew was that Lori had to come to him of her own free will. It was the only way he'd ever win her. Not that it would be easy. And not that this decision didn't hurt—it did. Hurt like hell. Scared him, too. Because there were no guarantees Lori wouldn't take off... like the wind, leaving harsh silence behind.

Still, to his way of thinking, he only had two choices here. He could either rescue her, which would mean marrying her against her will and trying to save her from the gossip and the censure of the hospital board about her pregnancy. Or he could give her the freedom and the baby she wanted so badly.

In the end, Travis knew what he had to do. And he knew when he'd have to do it. First there was the hearing to get through, and until then he'd do everything in his power to ease Lori's stress.

"You know, you're just about the only one in town who hasn't tried to give me advice," Lori told Homer. She was munching on a slice of bologna while he put the finishing touches on the built-in bookshelves he'd made for her. Normally Lori detested luncheon meat, but she'd had a strange taste for it since returning from Great Falls a week ago. No bread, just a slice of bologna.

"Advice?" Homer repeated with a shake of his head. "Don't believe in it."

Lori had to smile. "Thanks again for all the work you've done around here. The bookshelf looks great."

"Humph." Homer's often-mimicked-but-never-duplicated snort was even more disgruntled than usual. Lori couldn't help wondering if being stuck in town over the winter had the eccentric recluse chomping at the bit to return to prospecting in the mountains again. She had a feeling that he was itching to return to his hermitlike life-style.

After he left, Lori got to wondering about maturity and love, if people changed or if some things—like Homer's need for isolation—were as unalterable as the passage of time itself. Munching on blue-corn tortilla chips she ordered specially from Bozeman didn't provide her with any definitive answers, but did satisfy one of her cravings.

Interesting how these food cravings worked. And interesting how love worked. If only she could make up her mind about marrying Travis. But it was as if she were suspended in time, trapped like those insects in amber. With the hearing looming only a few weeks away Lori couldn't seem to make any decisions regarding her personal life.

Travis had been wonderfully kind and strangely distant. He checked on her every day, if not in person then by phone. He touched and impressed her by asking all kinds of intelligent questions, letting her know that he'd read the book she'd gotten for him. She wanted him to feel part of this pregnancy.

But what did Travis want? That was anyone's guess, because he wasn't saying anymore.

The next three weeks flew by for Lori. She spent a lot of time preparing her defense, gathering patient records she thought might be relevant. She'd considered hiring a lawyer, but decided that might look like she had something to hide.

The night before the hearing, she flaked out on her denim couch, eating the last of her blue-corn chips and salsa. She was thumbing through a maternity-wear catalog—which her cat kept trying to sit on—and half watching a talk show that featured outrageous stories, when the topic being covered hit her. *Women who remarry their ex-husbands.* She hit the sound button on her remote-control device.

None of the women's stories were similar to hers, but hearing them helped to crystallize her own thoughts, making her realize how different she was now than she'd been at eighteen, when she'd married Travis. In doing so, she had gone directly from her parent's house to Travis's. She'd

never been on her own, never been financially responsible
for herself. She'd felt completely dependent on Travis...and perhaps that's why she'd felt so threatened by his
love for the land. Because the land might take him away
from her—literally and figuratively.

She hadn't been able to form or sustain an equal partnership in her marriage because, at that point in her life, she
had never stood on her own two feet. Now she had, and she
was bringing that strength to the marriage, instead of de-
pendency. She'd resented Travis, even as she'd felt dependent on him.

Lori felt as if she'd finally fitted the last piece into one of
those complicated, thousand-piece puzzles. And now that
the picture was complete, she could see that while there was
no guarantee that any marriage would work out, she and
Travis didn't have the same relationship they'd had and
failed at before. She could see how they'd changed. Travis
was working hard to be patient. He'd shown that by holding her that night in Great Falls. And he'd stopped pushing
her to move back to the ranch with him.

"So, Demelza, now all I have to do is tell Travis. Tomorrow, right after the hearing," she told the purring cat.
"That's when I'll tell him...."

Sitting on his king-size bed, Errol asked Mary Jo, "Can
I count on your husband's vote tomorrow?"

Mary Jo's thoughts were elsewhere. The next big step in
her plans was approaching, and she was still mentally running over a few of the details. "What?"

"Your husband. Dugin Kincaid. The hospital board is
meeting tomorrow morning 8:45 sharp," Errol said impatiently.

"I thought board meetings started at 9 a.m.?"

"Not this one. I heard that that crazy old lady, Winona
Cobbs, is trying to put together a citizens' coalition to testify on the midwife's behalf. Everyone who's going to testify has to be there when the meeting begins."

"Fifteen minutes earlier than expected," Mary Jo said, nodding appreciatively. "Clever move, Errol."

"Thank you. Now, how about your husband's vote? You talked to him about this like I asked you to, right?"

Mary Jo nodded, although she hadn't spoken to Dugin, of course. What would be the point? "Actually, Dugin won't be able to attend tomorrow's meeting. He's got some ranch business to take care of, something that can't be postponed."

Mary Jo had been waiting for this moment for a long time. She wasn't about to alter her plans to fit into Errol's schedule. He hadn't picked up at all on that line she'd given him about Dugin's alleged mistreatment of her. Typical. When you wanted something done, you had to do it yourself. Mary Jo had learned that the hard way.

"What do you mean, he won't be at the board meeting? I was counting on his vote, Mary Jo."

His whining voice reminded her too strongly of Dugin's. "Well, Errol, strange as this may seem to you, the world doesn't turn on its axis to please you," she retorted tartly. Instead of helping her with her problem, Errol had instead become obsessed with getting rid of the midwife. Small potatoes compared to what Mary Jo had in mind.

"Mary Jo, that doesn't sound like you," Errol said. "Why even your voice sounded . . . strange."

"I must be getting a cold," she said in her more-customary docile voice.

"Well then, go home, take two aspirins and call me in the morning," Errol retorted.

Mary Jo recognized the signs of a man in a snit. She'd seen plenty of examples in her lifetime. It didn't matter to her what Errol thought or felt; Mary Jo was the one in the catbird seat. Soon she wouldn't be dependent on any man, for anything.

"We're starting now?" Lori asked in disbelief, checking her watch. "But it's fifteen minutes early."

"All the board members are here. At least all those who are coming," Mr. Freeze, the hospital administrator, told her. "I hate to keep them waiting."

Travis was there with her. He was dying to jump to her defense in what was clearly an attempt to railroad her. He checked her expression, harnessing his anger until he made sure that what he wanted to do wouldn't upset her more. Hell, what he wanted to do was stuff this guy's tie down his throat!

Putting her hand on Travis's arm, Lori said, "I'll start now, but I reserve the right to call witnesses for my defense."

"This isn't a trial," the administrator told her.

"No, it's a witch-hunt," she muttered after he'd walked away.

"Then put a spell on them," Travis said from her side. "Give 'em hell!"

Lori hoped to, and once inside the boardroom, she began by reading her opening statement. Besides, she needed to stall for time until her supporters showed up. She smoothed her hands down the skirt of her brick red suit. With it she wore a rose-colored blouse. On the lapel of the suit jacket was a silver stork pin Winona and the rest of her supporters had given her. Looking down at it now, she gained confidence. In addition, she wore a pair of Black Hills-gold earrings—a present from Travis—for good luck.

Clearing her throat, Lori consulted her notes and began. "In the sixteenth and seventeenth century, midwives were tortured and burned at the stake as witches." She could have added that, in her opinion, the reason the women healers were gotten rid of in this manner was to enable the patriarchal medical profession to rise and conquer. They were still doing it to this day; there wasn't a single woman physician on the panel listening to her hearing. "I'd like to think that we've come a long way since then."

"Is there some reason for this feminist speech?" Mr. Freeze interrupted her to inquire.

So much for putting a spell on them, Lori thought to herself as she skipped ahead to her last paragraph. "Every year more than 150,000 women in this country give birth to their babies with the help of nurse-midwives, and the numbers continue to grow."

"Fascinating I'm sure, but irrelevant to this case," the administrator said impatiently.

"I was attempting to inform the board in case they were not familiar with the history and role of midwives in the medical community," Lori explained.

"We don't have time for a complete history lesson here," the man declared.

"Then let me point out that current statistics indicate that births attended by midwives have lower cesarean rates and the infants have higher birth weights."

"We're here to deal with your specific case, not all the midwives in this country. Just one. You."

"Right." To Lori's relief, reinforcements arrived in the form of Winona and her entourage. There were suddenly more people than there were seats, and the room was filled to capacity. Lori had no idea that Winona would be bringing this many people, and the sight brought tears to her eyes.

"What's the meaning of this?" Mr. Freeze demanded. "There are no children allowed in this proceeding. Who let these children and babies in here? You're all going to have to leave."

"These people are here as part of Lori's defense," Kane Hunter declared.

"I'm sure Nurse Bains is very popular with her patients—"

"I do believe the board's regulations are clear on this point," Kane said. "Nurse Bains is allowed to have people testify on her behalf."

"Six people. No more. We don't have all day," Mr. Freeze stated.

Kane began her defense, listing the cases they'd worked on together and giving his professional opinion of her abilities.

"Dr. Hunter, isn't it true that you were practically engaged to Nurse Bains at one point?" Dr. Straker interrupted him to ask.

"What does that have to do with anything?" Kane countered.

"I'm merely pointing out that your interest isn't exactly...objective, shall we say?"

Travis noted that Kane looked ready to serve Straker's head on a platter. He'd have to stand in line. Travis wanted at the jerk first. But for Lori's sake, he kept his cool.

Watching her, he saw the stiff way she sat in her chair and prayed that the stress of this hearing wouldn't hurt her or the baby. Travis had tried to give Lori what moral support he could the past few weeks, keeping their conversations on the baby and Lori's health. She hadn't talked much about the hearing.

Lori was aware of Travis's presence and appreciated him being there. Deeply moved by the show of support she was receiving from so many quarters, she listened to the ensuing testimony.

"I've been asked to speak on behalf of a number of patients," Sarah said. "We could each tell you a story, but I'll tell you Debbi's. Her baby wouldn't be here today if it weren't for Lori. Because of Lori's caring involvement, and her close monitoring, it was discovered that the baby's movements had become very limited. Lori saw Debbi immediately, had an ultrasound done that day. It turned out that the baby's umbilical cord was wrapped around her neck and a C-section was called for. If it weren't for the good care Debbi got from Lori, the close attention, this story might have a very different ending. As it is, Debbi's daughter was born a month premature, but is now a happy and healthy two-year-old."

Debbi held her daughter up, while many in the audience applauded.

"There are dozens of other stories, some not as dramatic, but all as meaningful to us," Sarah said.

Next to speak was Mary Red Deer, who held her baby daughter in her arms. "I'm here on behalf of all the women on the res that Lori has helped, directly and indirectly. If it weren't for Lori, I wouldn't have decided to get my GED. She's a wonderful midwife and she helps people. I'm hoping to go to nursing school someday and it's all because of her."

Even Granger showed up. He was brief and succinct. "I quit smoking 'cause of this lady," he noted with an approving nod in her direction.

Sensing that the board was swinging to her side, Dr. Straker said, "That's all very well and good, but there's more at stake here than popularity. Aside from the questionable ethics of having an unwed mother giving birth-control and sex-education information to the youth of this city, there is a more serious matter that needs to be addressed. I'm speaking, of course, about the case involving the death of Marilee Taylor. What about that?"

"I'd like to answer that question," Ethan Walker said from the back of the room. "Marilee was my sister. I was there when Lori showed up that night and took control of the situation, though Marilee wasn't her patient. Lori saw someone in need and she acted. If Lori hadn't been there, I doubt Marilee's baby would be alive today."

Lori knew that Ethan and his wife, Kate, had subsequently adopted his baby niece, after a heated custody battle with the infant's grandparents.

"Were you in the room the entire time Nurse Bains treated your sister, Mr. Walker?" Dr. Straker demanded.

"No, but—"

"Then you can't testify as to what occurred while you were out of the room." Dr. Straker's voice reflected his dismissal of Ethan's statement.

"The door was open, I wasn't gone long and I could hear everything that was going on," Ethan insisted.

"Since you don't have any medical training, you'd hardly be qualified to know whether what was 'going on,' as you put it, was good medical treatment or not, and cannot testify to that effect.

"No, but I can testify as to what it feels like to be unjustly accused of something," Ethan retorted. "And that's what's happening here. I'd advise the board to be mighty careful about jumping to conclusions. My wife happens to be a circuit-court judge, and she took the morning off to listen to these proceedings."

"And I'm not impressed," Kate Randall Walker said tartly.

At her words, the board members began nervously shifting in their seats.

"The people who have signed these petitions are prepared to picket the hospital if you remove Lori from your staff," Sarah added, placing a stack of petitions before the board.

Fearing an uprising, the board quickly conferred among themselves. Their decision didn't take long to make. "In light of the testimony we've heard today, we've decided not to revoke Nurse Bains's status here at Whitehorn County Hospital," Mr. Freeze declared.

There was a spontaneous outburst of cheers and applause from the gathered crowd. Lori wasn't sure who hugged her first, but she was soon being greeted by one eager supporter after another, all excitedly exclaiming their pleasure at the outcome. Even as she was thanking them, Lori was searching the crowd for Travis. He'd been seated directly behind her during the hearing.

She turned to look for him and, in doing so, found herself in his arms. He hugged her, as the others had, but there was something desperate about this embrace. It wasn't celebratory. Instead it was tinged with sadness.

As Travis released her, he pressed something into her hand before walking away. As he did so, she looked down and realized he'd given her the missing amethyst earring. She knew what that meant—he was setting her free.

"Travis, wait!" But he didn't. And her beeper going off prevented her from following him.

Sixteen

Even as Lori headed for the nearest phone to answer her page, the sharp pain of Travis leaving her was like an aching void inside. News of the hearing's positive outcome had spread quickly, and she received several words of congratulations as she made her way to a phone. But her victory felt incredibly hollow without the man she loved there to share it with her.

As Lori stood with the phone at her ear, waiting to receive the message from her service, she scrambled for reasons why Travis had left the way he had. She'd gotten the feeling he was setting her free, but what if the truth was that he'd finally decided she wouldn't be a good wife for him, that she wouldn't be the helpmate he needed on the ranch? There were women in Whitehorn who would be much better ranch wives than she could ever be, she knew. And she'd worried about it.

Was that why he'd stopped pushing her to move back to the ranch with him—because he realized she wouldn't be a full partner in the many duties of running a ranch? She'd attributed his silence on that front to the fact that he was learning patience, but maybe it had become indifference. Not that he wouldn't always care for her in a certain way. After all, she was carrying his baby.

The bottom line was that Travis still hadn't said he loved her. He'd wanted to marry her, true, but that could well have been because of his overdeveloped sense of responsibility. He wasn't the kind of man to walk away from a baby he'd fathered. But she wanted more from him than that. She wanted his love.

His leaving just didn't make sense. Unless she'd been right in the first place. Was it possible that Travis had walked away because he thought he was giving her what she wanted—her freedom?

Lori's thoughts were interrupted by the information from her service. One of her patients was having contractions. Lori immediately called, and after listening attentively and asking questions, determined that the contractions were Braxton-Hicks, or false labor. "When was the last one?" she asked, making notes on a pad she kept in her jacket pocket.

"About forty minutes ago. I didn't want to call, but thought I'd better just to be sure."

"You did the right thing. It sounds like false labor, but I'll tell you what…if they should return and start coming closer together, then you give me a call back, okay? Or if you have any other questions, phone me. My service can reach me."

"Thanks, Lori."

"No problem."

That situation taken care of, Lori returned her attention to her own problems. Just when she thought everything was settled and things were finally going to be okay, her gruff cowboy decided to go noble on her. She loved him all the more for it. And she wasn't about to let him walk away from her now.

She needed him. Their baby needed them. Lori touched her fingertips to her stomach. "Don't worry, little one," she murmured softly. "Everything will work out, you'll see. As soon as I finish checking on a patient upstairs, I plan on having a long talk with your daddy."

Dr. Errol Straker watched Lori enter the elevator, mistily smiling that toothpaste-ad smile of hers. He still couldn't believe he'd lost his bid to get rid of her. He'd had it planned so well.

His thoughts were interrupted by the arrival of a burn victim in the emergency room. The man was in bad shape; Errol could see that right away. He barked out instructions

for the Medi-Vac to be called. Whitehorn County Hospital
didn't have the trauma burn unit that this patient was going to need. It took him a second or two to realize that the
patient was Dugin Kincaid.

"What are his vitals?" Errol asked the paramedic who'd
brought him in.

"Pressure is eighty over fifty, pulse one-forty, respira-
tory rate forty. Third-degree burns over fifty percent of his
body."

Dugin was in and out of consciousness, which was a
blessing. The most important thing now was to stabilize him
and keep him alive until the Medi-Vac helicopter got here to
take him to Billings. He was in bad shape, Straker thought,
but there was a good chance he'd survive his injuries. Within minutes Dugin was hooked up to a large IV, a blood
sample had been taken and oxygen was being given. After
completing his examination and ordering pain medication
to be administered, Errol returned his attention to the paramedic.

"What the hell happened to him?" he demanded.

"There was a fire out on the ranch. The barn. Got all the
animals out, but Mr. Kincaid was trapped inside. We almost didn't get to him in time."

"My husband," Errol heard Mary Jo wail from the hallway. "Tell me about my husband!"

Dugin moaned and whispered, "Mary Jo."

"They love each other so much," one of the nursing aides
whispered, tears in her eyes.

"Where's that damn Medi-Vac?" Errol shouted.

"There was a pileup on the interstate east of here, with
multiple injuries. The chopper ETA has been pushed back
thirty minutes," the paramedic told him.

Swearing under his breath, Errol muttered, "I better talk
to his wife." In the hallway he took Mary Jo aside, as if to
fill her in on her husband's medical condition, which he did
once they were in the relative privacy of a small consulting
room used for speaking to family members of those patients seriously hurt. "Your husband has been critically in-

jured. He's severely burned. We've done all we can for him here, and we're waiting for the medical-emergency helicopter to take him to Billings, where they've got a trauma burn unit that can treat him." And then he had to ask. "Mary Jo, you know when you were telling me how Dugin beat you? When I was examining him, I noticed a bruise on his head...."

"He must have gotten that when he blacked out and collapsed from the smoke inhalation," Mary Jo replied, her voice soft and shaken.

"No, it was a more-massive bruise than that. I know this is a silly question to ask, but you didn't...?"

Her eyes filled with tears. "How can you even ask such a thing?"

"I'm sorry. Forgive me for asking." Errol turned away as if to leave.

"Wait." She put her delicate hand on his arm. "You're not going to put anything on my husband's chart about his head injury, are you?"

"I have to."

"No, you don't." Her voice turned steely. "And if you know what's good for you, you won't. Because, you see, I've done a little background research on you, Errol, and I know all about that little 'incident' when you were a resident back in New Jersey. The one you paid money and went through a lot of effort to cover up."

Errol's eyes widened. "That was an accident," he exclaimed, sweat gathering above his upper lip. "They never proved that I was responsible for the death of that patient."

"Perhaps not. But I don't think you'd care for me to make the sordid story public, now would you?"

Errol Straker was speechless.

"I hear that California is lovely this time of year," Mary Jo continued. "Any time of year, actually. I think it would do your health a great deal of good to move on, as quickly as possible. Do you get my meaning?"

Errol nodded.

"Good." Returning her handkerchief to her face, she resumed the air of the distraught wife as she whispered, "Thank you for your help, Dr. Straker. I do believe I'll go to the hospital chapel to pray for my beloved husband's recovery."

"Lori, have you heard the news?" Lori was on her way out of the hospital when she ran into Eileen Wolf, one of the best trauma nurses.

"What news?" she asked absently, her thoughts consumed with Travis and relief at the fact that, as a result of the hearing, she hadn't scheduled any patients for the day. That meant she could head out to the ranch right away.

"It's so tragic," Eileen continued. "Dugin Kincaid was brought in to Emergency awhile ago in critical condition, badly burned. We thought we had him stabilized but...he died. His wife is in bad shape, as you can imagine. She wasn't injured in the blaze, but the news of her husband's death...well, she's taking it pretty hard. The poor woman. She's been through so much—you remember the scandal when that baby was left on Dugin's doorstep? And there was that guest who turned up dead at their wedding, not to mention poor Jeremiah's heart attack, and now Dugin. He and Mary Jo were so much in love...."

Lori knew what it was like to be so much in love. "How awful," she whispered.

Eileen nodded. "You know, it was the strangest thing...I thought Dr. Straker said something about a blow to the head, yet there was nothing on Dugin Kincaid's chart about that. And when I asked Dr. Straker about it, he practically bit *my* head off. Claimed he'd had enough of small-town yokels and that he didn't want to be affiliated with a place like this, can you imagine? Everyone knows that he was the one behind your getting called before the hospital board. Talk about being a sore loser."

"I'm just glad things turned out the way they did with the hearing," Lori murmured. "But how awful for Mary Jo, losing the man she loved...."

"I know, but you have to focus on the good news," Eileen advised. "The hearing went in your favor, and Straker the Streaker is on his way out. He just turned in his resignation. I guess the public defeat was too much for his ego."

"I guess so," Lori replied, surprised but pleased at the news. Now she needed one more piece of good news before all would be right in her world. She needed to find Travis.

Lori found Travis where she always did, in the barn on his ranch. She had so much to say that she didn't know where to begin. So she started with the news that was bound to rock Whitehorn.

"Dugin Kincaid was brought into the emergency room this morning," she said quietly. "Apparently there was a fire in the barn at his place. Anyway, for a while it looked like he'd make it. But then he died."

Though the brim of his hat shadowed his features, Lori could still see the shock on Travis's face.

She nodded her understanding. "I know. It makes you realize how tenuous our hold on life really is. And makes you realize how precious time is." Taking a deep breath and screwing up her courage, she huskily confessed, "I don't want to waste a moment longer without you, Travis. I want to spend my life with you, argue and love you, care for and be cared for by you."

"I want that, too."

"Then why did you leave me at the hearing like that?"

"Because I'd given you what you wanted," Travis said. "The baby. And your freedom."

Lori could well imagine what letting go had cost him. It wasn't in his macho nature. He'd been raised from an early age to take charge. To go after what he wanted.

"What if I said that the baby isn't all I want?" Lori murmured. "What if I said I wanted you, too? What would you say?"

"I'd say it took you long enough," he shakily growled, tenderly pulling her into his arms. There was a world of emotion in his embrace. For a few seconds, no words were spoken. Instead Lori listened to the beat of his heart and basked in the powerful reassurance of his strength.

"What made you change your mind?" he gruffly demanded, his breath stirring her hair.

She took a slight step back, still within the loosened circle of his arms, but far enough away to look up at him. "It finally hit me that I wasn't the same girl I was at eighteen. I've stood on my own two feet and been successful at it. While it isn't healthy for anyone to live only for other people, which is what I was guilty of when we were married before, it also isn't healthy for anyone to live solely for themselves. This time we've been apart, I've grown and changed. Sounds pretty simple when I say it like this, but it was something I had to work out."

"You're going to be growing and changing even more now that you're pregnant," Travis murmured, gently laying a hand on her stomach.

"And I want you to be here with me every step of the way," she assured him, placing her hand atop his. "I really think we can make it this time, Travis. And I think I can understand better, now that I'm going to be a parent, about your ties to the ranch. You've been working so hard to keep what you'd been given by your father, so that you could pass it on to your child. Our child."

"I love you," he whispered in her ear.

"I love you, too," she whispered back.

They sealed their vows with a kiss that reflected the emotion they'd just expressed. It had been so long since Lori had felt his lips on hers. Too long. She made up for lost time, as did Travis, reexploring every inch of her mouth as if for the first time. She responded by greeting his tongue with her own, trading seductive thrusts.

Passion soon swirled around them, reflected in the way he tightened his hold on her, bringing her flush against his hard, throbbing body.

Travis broke off their kiss long enough to mutter, "You're tired. You've had a rough day. You're not in the mood for—"

"Yes, I am," she whispered, taking him by the hand and leading him to the haystack in the far corner of the barn.

"We should go into the house," he said, even as he was undoing the buttons on her blouse.

"We will. Next time."

"Slim and the rest of the hands are out on the range," he said, his voice rough with barely suppressed passion. "Tex took a trip into town, so we won't be interrupted...."

"Mmm, hands," Lori whispered, distracted by the feel of his hands on her bare skin. "I've missed having you touch me."

"Same here, darlin'. Are you sure...?"

"I feel wonderful," she reassured him, taking a handful of his shirt in her capable hand and drawing him down to her on the soft bed of hay. "But I know something that will make me feel even better...."

He made her feel incredible. His impatience was laced with tenderness as he removed her jacket and peeled back her blouse. Her impatience was laced with love as she unsnapped his shirt and ran her hands over his bare skin. It had been so long...too long...since she'd touched him this way or been touched by him this way—with heated passion and indulgent delight.

After undoing her bra and cupping her bare breast in his work-roughened hand, Travis brushed his thumb over her nipple and smiled that wicked maverick smile of his at her immediate response. When his seductive mouth replaced his hand, she gloried in the magic he was creating. She threaded her fingers through his hair, whispering her pleasure as he slid his hand beneath her skirt. The garter belt surprised him—she saw that in his smoky blue eyes, dark with desire.

"Panty hose aren't comfortable anymore," she said.

"I may need some help navigating my way around this fancy stuff," he drawled.

"I don't think so," she murmured. "I think you know your way around just fine."

She shivered at the brush of his big hands on her skin as he grappled with the satiny garter fastener. "I feel like a bull in a china shop," he grumbled.

Reaching down to stroke him through his jeans, she cheekily noted, "You don't feel that way to me."

"How do I feel?" he growled.

"Ready. Hot. Hard. Shall I go on?" Her grin was saucy.

"We're not stopping here, that's for damn sure." His voice was dark with promises and matched his slow smile exactly. "Been practicing your Kegel exercises?"

Lori grinned in anticipation. "Absolutely."

"Show me...." Minutes later, their clothing removed, he came to her in one smooth, powerful thrust.

He held himself very still as he looked down into her eyes, a tinge of concern overriding the passion. "Everything okay?"

"No. Everything is *wonderful*. Or it will be when you start moving...ah, yes...yes!"

"Exercises," he reminded her, then groaned in pleasure as Lori demonstrated her exercises.

"Tighten and release," she whispered seductively. "I'm... oh, that feels *so* good...I'm working up...to doing this...a hundred times a day."

The pleasure rose. There was a stark moment of suspension before the free-fall of joy. As the waves of ecstasy pulsed through her, her satisfaction was sweetly sharp.

Afterward, he huskily muttered, "Did you really say a *hundred* times a day?"

She nodded.

"You do and I'll be a dead man."

"Yeah, but...you'll go...with a smile on your face."

He kissed the smile from her lips, lingering there to enjoy the taste and feel of her. When the kiss had been slowly and fully played out, he lifted his mouth a few inches to murmur, "Did you notice that this time we talked before making love?"

"We're definitely making headway here," Lori agreed languidly. Tipping back the black Stetson—*his* black Stetson—that she wore along with his work shirt, she provocatively noted, "After all this rolling in the hay, don't you think it's time you made an honest woman of me?"

His look was one of mock outrage as he sat back and whipped the hat from her head to his. "I'll have you know that I've had a blank marriage license burning a hole in my pocket for the past month!"

"That's not the only thing burning a hole in your pocket," she observed with a sassy grin. His hat and jeans were all he was wearing.

"Marry me, Lori Parker Bains."

"I thought you'd never ask." When he leaned down to kiss her, she murmured, "Did I tell you that we're going to have a daughter? Winona told me so, and she's never been wrong. She also told me you were the only man for me."

"Guess that psychic knew what she was talking about, after all," Travis admitted with a slow smile. "Some things are just meant to be."

MONTANA MAVERICKS

continues with

MAN WITH A PAST

by Celeste Hamilton

Available in June

Here's an exciting preview....

One

Jarred from his deep concentration by the dog's raucous barking in the front yard, Jonas Bishop peered out the window. His hands fisted in anger. Moments later, he barreled out his front door and down the walk. "What are you doing here?" he shouted.

On the other side of the black iron gate, reporter Elizabeth Monroe was pressed back against her car. "What am I doing?" she demanded. "What about this vicious creature?"

Jonas took hold of Raven's collar and dragged her back from the gate. "Hush, girl. It's okay." Dropping to his knee, he reassured the dog.

Darting an anxious look toward the dog, Elizabeth took a step toward the gate. She was wearing a navy blue skirt today. Simple and straight, it ended just above her knee, revealing legs that were long and well-shaped. And her conservative white blouse accented, rather than disguised, her slender but unmistakably feminine build. She presented an all-too-appealing picture to Jonas.

"What are you doing here?" he said tersely. "Snooping around?"

Elizabeth's shoulders straightened. "Why would I do that?"

"You tell me. We're naturally wary of strangers around here."

"Forgive me if I sound like a typical reporter, Mr. Bishop, but you act like a man who has something to hide."

Jonas bit the side of his mouth to keep from protesting too quickly. Damn, but this was one vexing woman.

She stepped up to the gate, close enough that Jonas could appreciate the sparkling gleam in her warm brown eyes and the rich shine of her honeyed hair.

"What's going on in there?" she asked with the husky chuckle that had taunted the edges of his memory all night. "What are you hiding, Mr. Bishop? What's a man like you doing in this town?"

A man like him.

What did she know?

"I don't know what you mean," he murmured when the silence had grown too long. "A man like what?"

"You're not a native. I asked around."

"So?"

"So, why are you here?"

"I like mountains."

She blinked. "What?"

"That's the reason I live here." He gestured toward the ragged peaks that ranged to the west. "I happen to think this is some of the most beautiful country in the world. That's why I live here."

Of course she didn't buy it. If anything, the speculative gleam in her eye sharpened. Jonas began to wish his dog was a little more vicious.

"All right. I guess I'll just have to put you on the list of mysteries in this town."

"A list?"

"There's too much smoke for me to believe there isn't a fire somewhere."

And she was drawn to the heat. Moth to the flame. *Hell.*

Jonas could think of one more cliché that applied. It had to do with holding your friends close, but your enemies even closer. The best thing he could do for himself was help her, show her there wasn't a story and then get her out of town.

"Miss Monroe—"

"Elizabeth, please, *Jonas.*" Her smile flashed.

Trying to ignore the effect that smile had on him, Jonas gestured toward the house. "Why don't you come in? Let's talk over these mysteries a bit more."

Elizabeth eagerly followed him inside, admiring the luxurious, but faintly austere decorations. He showed her around the first floor before ending up in the kitchen.

"So what do you think of my home?" Jonas asked as he poured her a glass of water.

"You mean this is the end of the tour?"

"I'm still working on the rest." He smiled easily and held the glass out.

Smiles transformed his features, Elizabeth decided. They lifted the mystery from his dark eyes. And deepened his formidable appeal.

Telling herself not to notice, she took the glass, her fingers brushing against his. His gaze flicked to hers, lingering for the briefest of moments. Then he turned to pour himself a drink.

Elizabeth took a hasty gulp of water, and attempted not to notice the way his faded jeans cupped his taut rear. Or how the worn seams of his denim shirt stretched over his shoulders. He was a supremely fit specimen of manhood.

Jonas gave her a quizzical glance as her cheeks reddened. Then he asked, "So what about your list?"

She looked up. "My list?"

"Of Whitehorn, Montana, mysteries."

She seized the subject gratefully. "This little town of yours is a mighty strange place."

"Surely we're not the only small town beset by some form of violence in this day and age. A few deaths—"

"A *few?*"

"All right, so there's a bit more going on than you might expect from a town this size. But it's all happened over the course of a few years."

"Odd things have happened here before the present crop."

"If you mean the bones that were found on the reservation—"

"And what about Wolf Boy Rawlings?" Elizabeth interrupted.

Jonas looked surprised. "Who told you about him?"

"Jessica McCallum mentioned it. It's not every town that has a boy who was supposedly cared for by wolves until he was found out in the woods."

"It's just a legend. One that I imagine Rafe would like to see put to rest."

"It's interesting that little Jennifer wasn't the only baby abandoned here. Surely you have to admit that's not something that happens every day. And what about Homer Gilmore's disappearance last year?"

"Homer is an eccentric. A hermit of sorts. He probably just lost his way up in the mountains."

"He thinks aliens tried to kidnap him."

"Isn't that a little lowbrow for your normal readership?"

"We're not interested in that, per se," Elizabeth protested. "It's just that, combined with everything else— Dugin Kincaid's barn catching on fire, his death, the bones, Ethan Walker's trial for murder, someone trying to blow up Nick Dean's car—this town seems very accident prone!"

"I think your entire interest in all of this crap is to entertain your readers at the expense of this town."

She clenched her hands. Her boss had also falsely accused her of becoming an entertainer rather than a journalist. "That's not true," she said, her voice thick with fury.

"You clearly have little regard for small-town life or the people who lead it. All you've done is question me about why I'd want to live here."

"But why would a rich man choose this place?"

"I told you why I chose it. Why should anyone require any other explanations?"

"Because I think you're lying."

Jonas sucked in his breath. "You know what I really don't understand? What gives you the right to even start asking questions about me? I'm a private citizen."

"Last time I checked, America has freedom of speech. I can ask you anything I want."

"Yes, you can ask."

"But you won't answer."

He started to say something but Elizabeth saw him bite back the comment. He took another deep breath. "I don't want to argue with you. But whether you think I belong here or not, this is my home. I like these people. They're accepting—"

"And you need to be accepted?"

A muscle began to twitch just above his right eye. "Is there any way you could *not* turn everything I say into another question?"

"If you have nothing to hide, what does it matter?"

"It matters because you irritate the hell out of me!"

The words exploded out of him, betraying a depth of fury Elizabeth hadn't expected.

"I'm sorry," he said. "I didn't mean to lose my cool."

"The press is obviously your hot button."

Again he started to speak but changed his mind. A slight smile touched his mouth. "I'm afraid to say anything. No matter what it is, you'll somehow turn it back on me."

His words painted a distinctly unflattering picture of her. Telling herself not to be foolish, she tried to shake off a sudden, deep sense of sadness. "I'm just curious," she told Jonas. "It's not just my job. It's who I am. If I weren't curious, I wouldn't have this job."

He touched her gently. "Elizabeth?" he murmured, his voice husky.

She felt like a kid on a ride at an amusement park. The speed was just beginning to accelerate, the circle just beginning to spin. She was just a little bit dizzy.

And she wanted off.

She stepped back, pulling her gaze from his face.

He moved back just as quickly.

"I have to go," she said.

"I'll see you out," he replied.

They didn't look at each other or say goodbye.

A minute later she was in her car, heading back to Amity boardinghouse. Halfway there, she stopped to gulp in several lungfuls of Montana air. Only then did the spinning really stop.